Virgin & Child

MAGGIE HAMAND

BARB
ICAN
PRESS

This paperback edition published by Barbican Press,
London and Los Angeles, 2022

First published in Great Britain by Barbican Press in 2020

Registered office: 1 Ashenden Road, London E5 0DP

www.barbicanpress.com

@barbicanpress1

Cover by Rawshock Design

Cover Painting: Timur D'Vatz

A CIP catalogue for this book is available from the British Library

ISBN: 978-1-909954-45-8

Typeset in Adobe Garamond

Typeset in India by Imprint Digital Ltd

Maggie Hamand is a London-based author and journalist. Her award-winning novel *The Resurrection of the Body* has been optioned for film and television. Maggie followed a degree in Biochemistry and a Master's in Theology with a PhD in Creative Writing, and lectures at the University of Hull. She is the author of the best-selling *Creative Writing for Dummies*. As a publisher, Maggie founded and ran the acclaimed independent The Maia Press. Maggie's home is in Hackney, while Normandy provides a French writing retreat.

Praise for Maggie Hamand's *Virgin & Child*

'This is a strange and strangely touching novel – written with great elegance and authority. It tackles "head on" some of the most challenging issues for the Roman Catholic Church around gender and sexuality and at the same time has some of the loveliest, most persuasive, writing about personal prayer that I have ever encountered in fiction.'

– Sara Maitland

'*Virgin & Child* cleverly merges crime with Catholicism and piety with a dangerous love. The novel is wonderfully original and absorbing, from the halls of the Vatican to its explosive conclusion.'

– Mary Flanagan

'Hamand has an acutely tuned ear for the innermost needs and yearnings of the human heart... *Virgin and Child* hovers exquisitely in terms of plot and style between the writings of Antony Burgess and Michael Arditti. Hamand goes on to relate a tale so humanely, so movingly and with such authorial depth and deftness that the reader would have to be a saint not to read it through in one enormous sitting... beautifully written and utterly transgressive.'

– *Morning Star*

'Who doesn't love an outrageous premise? Maggie Hamand delivers in her third novel, *Virgin and Child*. Pope Patrick is our protagonist, the first Irish pope. Controversy plagues him. Sex scandals, assassination attempts, secret gay liaisons, pro-choice protests. What follows is a surprisingly realistic and robust exploration of the church's view on femininity, abortion, the body, love and more.'

– Irish Times

'[Maggie Hamand] invokes thriller tropes, mixing them with science fiction-style speculation, journalistic observation and lyrical descriptions.'

– The Tablet

'Lively and sympathetic... expertly, she convinces us to the point where we willingly suspend disbelief.'

– Church Times

'This Vatican thriller is beautifully written with some extraordinary twists and turns.'

– Sidmouth Herald

'A thinking person's pageturner.'

– London Grip

'Beautifully written, it's articulate and compassionate... Thought provoking and unputdownable.'

– The Bookwormery

'The most conceptually striking novel I've read this year... nothing short of genius.'

– All Things Bookie

'Strangely moving and intensely thoughtful...'

– Northern Reader

'Part thriller, part mystery, part who-dun-it... a truly original story.'

– Promoting Crime Fiction

'Virgin & Child is a fantasy, but meticulous research, liturgical and anatomical, persuades us to accept it is based on facts.'

– Shots

'Lyrical and full of philosophical questions.'

– Ramblingmads

In memory of Anne

What help is it to me that Mary is full of grace, if I am not also full of grace? And what help is it to me that the Father gives birth to his Son unless I too give birth to him?

Meister Eckhart, 1260–1328,
translated by Matthew Fox

Chapter One

April 4th. Two days after the Feast of the Annunciation, the Wednesday general audience in St Peter's Square. The sky a piercing blue, and the colonnades sharp and white in the clear sunlight. The square in front of the great basilica thronged with people; tens of thousands of them, all gathered to see him, Pope Patrick, newly elected the first Irish pope.

The popemobile lurched forward and sped down the bright avenues of cobbles between the crowds of people, penned in behind the security barriers. Flags waved all around him and hands stretched out, mobile phones flashed and clicked. The people shouted his name joyfully, *Papa Patrizio! Papa Patrizio*! He heard it in English, in Spanish, *Papa Patricio*, in French, *Pape Patrice*, in Polish, *Papiez Patryk*!

Around him walked the security men in black suits, with impassive faces and guarded looks, muttering into concealed microphones.

He should be safe. Everyone who entered the square passed through the airport-style gates to be scanned and searched. Security cameras pointed at him from every corner, men patrolled on top of the colonnades with machine-guns, police in their blue uniforms and pill-box hats and Swiss Guards in their brilliant striped costumes stood everywhere. It was still so new to him. He must learn to let them slip into the background – it was the people, his flock, who should be the focus of his attention.

The popemobile swerved round a corner and abruptly stopped – he had to grab the handrail to steady himself. A crowd of Irish pilgrims to his left waved their flags, shouting his name. He leaned forward and took their hands, one by one, blessed them all, and an elderly woman, tears in her eyes, handed him a miniature bottle of Irish whiskey. He smiled and kissed it, slipped it into his pocket.

Stopping again near the fountains, he saw a young man in a wheelchair, pale-faced, his head lolling to one side, pressed up against the barrier. He gave a blessing and the man wriggled excitedly in response, flapping his arms. The woman holding the wheelchair wept and he leaned over and pressed her hand, murmuring a prayer. Then he sped back towards the gleaming façade of St Peter's. More cheers greeted him, bright flags and banners waving. The vehicle came to a stop below the steps that led up to the dais. To the right of the great doors, the cardinals stood in their black cassocks, their fuchsia-pink sashes flapping in a sudden gust of wind. The wooden cross and the white throne stood waiting under the canopy. He was already familiar with what would follow: the reading of the gospel in several languages, followed by his catechesis, the translations, the sung Paternoster and the blessing.

He took a deep breath and turned to look back over the square, saw the water stream off the fountains like a spray of liquid silver in the sunlight, two seagulls circle overhead and, in the distance, a plane pass between the colonnades. The crowd murmured expectantly and he heard the crackling of the walkie-talkies, an announcement booming out over the speakers in several languages. The air felt crisp and clear and the wind blew towards him from across the river – it carried faint sounds of angry voices chanting in the distance. They came from the direction of the Castel Sant'Angelo. Could the demonstrators be there already? He had been told there was no danger of them approaching the square.

He stepped down on to the stone paving and turned to walk up the steps to the dais. Someone called to him, and he saw a little baby in a pink-flowered suit held high up in the air above the crowd. Long arms passed her forward; she cried loudly, frantically waving her hands. Supposing they dropped her? He turned to the waist-high barriers which separated him from the people and held out his hands. A woman at the front leaned over and offered the baby to him.

The little girl had a shock of black hair, her face was red and angry, and her arms jerked with strange, random movements – was there something wrong with her? He held her awkwardly; there was no shawl, nothing to wrap her in. She was surprisingly heavy and strong as she wriggled and yelled in his arms. He tried to cradle her as he had seen mothers do, but the baby did not like it. Who was the mother? He wanted to hand her back before something awful happened, but he saw only a sea of staring faces. Well, he must bless her – but he had no free hands. The mother must have wanted this so much for her daughter, to bring her here and hand her over to strangers like this, so that one day she could say to her that she been blessed by the pope.

Well, he could not make the sign of the cross in blessing, but at least, he could kiss her.

His head bent down and his lips pressed against the hot forehead. The baby stopped crying for a moment, as if astonished at being touched; her brown eyes stared up at him; her clothes felt slightly damp, a strange sweet smell reached his nostrils. She jerked her little body backwards, screamed again loudly, squirmed so vigorously in his arms that he was afraid that he would drop her on to the hard stones. He looked around to summon one of the bodyguards.

The guard stepped forward, took the baby, and turned to the pilgrims. He heard them asking, where was the mother? No one seemed to know. People started to shout and turn to find her; the guard walked along the side of the barricade, holding up the baby, appealing to the people for help. The baby's cries were frantic now; a murmur of disquiet went through the crowd.

The guards turned away from Patrick, leaving him alone, standing close to the barricade. Someone pressed his hand, grabbed the hem of his sleeve. People murmured prayers, petitioned him, someone thrust a rosary into his hand, asked him to offer words of comfort.

Smartphones and cameras flashed in front of him, inches from his face; the corner of a flag trailed across his forehead. What should he do? It was getting out of control. Then a cry went up; it sounded like the mother had been found. A sharp movement in the crowd made him turn back towards them.

A woman was leaning over the barrier, a foot or so from him, wearing a bright red shawl. Unlike the other pilgrims, she was not looking at him – she was glancing around nervously. She turned to face him and he saw that she was not smiling; her mouth was set in a red, hard line. The shawl dropped to reveal bare shoulders and a low-cut vest, and the sight of so much bare flesh was shocking. Her skin was very pale, as pale as her face – she had long, chestnut-coloured hair and freckles. Why did her face make him feel so uneasy? Was there something wrong with her – was she mentally ill?

He saw the red scarf flashing through the air and suddenly she was over the barrier and hurling herself at him. Her white face was close to his, her mouth was drawn into a snarl; he saw her hand held up in the air. He ducked and felt the impact as she struck his cheek, slapped it hard with a strength that almost knocked him sideways. There was no pain; only shock – what was happening? He staggered; his glasses fell from his face and he grabbed at them. Her voice shrieked close to his ear:

'Murderer! Murderer!'

She grabbed his arm. Her fingers pinched his flesh and he cried out as her nails dug into his skin. He tried to move but all the strength seemed to have vanished from him.

'Murderer!' she yelled again in a high voice.

Her teeth were bared like a monster, like a fiend from hell – her spit sprayed out and struck his face. He tugged backwards, but she lurched after him, her mouth still open – it was as if she wanted to bite him. He had to stop her. He raised his own right hand and slapped her, hard, on the cheek.

The sound rang out. A silence had fallen over the crowd. He was aware of them all stunned and staring at him.

Where were the guards? Why had no one come to help him? He watched, detached, as the woman's hand released his arm and flew instinctively to her face; a small red bead of blood appeared at her nostril and started to run down to her lip.

She wiped the blood away with the back of her hand and examined it, her face blank with disbelief. Then she screamed again and threw herself forwards. This time a flash of black came from the left and a security guard grabbed her roughly, then there was a second man pushing him aside and together they twisted her round and pulled her to the ground in front of him. One of them took hold of her arms and jerked them violently behind her back. Everything was happening, now, in slow motion; Patrick watched them pin her down and grind her head on to the stone pavement. Her white face twisted to one side, smeared with blood.

'Don't hurt her!' he ordered them, but they had seized him too and were pushing him away from her. He stumbled, tripping over her red shawl, and he snatched hold of it as they pushed him backwards. He could still hear her shouting over and over, that same word, 'Murderer!'

Strong arms pulled him up on to the popemobile, then they pushed him to the floor and his bodyguards crowded all around him, cutting off the sight of the crowds. The vehicle whirred over the cobbles, the crowd were shouting above the sound of the electric engine, he could hear screams and cries of fear. He wanted to pause, to go back and reassure them, but the men would not let him. They reached the side of the square and he was hustled out of the sunlight and into a vast room, the hallway to the papal apartments. Here they finally let go of him and he could breathe.

He stood on a great expanse of marble floor, under high walls and columns and a great arched ceiling. His own pale reflection was shadowed in the patterned marble, so smooth it looked like water.

After the roar of people in the square the silence was oppressive; every sound was magnified, every whisper sounded like a giant hiss, every footfall rang out like a shot. There was no comfort in this room with its jagged gold surfaces, hard angles, wood and plaster and stone. They led him towards a red plush velvet seat under the window.

He should not have hit her.

Everything had been filmed. His action would be on camera. Of course, she had attacked him first. It was self-defence. But it is not what Christ would have had him do. The words of Matthew 5:39 admonished him: 'Do not resist an evildoer. But if anyone strikes you on the right cheek, turn the other also.'

He sat still, surrounded by security men, all talking at once as they listened to the voices in their earpieces. He touched his red-hot cheek. His hand was shaking. Where were his glasses? He must have lost them in the square. Was he injured? No, it was the shock of it.

It was his right cheek that she had struck. She must have been left-handed.

And that word, 'Murderer.' What could she mean? Could she have got in from the demonstration? It was those doctors, those women who aborted their children, who were murderers. What had *he* done?

The shawl in his hand, how red it was, a deep maroon, like dried blood.

Footsteps hurried towards him – a familiar figure in black, with a shock of white-blond hair and heavy glasses. Thank goodness, it was Father Alfonso, the second of his private secretaries. The priest bowed briefly and bent down to speak rapidly into his ear in his awkward, accented English. The audience, he said, had been abandoned. They would immediately review security arrangements. The woman had been arrested. Alfonso would come with him immediately to his private chambers – the police would like to speak to him. A doctor could come and see him if he wished.

Alfonso's face bore no expression – his glasses were so thick they shielded and distorted the dark eyes. All the same, his voice seemed softened with concern.

Patrick looked down at his arm. The woman's nails had torn his skin, there were long raised weals and a faint smear of blood, but he was sure he did not need to see a doctor.

'You should put something on those cuts, at least, Holy Father,' said Alfonso.

'No, I'm fine,' he said. 'I can't disappoint all these people. I must go back and continue with the audience.'

'It's too late,' said Alfonso. 'The square is being emptied and shut off. Everyone can be given tickets for another audience.'

'But the pilgrims. They have come from far – it will not be easy for all of them to come again.'

'Holy Father, I'm sorry, too.'

'Yes, of course; it can't be helped.'

'The Head of the Gendarmerie will come and talk to you.'

'Tell him to come to my office.'

They escorted him upstairs. At last he was alone, in the security of his rooms. How quickly he had become used to the papal apartments with their high painted ceilings, marble floors and the heavy, dark furniture. He realised that he was shaking – his feebleness disturbed him. The image of the small, screaming baby kept coming back to him, the awkward feel and unpleasant smell of her.

From inside his pocket he pulled out the miniature bottle of whiskey. The pale gold liquid was inviting; perhaps a drink would help. He unscrewed the top, took a gulp, and placed the bottle down on the polished surface of his desk with a satisfying little tap. What would he say to the policeman? It was he who felt guilty. He had hit a woman. But surely you were allowed to retaliate when hit? How much force were you allowed to use? Did he use too much? He saw again the drop of blood issuing from the woman's nostril.

Alfonso returned a few moments later with the Cardinal Secretary of State, Romano. On entering, Romano gave him a formal, deep bow.

A purple sash was pinched tightly around Romano's angular, narrow form. The thin face was lined with two thick ridges which ran from his nose to the sides of his mouth, and deep frown lines on his forehead gave him a look of perpetual disapproval. Romano's English was surprisingly poor, and he spoke with such a thick accent that it was sometimes difficult to understand him.

Patrick had been persuaded that keeping Romano in post was a good thing; he was a Vatican insider, he knew all the ropes – a traditionalist, deeply concerned about the integrity of the Church's moral teaching, especially on matters of sexuality and the family. Here, they were in agreement. But as the weeks had gone by, there were signs that Romano did not approve of him – that the cardinal sensed some weaknesses in him – that he thought he would have done better than he, Patrick, was doing. After all, Romano had narrowly missed becoming pope himself.

Yes, it had been a mistake to ask Romano to stay. How easy it would have been to simply let his appointment lapse with the departure of the previous pope. Now, it was much more difficult to think of a reason for him to go.

Romano bowed again. '*Sua Santità*, Your Holiness, we must immediately review the security arrangements. We have cancelled the audiences for the next weeks, and the Sunday outdoor Mass.'

'That is too much. I would prefer that they carry on as usual.'

'I have spoken to the Inspector General of the Vatican Gendarmerie, Pietro Giordano. He is in agreement.'

'I wish to speak to him now, Your Eminence.'

'*Santità*, he is coming.'

The door opened and Alfonso ushered the inspector in. Giordano was a small man, not in uniform but wearing a smart Italian suit. He bowed obsequiously several times, as if uncertain how to behave in the presence of the pope. Patrick indicated for him to sit in the chair opposite.

Giordano cleared his throat. 'Your Holiness, do you wish that we speak in English? I can speak well enough, I think.'

'Please.'

'The woman is being questioned but is refusing to say anything, Your Holiness. I think that we should also call in the Italian police. We are afraid she may be connected with the demonstration. This may not have been simply an opportunist attack – it may have been a deliberate, planned attempt to harm you.'

Patrick had been warned earlier about the demonstration. Twenty years ago, there had been a scandal when the bodies of aborted babies were thrown into the Tiber by hospitals that carried out this vile procedure. A few weeks ago, there had been a demonstration to remember these lost lives. Now, there was a counter-demonstration of women protesting their right to have easier abortions.

'There were ten thousand of them today,' the inspector said. 'Some of them are known to us. They are politically motivated, allied to far-left groups.'

Ten thousand. A large number, perhaps, but far fewer than those who had gathered in St Peter's Square. Patrick shook his head.

'I do not want to bring any charges. I am unhurt. I hope the woman has not been at all injured herself – the security men seemed a little rough with her. Must we bring in the Italian police? This is on Vatican territory.' Technically he had full judiciary authority and could pardon someone at any time, but he also knew that under the Lateran Treaty he did have to co-operate with the Italian police.

'We must do something, Your Holiness, or there will be an outrage. It will be on the global news broadcasts already. We cannot allow someone who has done something like this to simply walk free. It would set a terrible precedent.'

'Perhaps she is mentally ill, unstable. She certainly looked strange to me.'

Giordano nodded. 'If she is ill, then she must be admitted to hospital for an assessment. Well, we will see. We are investigating her background, to see if she has any terrorist links. She has an Irish passport.'

'So, Inspector, do I.'

Giordano coughed awkwardly and put his hand in front of his mouth. After a pause, Patrick asked, 'And the baby – did they find the mother? It didn't belong to the woman who attacked me, did it? Was the baby all right?'

The inspector looked confused for a moment; then he seemed to recall. 'Ah, yes. We questioned the mother at the scene. We thought it might have been a deliberate tactic, to distract the security guards, but it seems the two events were not connected.'

Giordano asked some detailed questions about what had happened; Patrick answered as well as he could. When he said that in the scuffle he had slapped the woman to try to get her to release his arm, the inspector looked up sharply and frowned. Romano's head swivelled and stared at him out of the corner of one eye, like a bird of prey.

Patrick held out his arm, pushing up his sleeve. The scratches looked angry, redder than they had done before. The inspector nodded, made a note.

'We should have photographs taken,' he said. 'This will help if there is a prosecution, or if she makes an accusation against you.'

An accusation? Against him? Might it come to that? This was incredible. It was he who had been attacked, he had a right to defend himself. But again, he felt an acute sense of discomfort, that he had acted wrongly. 'There were many witnesses,' Patrick said. 'They will have seen what happened.'

'Indeed, we are taking witness statements right now, Your Holiness.'

Romano turned to the inspector and said something rapidly in Italian. The inspector nodded. Patrick did not want to admit that he couldn't follow them; what a nuisance that today his private secretary, Thomas, who always translated for him, had gone to visit his sister.

'Is there anything else, Your Holiness?' The inspector was still watching him. Patrick had a pain behind his eyes, the beginnings of a headache; he wished that they would go away.

'I don't think so.' Then he remembered the red scarf. Where had he put it? He found it on the chair by his desk and handed it to the Inspector.

Why, when it left his hands, did he have a momentary feeling of regret?

The inspector retreated, shuffling backwards, still bowing. Father Alfonso showed him out and came back to the desk. 'Is there anything I can bring you, Holy Father?'

'Thank you, no.' If only they could leave him alone, just for a few minutes.

'How are you feeling, Holy Father? Shall I cancel your other appointments?'

'No. I will carry on as usual. Give me just an hour.' He picked up the little whiskey bottle and drained the liquid that remained. He could not help smiling at the look of strict disapproval on Alfonso's face.

'One of the pilgrims gave it to me,' Patrick said, though why he felt he had to excuse himself he didn't know. 'I thought I could use it.'

'Holy Father, that is not safe!' Alfonso said. 'It has not been screened. Something could have been in it.'

Patrick found himself smiling again. 'Father Alfonso, it is quite all right, there is no danger. It was given to me by an Irishwoman, not by a cardinal.'

Chapter Two

Loud knocking startled him from sleep. What time was it? It was already day and the pale early sunshine cast squares of light on the papered wall. He pulled himself out of bed and called out to them that he was coming. He had overslept. Had it been the sleeping pill he had taken in the night? He still felt its effects; all his limbs were heavy and lifeless as clay. Then, as he reached out for his clothes, a feeling of nausea washed over him.

It must be the shock of yesterday. He should not have struck the woman; he felt hot with shame.

He dressed hurriedly. His garments felt heavy in his hands and the material scraped against his arms and chest; his skin felt unusually sensitive. He felt a little dizzy and passed a hand across his forehead. Cool and dry – it did not feel as if he had a fever.

There was no time to wash or shave; he would have to do that later. He pushed his feet into his red cloth shoes and opened the door. His foot knocked against the corner of the tray that had been left there and he saw the black coffee, still untouched, slop on to the saucer. It would be cold now, anyway.

They were standing there, waiting, his two private secretaries, Archbishop Thomas Benini and Father Alfonso, looking down at the floor. Neither of them said a word; it was his custom to keep silence till after the seven o'clock Mass.

They walked down the long corridor to the private chapel, a little more briskly than was usual. As they entered Thomas whispered, 'Are you all right, Holy Father?'

Patrick wondered, did he look that bad? Thomas should not break the silence, even if he was concerned about him. He nodded his head slightly but did not answer.

He knelt before the altar, bowing his head in silent prayer. Fresh white Madonna lilies stood in a glass vase in front of him; their smell was so sweet that it was sickly, overpowering. He turned his head away.

The prayers in preparation for Mass took twenty minutes; then Thomas helped him into his vestments. His clothes felt heavy and uncomfortable, the smell of the lilies was stronger and more nauseating, and the texture of the bread and the sweetness of the wine were unpleasant on his tongue. Here, in the sacred mystery of the Mass, came the moment he could, at least in his soul, touch and taste God. But he felt nothing. Well, sometimes, this happened. His feelings did not after all have any impact on the working of the Eucharist; it was enough that it was done. He tried to concentrate on the prayers of thanksgiving after communion.

After Mass, Thomas went ahead of him to see if breakfast was ready. As Patrick walked back along the corridor, he saw Sister Veronica standing in front of his new portrait. It had been placed too high for her short frame and so she stood back from it, her face upturned.

'Why didn't you wake me this morning?' he asked her.

She started. He hadn't meant it to sound so abrupt.

'But I did, Holy Father,' she said softly, in her Spanish accent. 'When I brought your coffee at six. I knocked at the door and you answered me.'

Her voice was simple and unaffected, and she looked at him directly. It was impossible that she was lying.

'What did I say?'

'Oh, no words that I could hear. But it was your voice, Holy Father.'

'But I was not awake.'

'Perhaps,' she said, looking a little confused now, 'you went back to sleep again?'

Why was she being so insistent? He had certainly not been awake before they banged on the door, it was the noise that had woken him. What made her so confident she had heard him? Was it worth arguing about and perhaps upsetting Sister Veronica, on whom he relied for so much? But on the other hand, it was important to establish the truth.

'Sister Veronica,' he said, 'I was not awake. I could not have called out to you.'

'Well,' she said, 'you could have called out in your sleep. Perhaps that is what I heard.'

What was the matter with her? Why did she insist that she was right? Shouldn't she defer to him – had she forgotten who he was? 'I do not think that is very likely.'

'No, not likely,' she agreed. 'But it is possible.' She paused. 'I do have to check that you are awake, you know, Holy Father,' she added. 'Just in case…'

'In case of what?' He should not snap at her like this. This was not how he wanted to be, this was not worthy of him. What was the matter with him? She was looking at him, concerned.

'You know what I mean…' Her voice trailed away and she looked down at the floor.

'I'm afraid I do not.' But he did know what she meant – in case he was dead, like the unfortunate John Paul I, found propped up in his bed one morning, who journalists in their ignorance and desire to create salacious stories for their readers so falsely said, or implied, had been murdered.

Sister Veronica looked up at him unhappily. Her plump, rounded face looked like a pale moon surrounded by the halo of her veil. She had dark brown eyes which regarded him with the unshaken devotion of a dog. He put out his hands and caught hers in his. They were warm to the touch.

'I'm sorry,' he said, 'I don't feel entirely well this morning. Take no notice of me.' How was it possible, he thought, to be God's highest representative here on earth and yet still be plagued by such moods and moments of weakness?

Sister Veronica seemed relieved at his gesture. She turned back to his portrait. 'What do you think of it, Holy Father? This is not a good place to hang the picture, it needs more light.'

He had asked for it to be placed there deliberately, in the corridor, away from direct view. It was a present from his home town of Cork, and he was not sure he liked it. It must have been copied from a photograph, for he certainly had not sat for it. The painting, he felt, was slightly crude, and it made him look too handsome. His faded chestnut-coloured hair, which had whitened irregularly with age but barely thinned, was swept back from his forehead. His jaw was firmer than in life and a slight smile hung on his full lips. And the portrait had exaggerated the different colours of his eyes, which had drawn so much attention when he was a child; the left one was definitely hazel-brown, the right one blue.

'I will think about what to do with it,' he said, and walked on down the marble corridor.

He looked at his watch to check the time – his old, faithful watch with the faded leather strap, a gift from his father many years ago. This was his routine every day; Mass at seven, breakfast, dealing with his correspondence, then the morning audiences, lunch, a short walk, rest and contemplation, then going through documents that needed signature and talking to the heads of the Vatican offices.

Thomas was sitting at the breakfast table. His tight, dark curls were illuminated by the sunlight pouring in through the window. Somewhere in his past, he said, there was some African ancestry and his hair was the only trace of it. Thomas had an English mother and an Italian father, and his fluent Italian was a great help to Patrick while he struggled to gain command of the language. Though he was only a few years younger than Patrick, he looked far more than that. His sultry good looks, Patrick often thought, would not have gone amiss in a film star.

As principal private secretary and head of the papal household, a role for which the previous pope had given him the rank of arch-bishop, Thomas was there to help him with all his duties; what a blessing it was to have him close by, someone who had been secretary to the previous pope and knew how everything was done. Father Alfonso seemed cold and aloof in comparison, with his thick glasses, his air of disapproval and his awkward way of speaking. Right from the beginning, when Patrick had felt so bewildered and lost, he had asked Thomas if he would share with him in everything, from early Mass to breakfast and right through the day till he retired to bed. In all that time Thomas had hardly left the papal apartments – he had deserved his day off yesterday.

Thomas nodded as he approached, said '*Buongiorno*,' picked up the coffee pot, and poured the dark stream into his cup. This was a signal for Patrick to practise his Italian, but today he did not feel like it. The smell of the coffee and its bitter shock on his tongue usually helped him to full consciousness, but now, when he raised the gold-rimmed cup to his lips and the steam rose to his nostrils, the smell of it was off-putting. And when he sipped, the taste was sour and harsh, even metallic, almost like blood.

He put down his cup with irritation. Perhaps they were using a new type of coffee, an inferior one.

Thomas had poured himself a cup but not tasted it. Patrick said, 'The coffee. It's different.'

Thomas raised his own cup. 'No, it seems the same, Holy Father.'

Patrick frowned. 'Try mine.'

Thomas hesitated, then took the cup. He sipped it and lowered it gently back on to the saucer. 'It tastes good to me, Holy Father. I'll ask if they have changed the source.' And then he smiled and added, as an afterthought, 'Why, you don't think it's poisoned, do you?'

Patrick shook his head. He thought of his stupid joke last night, with Father Alfonso. He was a little off-colour, that was all.

He took a slice of toast, buttered it, and smeared it with jam. Surprisingly, when he ate, the nausea seemed to vanish, and he realised that he was hungry. He munched a second piece of toast as Thomas opened the morning papers and laid them on the table for him.

The lead was, of course, the attack yesterday. He looked at the blurred image of the woman wrestling with him. There was no mention of his striking of her; the English language paper said that he had 'managed to free himself before the woman struck again'. *L'Osservatore Romano* did not mention his action at all. *Il Messaggero* and *La Repubblica* said that he had 'defended himself until the security staff came to his aid'. Patrick was surprised by the intensity of his relief. He inclined his head and put the papers to one side.

'I don't need to read all this. Is there anything else?'

'You won't like this one,' said Thomas, as he passed him the copy of *The Irish Times*.

The front-page article concerned the recent change in Ireland's abortion laws. This was of the deepest concern to him; his native country had been one of the few left in the developed world where the unborn child was protected. Now, even this had been swept away, and he saw the authority of the church fading. Was there any hope of reversing this? He doubted it. Two lawyers were bringing a legal challenge but it did not look very hopeful.

There had been a recent, tragic event. A mother-to-be had died in hospital – her lawyer and her husband argued that her life could have been saved if only she had been allowed the abortion she had requested. She had not wanted to lose the child, but it was the only way to preserve her life. It was a hard case, he accepted; but hard cases make bad laws. And now the pro-abortion lobby had seized on it as ammunition for a wider change in the law. This was dangerous. The Second Vatican Council had defined abortion, together with infanticide, as 'an unspeakable crime'. Nothing could justify it.

He folded the paper and stood up. The room seemed to tilt sideways; he had to sit down again, heavily. He felt as if he had fallen asleep for a moment and been woken by the loud scrape of the chair legs on the floor. Thomas was kneeling beside him. 'Are you all right, Holy Father?'

Clearly he was more affected by yesterday's events than he thought. He rose again, put out his arm to steady himself against the wall. 'It's nothing. I'm sorry. Well, to work.'

By half-past eight, he was at his desk. On its dark, polished surface stood a silver crucifix, an ornate lamp, and an elaborate old inkwell. Sister Veronica had placed a little vase of early roses on the left-hand corner; a sweet scent came from them. Above his desk hung a golden icon of the Virgin and Child. Her eyes looked lovingly down at the baby, whose face was pressed against her own. His little hand reached out to rest on her breast, while hers was lifted up to caress him. It was an image of such tenderness and devotion that it never failed to touch his heart.

Thomas stood behind him, a sheaf of papers in his hand. 'These are the things I think you should see, Holy Father, as a matter of some urgency. Romano has asked me to ensure that you are up to date with all of this.'

First there was the post, a huge pile of it. Thomas had sorted the letters into order of importance. Letters from heads of state, etc. Obsequious messages beginning: 'Most Holy Father,' and continuing with such phrases as: 'Rejoicing at the thought of being able to enjoy the comfort of your fatherly benevolence'... 'May the Holy Spirit continue to assist you in your sublime ministry...'

He put them aside impatiently; he was still not used to all this adulation. The letters were a waste of time. Next there was his schedule for the day; a working lunch with the Cardinal Secretary of State and the head of the Vatican press office, and in the afternoon, an audience with an African head of state with whom he must talk banalities, and then personal audiences with two bishops. Then there was a list of occasions for which he had to write sermons, homilies, speeches. He flipped through papers concerning the essential and continuing reforms of the Vatican Bank, another issue that Romano had highlighted. Sometimes he wondered if the man wanted to work him into an early grave.

'Holy Father, there are some responses here to your proposed reforms to the Curia. They are not very encouraging, I'm afraid.'

'Well, I expected that.'

The Curia – the Secretariat of State, nine Congregations, three Tribunals, eleven Pontifical Councils, and seven Pontifical Commissions, all churning out endless reports and papers, with a complete lack of communication and co-ordination. No one could possibly keep track of it all. Wars were waged between different cardinals jostling for power within the system. He, as an outsider, could not hope to understand it. And Romano had advised against too rapid reform – perhaps, after all, he had been right. He put the letters to one side.

He could not help thinking of the woman in the square. What had happened to her? Why had he struck her?

'And the sex abuse scandal, you wanted this prioritised, Holy Father. The proposals for your Committee have been welcomed. Here are some suggestions about the membership.'

'Let me see.'

He scrutinised the list of names, ticked some, put a question mark next to others. It was a tricky problem. He had to give justice to the victims without further tarnishing the reputation of the Church. Most important was to make sure it didn't happen again in the future. His proposed panel of experts would provide codes of conduct for clergymen, guidelines for Church officials and better checks for the selection and training of priests.

He realised that he had been sitting, staring at the papers, for a long time. He could not concentrate. His right hand was trembling; he rested it on the desk. Thomas cleared his throat, and said in a voice of concern: 'If you are not feeling yourself, Holy Father, we can look at all this tomorrow. We can postpone some of these meetings... perhaps the lunch.'

'No. I will carry on as usual. But, to be sure, I am not in the mood for dealing with these letters. I have an hour or so before the lunch, so I will rest first and recover myself.'

Thomas turned to go, but then Patrick remembered. 'Thomas, those sleeping pills I asked you to get for me.'

'They were too strong, Holy Father. You would have to see the doctor and get them on prescription.'

'Well, I still have a few left. I think I will need one tonight. No, please wait. There is something else I want to ask you.'

'Ask me?'

'I have it in mind,' Patrick said, 'to write a spiritual diary. This is a private diary, for myself alone. I have always written, and it is important for me to do this. But it is not for publication, not for posterity.'

'Of course, if you wish it, Holy Father.'

'If anything should happen to me, I ask you to destroy it. At once. You must promise me.'

Thomas looked concerned, bewildered, almost. 'But surely your thoughts –'

'My thoughts are as unworthy as anyone's. I could not be honest if I thought anyone would read what I write. This is between me and God alone. I will leave it here – on this bookshelf, behind my St Augustine. You understand – on my death, you must destroy it instantly.'

Thomas looked puzzled. For a moment, Patrick thought that he would say something. Then he nodded. 'Of course. If it is your wish... You have my word, Holy Father.' Then he left the room, closing the door quietly behind him.

Chapter Three

Finally, he was alone. He lay on his back on the carved wooden bed and stared up at the chandelier on the ceiling. Dust motes circled in the bright air. It was still hard to believe that he was pope, and that the people loved him – Pope Patrick. Yes, that was his name, his birth name, and his name as pope – the first, the only, Irish pope. They came to him, after he had been chosen, bowing, and asked him in that solemn moment, 'By which name do you wish to be called?' He had not thought he would be elected; he had no other name ready but his own. And it was, after all, the name of a great saint. They told him the last pope to use his baptismal name was Marcellus II in 1555. Well, it did not matter if he set a new precedent. It seemed such an immense honour, and he was overwhelmed; that not only had the cardinals chosen him, but God also. Was he worthy? Was he capable? Should he, as he had once thought, refuse? But the message from the Gospel was clear – Mary had accepted the vocation offered to her, Jesus had accepted the cross. He could not avoid what God had chosen for him.

When they asked him the question, 'Do you accept your canonical election as Supreme Pontiff?' he had answered, 'Yes'. And then, the Room of Tears with its low vaulted ceiling where he was robed in his white vestments, the moment of silent prayer in the chapel. He felt God's hand on him then, propelling him to the window where he appeared to the crowds for the first time. He stood there, and the gauze curtains suddenly filled with wind and a gust of air blew them apart as if the spirit of God himself was moving them. As he stepped out the roar went up, perhaps a hundred thousand voices, clamouring his name. It was a moment of sheer exultation that he would not forget.

Of course he had accepted. They chose him as a contrast to his predecessor. He was young, only fifty-five, with years ahead of him – three years younger even than John Paul II. They wanted someone who would adhere to the traditions of the Church, yet set a strong example of prayer and spirituality. God had chosen him for a reason – there were things he had long wanted to do, from his days in the Marian order whose mission was to 'think as Mary, judge as Mary, feel and act as Mary in all things'. Mary had never been given full recognition in Catholic doctrine – that she was, with Christ, our co-redeemer. How close the Second Vatican Council came to declaring this doctrine! It was unfinished business.

Restless, he rose from the bed, crossed to his little, private desk, and took out the diary. He ran his hand across the soft brown leather cover, and turned the creamy white pages. He held his black fountain pen poised above the page. To make the first mark was difficult. He did not want to make an error, a black smudge.

He sat in silence for a long time, waiting for God's hand to guide him.

Then he began to write.

The table was laid ready for lunch – the crisp white cloth, the gilt-edged plates with their papal crest, the silver cutlery, the cut glass. He declined a glass of wine, and asked for water instead. Romano sat opposite him; the head of the press office, the quietly distinguished Salvatore Bianchi with his silver-white hair, was on his right, holding a glass of Chianti.

The agenda for the meeting had inevitably been changed in view of the previous morning's attack. Bianchi was full of sympathy. He had seen the security footage, and thought the woman had looked mad. They were waiting for more details from the police.

Patrick nodded. What, exactly, had Bianchi seen? How did it look, on the cameras? Should he say anything? Perhaps it was best.

'I'm afraid I struck her, trying to make her let go.'

'Your Holiness, of course you had a right to defend yourself. These things are instinctive. It does not look as if you hit her very hard. But we stream these audiences live and some people may have recorded it. In slow-motion it might not look so good… it's true, some people might use it against you. It would be best to have a statement from you for the press.'

'Of course. Say that I forgive her, that I am praying for her…' He did not know if he should say that he asked her also to forgive him.

Bianchi nodded. 'I will send you a draft for approval.'

Romano leaned forward across the table. 'The attack has urgent security implications. It is important to discuss these. It is clear that we need to limit our public audiences.'

'I completely disagree.'

'This may not be an isolated incident. This woman may be linked to terrorism.'

'Then it is even more important not to give in to it.'

'We cannot expose you to this kind of danger, *Santità*. To lose the head of the Church in these uncertain times would be a catastrophe. I –'

He could not let this go on any longer. 'I think, Eminence, this is a debate for another day.'

Romano's face assumed a dark, angry look. It was Thomas who smoothed things over. He tapped Romano's elbow and engaged him with some other topic. It was fascinating to watch Thomas speak Italian; his whole face, his voice, his body language changed as if there were two distinct personalities who lived inside him, the quiet English Thomas and the flamboyant Italian Tommaso.

Sister Veronica came and served them the vegetable soup, delicately scented and sprinkled with parsley. Patrick spooned it into his mouth. He wanted to get away from the subject of the attack, back to the agenda for which he had called the meeting. He turned to Bianchi.

'It's important that we do not get waylaid with minor issues such as this attack yesterday, or with petty scandals. We must concentrate on putting across the Church's core mission, to state clearly and unequivocally that God and Christ sustain all things and that faith brings hope, joy and love in unsurpassable measure.'

'Of course,' said Bianchi, nodding vigorously. 'This is indeed the core message.' He dipped the bread into his soup and raised it to his lips. Patrick watched as two small drops fell on to the white tablecloth.

Why was he so distracted? He came back to the point. 'It's too easy for those outside the faith to ridicule the language of dogma, and for the Catholic Church to be perceived as a narrow, male-dictated morality. Of course it is important for the Church to advise on matters of faith and morals; this will continue as it has always done, but we must also be clear that people in the world outside do not see that what Christianity brings is primarily a message of joy and love.'

Romano glanced across the table at Bianchi and then back again. Romano finished his soup and placed the spoon carefully back in the empty bowl.

'Let me understand, *Santità*... you are seeking a change in emphasis?'

'Exactly.'

He saw them exchange glances across the table again, and then a silence fell.

'The problem is,' said Bianchi, as if he was speaking to a small child, 'that it is not that simple. We put out positive statements such as you have just given us every day, but they are ignored. The worldwide media does not report it. They are only interested in reporting on scandals and division.'

'Well, we must try to change that.'

Romano cleared his throat, 'Exactly, how, *Santità*?'

Romano seemed to block him at every turn. He seemed interested only in the detail, in the paperwork, in imprisoning him behind his paper-laden desk, not in the wider mission of the Church. There was a long silence; it was Thomas who broke it. 'More soup, anyone?'

Prayer was not meant to be easy or satisfying. Rather it was an effort of the will, a desire to plumb your own depths and expose your own secrets and desires in order to discern God's will. It was an exercise in self-examination. This is what St Augustine must have meant when he said that it was in your own interiority that you found God, that God was 'closer to me than I am to myself'.

He examined his response to the woman who attacked him. Why had he struck her? Had it really been in self-defence? Or was it in anger, in retaliation? Had he, for an instant, felt hatred for her? Did he see in her, as in other women, an echo of his mother, who had failed to care for him as he had wanted?

He prayed until his body swayed with fatigue, then went back to his bed. On the bedside table lay the tiny gold cross his mother had given him; he wore it daily, on a fine chain under his clothing. Next to it, the little jar of sleeping pills. He would wait, always, till the early hours, in the hope that he would fall asleep naturally. But without one, he knew sleep would not come tonight. He tipped a tablet on to his palm. It would be a pity if he could not get any more of them.

The faint bitter taste of the tablet, and a faint metallic tang to the water. He grimaced, then lay down, waiting for the drug to work.

He woke with a start.

It was still dark.

The bed was rumpled as if he had been tossing and turning in his sleep and his nightgown was wound up around his waist. He sat up and turned on the light. In his dream, someone had been in the room with him. It felt so real that he looked round, half expecting to see someone; there was no one there. No one could have been there. He had dreamed – he did not want to think about what he had dreamed. And this had happened to him before, a few nights ago. He felt sick.

His limbs were heavy and his head befuddled with the effects of the sleeping pill. But he did not think he could go back to sleep.

The dream. It had come back to him, several times, and each time, he felt more afraid. Why was this happening to him? Why, after all these years of calm, in which no sexual thoughts had intruded into his mind, was he being tempted? Why now, when he had become pope?

In the dream, someone was in bed with him. He felt the warmth of the body and the hardness of limbs pressed against him. Then hands began to stroke his back. He knew it was wrong, that he should ask whoever it was to stop, but the sensation was so delicious, he could not. As the hands continued stroking, desire began to spread – a desire to become closer, to give in, to surrender. Then lips were pressed against his skin and melted into him. He felt an overwhelming joy at this sensation, and at the same time, a terrible fear.

He'd woken then in a fever, just as now, calling out loudly, his heart knotted with pain.

Was he ill? Was it a hallucination, brought on by stress? Was he feverish? He pressed his palm over his forehead but it seemed quite cool.

He couldn't go back to bed and run the risk of another dream like this. Instead, he went to his desk, took out the diary, and began to write.

He thought of those words that open the Song of Songs: *Let him kiss me with the kisses of his mouth: for your love is better than wine.*

The sickness he had felt the previous day had not gone away. When he rose and shaved before Mass, he retched, though there was nothing in his stomach to bring up. What was the matter? He was never sick. It was not an ordinary nausea; he felt as if he had been poisoned. But that was surely not possible. He ate the same food as the others in the papal household. Thomas almost always ate with him. The nuns prepared the food; much of it came from the Vatican's private organic farm at Castel Gandolfo. He drank only bottled water. It would not be possible for anyone to poison him without the active co-operation of everyone surrounding him and that was unthinkable.

He thought again of the miniature bottle of whiskey. The seal had been intact; it could surely not have been poisoned. Or could it? He went to his desk to see if the bottle was still there; it was not. He searched through the waste-paper bin. It must have been removed, taken out with the household rubbish; it was too late to ask about it now.

Perhaps he was allergic to the sleeping pills. He would stop taking them. He did not want to go and see a doctor; he did not trust doctors. The thought of seeing them filled him with anxiety.

After breakfast, he went to his office. Thomas came in, a sheaf of papers in his hand. He had to plan ahead for a meeting with the head of the Pontifical Council for the Family, which had its annual meeting soon. He glanced at the briefing paper.

Thomas sat down, facing him. The bright sunshine which came in through the window opposite lit up his handsome face, which looked at him, calm and open.

'There's a real opportunity here to deal forcefully with this issue of abortion,' Patrick said. 'I am more and more troubled by it. We need to find new ways to speak about it.'

'It is intrinsically tied up with the question of women,' said Thomas. 'Once women seek to be like men –'

'Exactly.' It was wonderful that he and Thomas were so much in accord, that they knew one another's thoughts before they had finished speaking them.

'Pope John Paul's encyclical, *Evangelium Vitae*, has said everything that needs to be said on this subject,' he said. 'But the message is not getting through. We need to find a way to communicate these time-less truths in a language that will speak to people of all kinds today. And perhaps we have not gone far enough with affirming the full human dignity of the unborn, right from the very beginning of life.'

Each human soul pre-existed in the mind of God. Each human soul was equally loved by God. Even if it was destined for perdition? Yes, even so. All are redeemed in Christ, but all can reject their own salvation.

But what of those who die unborn? Who have not been baptised, have not known Christ, but have not rejected Him either?

Here was a problem, one that the Church had not fully addressed or found an answer to. Well, he would address it. In the modern world, when so many babies were aborted, aided by those who were the very people who should protect them, their mothers, it was essential to speak out.

Even as the pope, he must go to confession. Usually he went every fourteen days. The Vatican appointed a Preacher of the Pontifical Household, a member of the Capuchin order, as his confessor.

He sat in the dark interior of the room, the secret place where he could lay bare all his faults. Not for him, now, the dark wooden box with the grille that he had used in his childhood, but two plain wooden chairs placed close to one another, side by side. He began, as always, with the formula: 'Father, I have sinned.' He was aware of this, every day. He, the head of the Church, who spent much of his day in prayer, who had dedicated himself and his life totally to God and his Church – even he could not rid himself of anger, of envy, of unkind thoughts, or petty irritations. He thought of the things he usually said. 'I have at times been inattentive at Mass. I have been impatient, angry, proud. I have wished ill of another. I have been fearful, have not trusted and loved God enough.' Now he could add to this: 'I have had impure thoughts.'

How could he even begin to confess the thoughts that he had? Even though the seal of the confessional was inviolable, he was afraid to speak. He knew that his confession should be plain, entire and prudent, neither obscuring his faults, nor concealing anything wilfully, nor saying what would be prejudicial to a third person. What could he say?

'I have had erotic dreams. These are not my fault, but I enjoyed them and afterwards, when I thought about them, I enjoyed the memory of them.'

Mercifully the Capuchin did not probe him with questions. He laid his hand over his head and said, 'Through this sacrament of penance you die with Christ and rise to be renewed in the Paschal mystery. I absolve you from your sins.'

As always, the blessed relief, the feeling of being washed clean, of being whole again.

Today, the third Sunday of Easter. He was to say a High Mass at St John in Lateran. His beloved Tridentine Mass, as the Mass should be.

The attendants helped him put on the vestments. He loved the richness of the fabrics and the embroidery, the heaviness of the robes and the way they moved as he walked, the weight of the mitre on his head and the gold of his staff heavy in his hand. No one would ever take these precious things away from him; they were his for his mortal life, like the painted walls of the palace, the gorgeous tapestries, the beautiful paintings, the marble floors, the huge carved doors, the ornate wooden furniture. He enjoyed these things every day – it would be hard now for him to lead a life where he was not surrounded by physical beauty. It was, he knew, a fault in him.

He was ready, but already he was feeling sick. The nausea came over him in waves of heat, leaving him shivery and cold. Perhaps he was getting flu. At the entrance to the cathedral, behind the long procession of cardinals, bishops and prelates, he received the holy water and sprinkled the clergy and those standing nearby. The holy water might cure him of the sickness. He prayed before the Blessed Sacrament and then went to the throne to vest. The Office of Terce was sung while the vesting took place.

> *O God, Come to my aid.*
> *O Lord, make haste to help me.*

During the singing of the psalms he read the prayers of preparation. His buskins and sandals were put on, and then he sang the prayer of terce. His garments were removed as far as the cincture, he washed his hands, then he put on the other vestments, kissing the sign of the cross on each one, ending with the mitre and the ring. The procession, headed by the censer-bearer, cross-bearer and the acolytes, made its way to the main altar.

Nine acolytes and clerics ministered the book, the mitre, the bugia, the crosier and censer, two candles, the gremiale, and the cruets, and four ministers in turn washed his hands. As he carried out the familiar actions, he felt bewildered. Something had gone wrong. What were all these people doing? What would happen if he lost track of what he was doing, did something in the wrong order? Surely they would help him? Seated on his throne, he struggled to listen as they read the epistle, the Gradual and the Gospel, then he gave the kiss of peace to each of his five ministers. The strong scent of incense dizzied him, the singing reverberated around the massive cathedral, built up layer upon layer until it seemed to him to be a wall of solid sound.

He came to the offertory prayers, which were said in secret before the altar with his back to the congregation. Something strange was happening to him. His head felt light and full of air, as if it were expanding. Was he levitating like St Teresa of Avila, whose fellow sisters held on to her to prevent her from rising from the ground? The solid marble was there beneath his feet – he would hurt himself if he fell on it. The words, known through endless repetition, began to come out oddly, so he said them under his breath so that others would not hear him. But God would hear. How could he conduct the Mass, if he said the wrong words? He must stop at once. But now the great cathedral was tilting beneath him, and he was looking up, up into the great dome, and tendrils of smoke from the incense drifted into the lofty space above him...

They were looking down at him. He was lying on his back. He had no idea how he had come to be there. The music sounded faint now, as if from a long way off. He tried to get to his feet but his limbs would not co-ordinate. They were helping him, picking him up and carrying him back to the safety of his throne. The Mass continued without him. Figures in their golden robes were bobbing up and down in front of the altar. What were they doing? What could it all mean? None of it made any sense. He must continue, show everyone that he was in command of himself, but he was afraid that if he got to his feet he would fall again. He could see the headlines: 'Pope Patrick collapses at Mass.' No, he must get up again.

They brought the host and the chalice to him on the throne. The dizziness had passed and the actions and the words came back to him. He divided the other part of the host, gave communion to the deacon and subdeacon, gave them the kiss of peace and received the wine of the purification from another chalice and washed his fingers in a little cup. His strength returned as he rose to his feet and returned to the altar to finish the Mass.

Afterwards, a car took him back to the Vatican. He passed through crowded streets, looking at the tourists with their mobile phones, the hordes of shoppers with their carrier bags stuffed with purchases, staring into windows full of shoes and fashionable clothes. Shopping had become for them their ritual, their Eucharist the ringing of the tills. They seemed to him to move without purpose, scurrying backwards and forwards like insects when the nest is disturbed. What was it all about? Why did he feel so separate from them? What did they and their secular lifestyle have to do with him?

It was a relief to be back in his rooms. He lay on his bed. A heaviness filled his limbs and he thought that he could sleep. He could not allow himself to be ill. He must do something. Yet he was afraid to confess his weakness to anyone. But fainting during one of the major services – that could not happen again. Patrick was told the doctor had been summoned, but he'd refused to see him and asked them to send him away again. He did not even know who the doctor was – he had never seen one here, not even for a check-up – his health had always been too good. Though, thinking about it, he didn't understand why they didn't give a pope a mandatory health check when he took office, especially after what had happened to poor Albino Luciani, John Paul I. Perhaps, in the morning, he should ask Thomas to call the doctor after all.

He had hardly been to see a doctor in his life. His mother had disliked them. She had preferred the old remedies, the nuns with their cures and prayers. There was one occasion when, as a child, he had been to the doctor – he recalled it clearly. He had been embarrassed and refused to go again. He remembered that his mother did not try to persuade him. She could not force him to do anything – in the end she had always given in to him. He saw her now, a thin, pale woman, with wispy flyaway hair and that constantly downturned mouth.

He was drifting towards sleep.

He remembered his mother, so proud at his first communion. Kneeling at the altar rail, in a line of others, watching the priest advancing, coming closer and closer, handing out the wafers of bread in a repetitive, swift movement, saying again and again, 'The Body of Christ, the Body of Christ.' His heart beat faster as the priest approached and he held up his cupped hands to receive the wafer. Watching the bread being dispensed was like, for a moment, seeing the endless self-giving of God, and he longed to take part in it. Then the priest reached him and placed the wafer in his palm and he saw it there, a perfect little disc, and for a moment he was afraid as he took hold of it and raised it to his lips that he would drop the precious thing. It rested there for a moment before he put it in his mouth and swallowed. And then the cold rim of the chalice and the sip of sweet, sickly wine, and it was over. He rested there for a moment like the others, waiting for something to happen, for some powerful emotion or a great realisation to sweep over him, but there was nothing. Yet he had written later, he remembered, that he had felt a calm, spacious emptiness, a sudden opening up into the divine nothingness.

At breakfast the next day, he did not need to raise the issue of contacting the doctor; Thomas was insisting on it.

He still felt reluctant. 'Thomas, I do not think it is necessary. I am a little under the weather but it is nothing.'

'Holy Father, if you will not, I will call them myself.'

'It was nothing, just an attack of faintness.'

'There must have been a reason for it. It is not like you. You have so much to do, you must be in good health.'

'I am in good health. It is only a trifle, probably just a virus.' Why was he not admitting, even to Thomas, how anxious he felt, that he was worried deep down that there might be something seriously wrong? It was as if there was something shameful about it.

'Holy Father, we can't have it happening again,' Thomas said. 'It's not normal to faint like that, for no reason. I would not be able to forgive myself if anything happened to you and I had not persuaded you to have a medical check.'

'Yes, of course.' He was being selfish. The Church needed him; if there was anything wrong, it should be treated. Why then did he feel such a sense of alarm? Surely God would not have chosen him for this role and then allow him to become seriously ill, rendering him unable to perform it?

Thomas cleared his throat. 'There's another thing I want to raise with you, Holy Father. That woman who attacked you, she has asked to see you privately.' He sounded dismissive, protective. 'Of course, I told them it was impossible.'

'No, I would like to see her.'

'She's in hospital, being assessed. In the psychiatric ward. To see if she is fit to stand trial. I do not think it would be at all a good idea to see her. She may be insane. She may be dangerous.'

'If she has asked to see me, then I wish to see her. Does she have a name?'

Thomas hesitated. 'Well, it seems that she is claiming to be related to you. To your father's cousin.'

'His cousin? On which side?'

'The Connellys. From Newport, County Mayo.'

'Let me see. Mary?'

'The young woman is called Siobhan.'

'Siobhan.' How astonishing. Mary's daughter, the middle of five daughters. He'd met her once or twice, at a wedding and a funeral long ago. A chestnut-haired girl with pale skin and deep grey eyes. The one who was always in trouble, the one who could only get any attention by playing up. No wonder she had drawn his attention so forcefully – her face must have been familiar.

He had a memory then, of sitting at a table with her at her elder sister's wedding. She must have been about eight. Quite inexplicably, when a slice of cake was put in front of her, she refused to eat it but crushed it into a pile of crumbs which she scattered under the table. He recalled the expression on her face when she did this; a wild, gleeful face. And then later, he remembered her running and dancing over the grass on the huge lawn below the big house, and how it started raining and she had continued to dance, and then she took off her sodden clothes and danced with her body naked in the rain. How shocked they all were. Perhaps it was not so surprising that she had ended up this way.

But she went to England, to art school, he thought, and got married there, to a Polish sculptor; that's right, a man with no money but a lot of talent, an intense, a driven man. Mary had told him that the marriage had been difficult.

'I remember Siobhan,' he told Thomas. 'I will go and see her. I will go in a private capacity, of course. I don't want anyone to know about this, especially not the press. Can this be arranged?

'If you wish it, Holy Father. I will see what I can do.'

Chapter Four

The weather had changed. It had been raining on and off all day and now, as the car approached the hospital, a watery rainbow appeared over the squat, ugly building. The car passed under the arch and drew up by a side entrance. The security men opened the door for him and walked beside him, up the concrete stairs and along a narrow corridor. Although Patrick had asked that no one be told he was coming, something must have leaked, because he saw faces popping briefly out from behind the doors ahead of him and as he passed the rooms, the doors were open and he saw people glancing up at him.

They took him into a bare, tiled room, a room with a desk and table in it. The doctor was a woman in her mid-forties with greying hair and a tired expression on her face. She made some awkward kind of bob and then looked as if she instantly regretted this. Her eyes seemed hostile, but he could see she was also in awe of him. She clutched a bulky file closely across her chest.

'I will also be present during the interview in case the patient becomes agitated,' she said, and then added 'Your Holiness,' as if reluctant to do so. 'Someone will also stand by the door to watch and ensure you are safe. Your own security men may stay outside.' Then she stood there, uneasy, as if she had no idea how she should continue to conduct herself in his presence.

Two men brought Siobhan in, and sat her on the chair in front of him. He recognised the pale skin and chestnut hair, which was now pulled back severely from her face and fastened in a pony tail. Only one stray lock fell forward across her eyes. She looked confused, her movements slow and awkward, as if she had been drugged. The two men went and stood on either side of the door, like guards or executioners. Siobhan made no eye contact with him, but sat on the chair in front of him, staring at her lap. Her skin was even paler than he remembered, so white it was almost the colour of her white blouse and the white tiles on the walls. Her dark grey eyes were sunken in her face, the skin around them was dark as if she had two black eyes, and there was a fading bruise on her cheek. Could he have hit her so hard that he had marked her? Or was it from when the security guards had pushed her on to the ground?

She looked as if she was exhausted or had been weeping for a long time.

'I want to talk to him alone,' she said, glancing at the doctor.

'I'm sorry, that won't be possible.'

Siobhan raised her eyes briefly to his, and then dropped them again. Her eyes glittered fiercely – it was as if she had stabbed him with them. He opened his mouth to speak, but then closed it again. It was best to let her speak first.

'Yes, I am your cousin, Patrick,' she said. 'It's a long time since I have seen you, I can't remember when, can you? No, I don't want you to say anything,' she said, as he opened his mouth to speak. 'I don't want your mindless platitudes. I want you to listen to me, really listen. Are you prepared to listen to me?'

'To be sure, Siobhan, I'll listen.' He turned to the doctor, who stood behind him. 'How long do we have?'

The doctor looked at her watch. 'Perhaps half an hour? That will be enough for her I think.' Again the slight pause. 'Your Holiness.'

'You're wondering why I did it,' Siobhan said. 'I'll tell you why. Did you read in the papers about the woman who died, recently, before the law changed because she was refused an abortion?'

'Indeed, I remember the case well. I –'

'Except that she was not a 'case,'' said Siobhan roughly. 'She was a living, breathing, human being. Her name was Aisling and I knew her. She was at school with me. She was – so bright, so full of life.'

He opened his mouth to speak but she held up her hand. He remembered his promise to listen and was silent.

'It is not just her. Every year, fifty thousand women around the world die from illegal abortions. Fifty thousand women. Can you imagine that? And that doesn't count all the other problems that they suffer if they are lucky enough not to die. Infections. Infertility. Let alone the disgrace, which causes some to go on and kill themselves. As far as I'm concerned, anyone who opposes safe, legal abortion is complicit in their death.'

So that was why she had shouted 'murderer'. He had heard these arguments so many times, he felt weary. Would he have to listen to it all again? 'It is a terrible tragedy —' he began, almost automatically, but she cut him off.

'You said you'd listen. If you don't listen I'll ask them to take me back to my room now.'

He said nothing, and merely spread his arms out in a gesture that invited her to carry on speaking.

'Many of these women,' she said, 'Did not want to be pregnant, they did not choose it. They may have been married to someone they didn't want to marry. They may be too young to have a child, or too old. They may have been raped. They are desperate. Can you understand what that feels like? No, how could you. You are not a woman. But that is not all. You say a human embryo is a full human life from the moment of conception. But that's not true. How could it be true? Every year, millions of eggs are fertilised but never implant in the womb and they're washed away down the toilet without the woman ever knowing she is pregnant. But these are a full human life! So why don't we have a Requiem Mass for them? Why don't you ask women to collect all their menstrual blood in case there's a foetus in there somewhere? Why aren't bloody sanitary towels put into coffins and taken into churches so there can be a Requiem Mass for them? Why? Can you answer me? Why?'

He started to speak but she swept on, her eyes blazing now, alive and sparkling for the first time since she had entered the room.

'I have had six miscarriages,' she said. 'Six! I can conceive but it seems I can't hold on to them. All lost before twelve weeks. Did anybody care about them? Did anybody bury them? Most of them happened at home, one in a supermarket, one in the hospital. I asked the hospital if I could keep the foetus but they said it was impossible. Why? Why don't you care about this? Why don't you go round the hospitals, collecting all the aborted foetuses and putting them in special coffins and saying a Requiem Mass over them and –'

She stopped speaking suddenly.

'But why do I waste my breath,' she said. 'You could never understand.'

He opened his mouth to speak but then shut it again. Whatever he said, she would not want to hear it. His heart went out to her for this terrible tragedy, that she had lost all her children. But he didn't understand why she was angry about abortions. If she had lost her own children, surely she would know how precious each human life was, how –

'I know what you're thinking,' she said. 'Why would I, who want a child so much, sympathise with women who don't? It's because I see the hypocrisy of it all. You are not concerned with women who lose their babies through a *natural* abortion. No, you couldn't care about that at all! All you care about is when women take *control*, if they *choose* to end a pregnancy rather than let God choose to end it for them! Do you know how many miscarriages there are? Do you know that at least one in four pregnancies miscarries? And if you count fertilised eggs, about half of all of them fail to progress? Did you know that? It's a medical fact, you can check it if you don't believe me. It's a real slaughter of the innocents, isn't it? Surely it puts Herod to shame! Why would God want to slaughter so many babies every year? Can you answer me that? Can you?'

He was silent, watching her. She had asked him to listen; he would listen. She stared at him for a few moments, as if challenging him to speak, but just as he opened his mouth to say something she began again.

'And these babies are not baptised, are they? Why not? Why, as soon as a woman knows she is pregnant, doesn't she have some form of baptism for the baby in the womb? Why can't that be arranged? Why didn't anybody ever think about that? Answer me!'

She had stopped finally, and he said, 'But they *have* thought of that, Siobhan. A baby cannot be baptised in the womb. We trust any baby who dies unbaptised to God's love and mercy.'

'God's love and mercy! And what does that mean? Tell me why God's love and mercy would allow the death of so many children?'

He shook his head. There was no answer to this question. He saw how desperate she was, how the grief for her lost children had made her bitter and deranged. 'Siobhan, I grieve for you in your loss. We can say a Mass. We can pray for your babies. We have some beautiful prayers for those who have suffered miscarriages –'

'I don't want your prayers,' she said. 'What use are prayers to me? I have finished with religion. In fact, I am going to fight religion. I am going to challenge you all, wherever you are. I am going to go into churches and disrupt Masses. I am going to write to every cardinal, go to every –' and she stopped, suddenly. 'You are such hypocrites, all of you,' she said. 'You pretend to be so holy and you are no better than anyone else. Look at you. After all you hit me – me, a woman. What was that about turning the other cheek?'

He had been waiting for this. He shut his eyes, opened them again. She stared into his eyes and he realised, with a shock, that it was some time since anyone had looked at him so directly. He felt as if there was some understanding that passed between them.

'I am truly sorry for this, Siobhan,' he said. 'You were hurting my arm, I wanted you to let go of me.'

'So you think it was justified?'

'I am sorry that I hurt you.'

'Well,' she said. 'It is something that I can get you to apologise for that even if you will not apologise for murdering women.'

'We do not murder women, Siobhan.'

'You might as well,' she said. 'They die, anyway. Anyway it's no use. I've wasted my time, haven't I? I have this one chance to meet the pope himself, my cousin, Pope Patrick, to tell him everything I want to say, but in fact it's no use. There's nothing I can say to you.'

'I hope that you will receive help, here. I have asked that they do not bring charges against you, but it is not in my hands.'

'I don't want help. I don't care what happens to me, I don't care if I am in prison, I will be a martyr for my cause, but I'm afraid that they will say I am mad. I'm afraid that they will drug me up and keep me here.'

The doctor had started to look impatient and glance at her watch. He realised that it was time to end the conversation.

'I am glad that I saw you, Siobhan. I understand now, why you are so upset. You can write to me, at any time. Please, do write to me. I will pray for you.'

He expected her to say again, I don't want your prayers, but she was silent. Then she said, in a tone that could have been ironic, 'By all means, pray for me, cousin Patrick. I think that I may need it.'

He and Thomas prayed together, late in the evening, in his bedchamber. He loved this time, when the day was over and the two of them knelt, side by side, entering a calm state where time did not seem to pass at all, when he was acutely aware of everything around him and yet strangely removed from it. This, he believed, was the most important part of his papacy, the place where he found the strength to carry on, where he could be still and silent. There was no need to pray now with any words; had not Jesus said that we should not babble on like pagans, for our Father in heaven knows what you need before you ask him? And St Paul had written that we do not know how to pray as we ought, but that very Spirit intercedes with sighs too deep for words. Too often for him, there were words, the Vatican was drowning in them. Words, important though they were, could never define or encompass or explain divine things. It was in this silence that he could feel his own presence, just as he was and not as pope, the presence of Thomas beside him, and beyond them both the presence of God.

Patrick could not sleep. Siobhan's words had troubled him, deeply. As a man, he knew so little of the other sex, of women's bodies. He knew the facts, but he sensed something dark and mysterious about them. And what could cause a woman to have so many miscarriages? He could understand her bitterness, but to turn this in favour of abortion seemed perverse. Did she secretly wish for other women to go through the pain that she had suffered?

Her words about the fate of unborn babies troubled him. Catholic teaching was uncompromising on this point, that all who depart this life without baptism are perpetually excluded from the vision of God. He knew that Siobhan would have read the 1992 *Catechism of the Catholic Church.* This made it clear that there is hope of salvation for children who have died without baptism. But, he had to admit, it was only a hope, not a certainty.

The history of church doctrine on their fate was confused. The Greek Fathers seemed to have given little thought to the fate of unbaptised children who died, which must have been common at a time when adult baptism was the norm. But of course it was not the Greek Fathers who had developed the doctrine of original sin. That was St Augustine, in countering the heretic Pelagius. It was Augustine who said that unbaptised infants were consigned to hell – for though they might have no personal sin, they all carried Adam's sin. Then, later, Abelard softened this harsh doctrine with his idea that these infants did not suffer the torments of hell, though they would not enjoy the Beatific Vision. Thomas Aquinas took this further, saying that infants who died without baptism did not know what they were deprived of, and so they did not suffer from the privation of this vision. This then led to the idea of 'limbo', the place where these infants rested for eternity.

But in the twentieth century the idea of limbo had seemed increasingly unacceptable, and at the Second Vatican Council it was decided that God does not deny the possibility of salvation to those who, without any fault of their own, do not yet have an explicit knowledge of Him. God is not limited by a physical sacrament. He can therefore give the grace of baptism without the sacrament being conferred, and this fact should be borne in mind in situations when baptism was impossible.

There were reasons for 'prayerful hope', rather than certain knowledge. But still, for the ordinary believer, there was a lack of clarity. As more and more innocent infants died as a result of abortion, no one could deny that this was becoming an urgent pastoral issue.

He rose from his bed, and drew out his diary, intending to clarify his thoughts. Could this be the subject of his first encyclical? He smoothed down the page, drew a line under his last entry. But nothing came to him. He was tired, too tired to think clearly. He would look at it again in the morning. But no, he must write something. He lifted the pen and, as he turned the page, his eye flickered upwards for a moment; he saw that Sister Veronica was standing in the doorway.

He slowly shut the diary and slipped it under some papers on his desk. The nun came a little closer. He saw her look down at the papers and did not think he had imagined that a flicker of curiosity passed across her face.

'I saw your light was on, Holy Father. I also could not sleep. I thought I would make myself an infusion. Would you like me to fetch you something to drink?'

'Thank you, I am fine. I will go back to bed now.'

With a little nod, she turned and left him. When she reached the door, he found himself calling, 'Sister Veronica?'

'Yes?' She came back towards him.

'Sister Veronica, something is puzzling me. What do you think happens to the souls of those babies who are not baptised?'

Sister Veronica smiled. 'Oh,' she said, 'They must go to God. Did our Lord say, 'Let the little children come to me, and do not stop them? Holy Father, in those days they were not baptised.'

How simple it was, for her. He thanked her and dismissed her. He stared down at the diary on his desk.

The bookshelf was not a good place to keep the diary. He thought of other places – his desk drawer, the wardrobe – but he dismissed them as too obvious. He kept nothing locked; there was no need. In the end he put it back where it was, sliding it into position between two other dark volumes, where its thin black spine would not be noticed. Where else to hide it but in full view? There was little chance that someone would find it accidentally, and no one who was looking for his diary would search for it there.

The fourth Sunday of Easter – an open-air Mass in St Peter's Square. Tight security everywhere; a helicopter flew overhead at the beginning of the service, drowning out the singing as they processed to the altar. Mercifully, it departed after twenty minutes, well before the consecration of the host; he loved the intense silence that fell as the bell rang out and he lifted up the wafer and every head in the square bowed. At this moment even the children were quiet; even they sensed that something mystical was happening.

He took his energy from the crowd; they fed and sustained him. They made him who he was; without them, he was nothing, nothing at all.

On Monday morning, Inspector General Giordano came to see him. He sat awkwardly in front of Patrick at the desk in the library; Thomas stood nearby, ready to translate if needed.

'To update you, Your Holiness. Your assailant, Siobhan Connelly, as I believe you know, is being assessed in the mental hospital. We will be awaiting the findings before we proceed with any prosecution.'

Had someone told him about his visit? 'When I spoke to her she did not seem to be mentally ill. She seemed perfectly lucid to me. She is angry and grief-stricken, not mad. If we pathologise every evil act, we are denying the human person any free will.'

'Your Holiness, forgive me, I am not here to have a theological or philosophical argument. I am here to investigate a crime and to protect you from harm.'

He could only concede this point with a silent nod. 'I simply ask that she be treated with compassion.'

'I will ensure that, Your Holiness. You asked that I keep you informed, and I am doing what you asked me.'

'Of course, I am very grateful.'

'There is another matter, Your Holiness, which we must discuss. It is important that we review security for your person. There have been a number of threats made against you from several sources.'

'Threats? Where from?'

'The Cardinal Secretary of State, his Eminence the Cardinal Romano, has passed these to me.'

'Romano? When? I have heard nothing of these threats.'

Giordano looked embarrassed. 'Perhaps His Eminence did not wish to alarm you. Occasional threats are not uncommon, Your Holiness, but this time there have been several and we cannot ignore this. At any rate, we recommend that you do not continue with the tour of St Peter's Square before the Wednesday audience and the Sunday Mass. And we suggest you have a see-through bulletproof screen in front of you on the podium.'

'Absolutely not. This is impossible. I must be able to minister to my people. I must be able to interact with the pilgrims. We cannot let ourselves be defeated by these threats.' He suspected – perhaps it was an unworthy thought, but it came to him all the same – that Romano was jealous of his rapport with the crowds and wanted to put a stop to it. 'I will not change my routine. This is my last word on the subject. I will speak to Romano at once. Now, if you will excuse me.'

As soon as Giordano had gone Patrick asked Thomas to summon Romano. He came, within the hour. He did not seem happy.

'We have, *Santità*, had numerous threats, not just against your person,' he said. 'I have just received this letter.' And he placed a piece of paper in his hands.

It was printed, in a common typeface, on one side of A4 paper.

Your Holiness,
I am a friend of Siobhan Connelly. I was present at the general audience on Wednesday. I have in my possession footage from my mobile phone which clearly shows you striking Siobhan with some force. If she is not released I will take it to the newspapers and if they do not use it I will put it on YouTube so the world can see it. In the next few days I will send a computer file to the Vatican News service. I will use a temporary email account so as to preserve my identity.

He turned the paper over. That was all. There was no name, no signature, no clue as to the sender.

'It was posted in Rome,' said Romano. 'I fear this may be part of a wider conspiracy.'

'How could anyone take this seriously? It is nonsense.'

'*Santità*, I hope so. We must ask to see the footage. It may be damaging.'

'Have you told the police?'

Romano hesitated. 'No, *Santità*, not yet. Should I?'

He hesitated. His instinct was to keep this within the Vatican. 'Can they find out who the writer is?'

'I don't know. If they do send a file, perhaps the police will be able to identify the phone. I don't know about these things. There were tens of thousands present in the square. The police cannot check them all. They can of course examine the official footage, but it is unlikely that it will be clear enough.'

'If you have seen the footage, then you will see that I have done nothing wrong.'

'Of course, *Santità*. But you know how these things are. Depending on how it is cut, depending on the angle… it may look very different. It may be very damaging.'

This was getting out of hand. 'I have said before, I do not want to bring a prosecution, in any case. The event was trivial. Neither I nor the woman were injured.'

'We cannot let it seem as if you were bribed into releasing her, that you had something to fear.'

'That is not what I meant.' He was beginning to feel ill. Why had he asked to see Romano? He looked at his watch. He had to go to see the doctor. 'Let us do nothing for now. We should wait till whoever it is sends the footage. Perhaps this is a bluff and there is no footage.'

'I do not think it wise to withhold anything from the police.'

'Very well, Your Eminence. Do as you think best.' He nearly added, 'You always do.' But fortunately he stopped himself before the words issued from his lips.

Chapter Five

The Vatican Health Centre was housed in an ugly modern building in the business sector. Patrick felt self-conscious as he approached the entrance. Would everyone be wondering why he was there, whether there was something seriously wrong with him? He was met at the door by a young nun who took him up in the lift to the second floor, walking along a series of corridors to his doctor's office. At the door she hesitated, bowing her head shyly, and then left him.

Dr Conti rose and bowed deeply as he entered. He was a small man, with short, dark hair, just beginning to go grey at the temples. He indicated a chair facing the desk and, after Patrick had sat down, sat himself in the chair opposite.

Patrick looked around the room, at a grey filing cabinet, a wall planner, a small crucifix behind Conti on the wall. Sunlight filtered in through a gauze curtain.

'Please, Your Holiness,' Dr Conti said. 'How can I help you?'

Patrick explained his symptoms.

The doctor's manner was calm and reassuring as he took some notes. 'It could be a variety of things,' he said. 'A fall in blood pressure, stress, emotional shock after what happened the other day.' He looked up from his desk. '*Heterochromia iridum*,' he said, focusing on Patrick's eyes as if he was looking at them instead of into them. 'How very interesting.'

'I'm sorry?'

'Your different-coloured eyes,' the doctor said. 'They are quite unusual.'

'So I am often told. Why do they happen?'

'You have had them since birth? Or did the colour change later? Did you have any kind of injury to the eye?'

'No, from birth, I am told.'

'Well, this can be inherited. There are other reasons, I can't say in your case, but you have had the eyes looked at?'

'I have had regular eye tests, yes, and a scan of the retina.'

'Good. That's a wise precaution. Still, that's not why you have come to me.' Dr Conti asked, a little tentatively, if he could examine him. He came around from his side of the desk and, in his smooth, professional manner, he shone a bright light into both of Patrick's eyes. He took his temperature, then he asked if he could take his blood pressure. Patrick was not used to being touched. He felt awkward as he pushed up the voluminous garments and let the doctor fit the cuff round his upper arm. The machine whirred; the pressure tightened, then released. Dr Conti removed the cuff.

'Your blood pressure is quite low – it's just within the normal range. That is quite healthy, but it could explain the fainting.'

Dr Conti remained thoughtful for a moment, looking at him. Then he asked Patrick to go behind the screen, to remove his white cassock and undergarments and sit on the couch so that he could listen to his heart and lungs with a stethoscope. Without his protective clothing Patrick no longer felt like a pope, but like a vulnerable, exposed child.

The metal disc was cold at first but slowly warmed as the doctor moved it all around his torso. When he had finished, and Patrick was fully dressed again, he went back to sit opposite the doctor.

Conti sat back in his chair and regarded him carefully. 'Any other symptoms?'

'Nothing much. Sometimes the nausea is worse than at others. I feel more tired than usual, sometimes have difficulty concentrating.'

'I can find nothing wrong with you. Most likely it's a virus. You are not overworked? You must have much to do – can you take things a little more slowly?'

'I thrive on work. And I have time for prayer and meditation, and a rest after lunch.'

'Do you sleep well?'

'Not always.' He did not want to tell the doctor about the sleeping pills he had brought with him from Ireland. It did not matter, because he had decided not to take them again.

Conti smiled, as if to reassure him. 'We'll do some blood tests and take a urine sample, just in case. After all, we can't take any risks with your health.' He paused. 'And then there is the question of the – of the unfortunate attack the other day. Is that when the symptoms started? Sometimes an event like this can be a real shock to the body.'

The blood was taken quickly and painlessly, the dark purple liquid drawn off into several tubes which the doctor labelled and laid out neatly on his desk. For the urine, the doctor gave him a little plastic cup to take into the toilet cubicle opposite the room.

'I'll let you know the results in a few days,' he said. 'It's nothing to worry about, I am certain.'

He had mislaid his mother's little cross.

He had last seen it a few days ago. He remembered that he had left it by his bed, but because of his sickness, because of the attack, he had delayed looking for it. He knew it must be there somewhere, but he could not find it. He had searched in the room, his desk, among all his things. Could someone have moved it? Sister Veronica, perhaps, or one of the people who had come to change his bedding or to clean the room? He asked but no one had seen it.

It was very small. Could it have fallen on the floor, or could someone have swept it up without noticing?

Missing the cross made him think of his mother. Three months he had been here, and hardly thought of her. She had given it to him when he was young; it had belonged to his grandmother and his mother had handed it to him as a memento after she had died.

He remembered it as a very grown-up thing. Perhaps he was about twelve. His mother, on returning from the hospital, had started weeping, and he had put his arms around her and comforted her. She had sobbed on his shoulder till his shirt was wet with tears. He remembered his anger that he had comforted her, when so often as a child she had refused to give him comfort when he needed her.

She showed him then the little plastic bag they had given her in the hospital, containing her mother's personal effects. She tipped the objects on to the table; an old lipstick, an unused handkerchief smelling faintly of a sweet, old-fashioned perfume, a rosary, and the little cross and chain. His mother held it up and dropped it into his palm.

'There,' she said. 'That is for you, to remember her by.'

It was strange that it reminded him of his mother, not his grandmother. She had given him so little, this one thing stood out.

'Look,' said Father Alfonso, coming into his office, 'There is trouble.' And he handed Patrick two letters.

Both letters were anonymous; the first sent to Alfonso, the second addressed to him as pope. Both were handwritten, in different scripts.

Reverend Monsignor, after many prayers and meditations I have decided that I must inform you of a scandal which, I believe, is shortly to break and which the Holy Father, in his role as pastor of the Universal Church, may need to be aware of. I have considered whether this is a violation of confidentiality rules, but I believe that confidentiality is about to be breached by reports that are likely to appear imminently in the press.

The situation that I have become aware of is that a certain archbishop, who I will not name at this point, was caught in a compromising situation with another senior cleric, a situation incompatible with his priestly condition. Evidence also exists that he has visited male and transsexual prostitutes here in Rome. Several people other than myself know about this and I do not think that it can be kept secret any longer.

The second letter clearly addressed the same problem.

Most Holy Father,

I have received from the Secretary of State evidence of a confidential and personal letter making unjustified and regrettable claims, which threaten to drag the name of the Holy Church through the mud. I am deeply concerned about these false claims. I do not say this just for myself, but at a time when religious practice is declining in the Western world, this is the worst possible time for such claims to be made public.

Knowing that I have always acted with fidelity and wisdom in the service of the Holy Church, please accept, Your Holiness, my feelings of profound veneration and filial devotion. I regret that I do not feel able to identify myself for fear of the unpleasant and unjustified repercussions that may result.

He dropped the letters from his hands as if they were poisoned, then watched as Alfonso bent down and picked them up.

Patrick turned to Thomas, who was standing by the window, looking at his mobile phone, appearing not to be aware of what they were discussing. Thomas came over, slipping the phone into his pocket. He read the letters and then looked up disdainfully.

Patrick asked, 'What should I do?'

'Perhaps it is best to do nothing, Holy Father.'

Father Alfonso disagreed. 'We cannot have this kind of immorality in the Church going unpunished. If it reaches the papers, and he is identified, he must go.'

'Of course. *If* it reaches the papers. This may be an empty threat.'

'You think this "are likely to" is a threat?'

'It may be. I have no idea.'

'Stop!' Patrick held up his hands to them both. 'I had better investigate this.'

Thomas was shaking his head. 'Holy Father, perhaps it is best not to get involved. Let the Secretary of State deal with it. It is better if you talk to him, and let him handle it.'

Patrick turned to Father Alfonso. 'Thomas is right. Why did you show me these letters? They have not even had the courage to identify themselves. I will not deal with idle rumours.'

'I did not want to conceal anything from you, Holy Father.' Alfonso's voice sounded cold with repressed anger.

'That does not mean I have to see every piece of tittle-tattle that is addressed to me.'

'I am sorry to have troubled you, Holy Father.' Alfonso reached out his hand to Thomas for the letters. 'I will take them.'

'No, I have them. I will do what the Holy Father commands me.'

Patrick watched as Alfonso hesitated, thinking for a moment that he might even reach out and snatch them out of Thomas's hand. But then Alfonso simply nodded. 'Very well.' He turned and, glancing at Thomas with a cold look, left the room.

What was that all about? There was something amiss between those two; that was clear.

It was impossible, this situation of homosexual priests. It was impossible to act against them, because there were so many of them. He had read absurd estimates, that as many as a third of the clergy were homosexual; he did not believe this could be true, but even if it were a small number, only two or three per cent, that was still too many. Of course, if they were celibate, this did not matter so much, but many seemed incapable of celibacy.

For many years debates had been going on within the Church as to whether homosexual men should be admitted to the priesthood.

In an ideal world, perhaps they should not be, but with the acute shortage of priests beginning to reach crisis proportions, it did not seem possible. And who was to judge if a man was homosexual if he did not admit it? It had already been decided that those who had been active homosexuals, or whose homosexuality was 'deeply seated' or who supported the 'gay culture', should not be ordained, but that of course was no help in dealing with those who already had been ordained.

He tried to examine his own feelings. Now that civil society in so many countries recognised so-called 'marriage' between two men or two women it had become much harder for the Church. Civil society had taken the moral high ground – how could love between two people who wanted to commit themselves to one another be wrong? Of course, homosexual people should be treated with compassion and mercy, as should all people. But that did not mean such relationships should be approved, let alone be raised to the status of marriage!

He tried not to imagine these people having sex. He tried not to imagine anyone having sex – it repelled him. His distaste went back to his childhood. At school, everyone had been terrified of sex, the girls especially. No adult ever spoke about it. He remembered Father Benedict took them for sex education, and his timidity and anxiety communicated itself instantly to the class. He thought about the pictures in their biology text book, which the boys pored over afterwards, when no one was watching them. He thought that they must have exaggerated the size of the male organ to make the details clearer, or that perhaps an adult penis grew to that size. All Father Benedict ever said was, 'We understand your bodies are changing, and boys' bodies are changing just like girls.' But he never explained what changes they should expect. He looked at his own body sometimes when he was lying in the bath, but it didn't seem to be changing very much, except that he was getting taller and wider and bits of him gradually rose above the water-line.

Some of the boys went behind the Marian grotto in the school grounds and he did not know what they did there. Sometimes they went alone, sometimes a girl or two would go with them. Sometimes the boys would 'date' a girl and then there would be talk of 'shifting'. He heard one of the girls saying to her friend, 'So, did you shift him, then?' He had no idea what shifting was, but he knew it was sexual – perhaps a kiss or a touch. He never had any desire to go near the girls himself.

'Holy Father?'

He started. Thomas was standing in front of him, holding the letters.

'What shall I do with them?'

'You are right. I will do nothing. Give them to the Cardinal Secretary of State, let him deal with it.'

Sunday morning; the midday Angelus prayers. The red hanging was draped from the balcony in readiness and then Patrick stepped forwards through the gauze curtains, holding up his hand in blessing. It was raining; below him was a sea of umbrellas, and when he spoke they waved and trembled in response. He heard the voices of the faithful in union with him as he prayed, 'The Angel of the Lord declared unto Mary, and she conceived of the Holy Spirit. Hail Mary, full of grace... blessed be the fruit of thy womb...'

After the prayer, he gave a brief address. The crowd waved and cheered. So many were coming to see him, he was told, that they had to restrict entry and the crowds spilled out down the Via della Conciliazione. Why did they love him? No one had loved him like this before. How could he be worthy of their adulation?

In the morning, Bianchi called him.

'I need to see you urgently. Do you have any time this morning?'

There was time in his schedule just before lunch. Bianchi came to him in the library and opened his fist to reveal a small memory stick.

'May we look at this together, in your office?'

The three of them, he, Bianchi and Thomas, crowded round the computer screen. It was the footage from the Wednesday audience, blurred, the camera unsteady. Unlike the official footage, this was taken from behind the woman, so that he could only see a mass of chestnut hair and her red shawl flying as she leapt across the barrier. His own face, however, was looking right at him. And he, like the others around him, winced when he saw the expression of ferocity on his face when he lifted his hand and struck the woman's cheek. And then there was a blur of action as the security men pushed her to the floor and ground her bleeding face into the paving stones.

No, it did not look good.

Bianchi retrieved the memory stick and said there had been no message with it. Patrick told him about the letter Romano had received earlier.

'Well, perhaps there is no need to worry. I understand that no charges are to be brought against the woman, Siobhan Connelly. She has been assessed by a psychiatrist and seems to be suffering from a severe depression. She may have had a psychotic episode.'

'But she is in hospital?'

'I understand she may travel home to be treated in Ireland.'

'What do we do then?'

'I think that we just wait. Perhaps this will come to nothing. Even if this video does get released, there may be no publicity. Not everything, Your Holiness, goes viral. We could, in any case, deny it; it is so easy to fake such footage nowadays. I think that it would not affect you seriously. It is best to ignore it.' Bianchi slipped the memory stick into his pocket.

Patrick still felt nervous. 'But the police? Should we pass this to them? Perhaps this memory stick is numbered, perhaps the file can somehow be traced?'

'Perhaps, Your Holiness, but that might draw too much attention to this. I really don't think that will be necessary. But of course I leave that to you.'

Of course; Bianchi was right. The matter was better left alone. 'Let's leave it then, unless we hear further.'

Bianchi nodded in agreement. 'I think, Your Holiness, that this is very wise.'

Thomas told him there was a phone call, from his cousin in Ireland, Mary Connelly. She was asking to speak to him.

He took the call.

'Holy Father, it is me, Mary Connelly, you remember... I hope to be sure you do not mind... It is such an honour... How proud we were to hear you had become our pope!'

He was surprised by the strength of his reaction to her voice. It reminded him acutely of home. He must have last seen Mary at a family Christmas, in his grandfather's house. He could imagine himself back there, in the dark-panelled living room, in front of a struggling fire.

The words spilled out of her, as if she was afraid she would only have a few minutes in which to say them. 'Holy Father... I am coming to Rome to see Siobhan. I am taking her home from the hospital. Of course I would like to – I completely understand if it's not possible for me to see you... you must be so busy...'

'Of course I will see you, Mary, it would be a pleasure.'

'It would be so wonderful, thank you, thank you. It is a little difficult... I can come on Ryanair, that is cheap enough, if I bring no baggage, but I have nowhere to stay. I could find a cheap hotel, but I wondered... is there some place I could stay, some hostel in the Vatican, some convent nearby... I don't want to presume, of course...'

'I will see what I can do for you. Hold on.'

He passed the phone to Thomas, who introduced himself, then said: 'We can recommend rooms in the Istituto Santissima Bambina. It's just outside the Vatican. We will arrange everything for you and I am sure you will find it very peaceful and comfortable.'

He returned to his desk. There were letters he must respond to, his encyclical to write. As soon as he started to make some notes on this, Thomas came back into his room. His face gave away that it was something troubling.

'Holy Father, I am sorry to disturb you. Dr Conti is on the phone. He says it is urgent that you should speak to him.'

Urgent? This was intolerable. Was he never to get any work done with all these interruptions? 'Very well, put the call through.'

Dr Conti's voice sounded cool and detached. 'Your Holiness, I am sorry to disturb you. I think there's been a mix-up with the blood tests. They must have crossed them over with someone else's in the laboratory. Can you come in again for me to repeat them as soon as possible? And just in case, while we are waiting… I'd like to arrange for you to have a scan.'

Chapter Six

So, it was as he feared. Something was wrong. They were worried. He had not been imagining it. Patrick felt a tight band draw across his temples. Yet – he must not be afraid. Everything was the will of God. What would unfold would unfold.

He was aware of Thomas still standing in the doorway. 'Holy Father?'

'I must see the doctor, right away.'

'Is anything wrong?'

'I hope not.'

Thomas said he would go with him and together they left the building and crossed the courtyard. Patrick did not say anything; there was nothing to say. He was acutely aware of Thomas's presence next to him; he wanted to reach out, to say something reassuring, but found that he could not. Thomas left him at the entrance and when he arrived, he was told to wait as Dr Conti was with someone. He was asked to sit for a few moments in the corridor – he, wait, whom others waited on! His nerves overwhelmed him. It was cancer, he was convinced of it. That was what he had felt these past few days, that something was invading him, taking over his body from the inside. In a few days, perhaps everything would have changed. He would not be the person he was. Would his faith alter? How would people regard him, with pity or with fear? Would they start plotting who would follow him, who would fill certain roles when he was too ill to carry on? Would they cancel events, make statements, ask for prayers? Would they expect him, as his predecessor did, to step down when he could no longer function? Or would he carry on to the end, as John Paul II had done?

He realised with complete certainty that he did not want anyone to know that he was ill. He did not want to be prayed for. He did not want pity or hope. He did not want anything, except not to be ill. He continued to pray silently.

A priest walked out of the doctor's office, seemed startled to see him, then bowed his head and walked on by. Dr Conti called him in.

'I think I should examine you again, more thoroughly,' he said. 'Will that be all right?'

'Of course.'

First, his blood pressure; the whirr of the machine and the comforting pressure of the cuff. Blood tests, the rolling up of his sleeve, the ligature around his upper arm, the sharp prick in his inner elbow. His heartbeat; his lungs; the cool stethoscope against his flesh. Then, 'Would you mind undressing and lying on the couch for me?' So calm, so professional. Hidden behind the curtain, Patrick fumbled at his robes with nervous fingers, then lay down and shut his eyes. He heard footsteps approach. He felt Dr Conti examining him, pressing his hands firmly over his abdomen. He thought he heard a sharp intake of breath. Then the doctor asked, 'Do you mind if I examine you internally?'

'You mean – for the prostate?'

'Yes, that and – let me see.'

Patrick's heart beat faster. He knew he couldn't refuse, that this would seem odd. The doctor simply wanted to help him, to make a diagnosis and then to treat him appropriately. But he could not detach himself from the feeling that these parts of himself were dirty, sinful. Of course, that should not be, he knew that. But he could not help recalling that his mother had always seemed ashamed of him and had hated to ever see him naked. For a moment he saw himself back in the bathroom in his house in Cork, shivering with cold as he stood in the bathtub, his father stepping into the room and his mother grabbing the towel and hastily wrapping it around him as if there was something she wished to cover up.

The doctor put on a plastic glove and asked him to raise his legs. He said, 'This may be a little uncomfortable, but it will not take long.' He kept his eyes firmly shut, trying to detach himself from the strange sensations. It was not painful, but uncomfortable and strange. He felt the doctor's finger pushing inside him, moving around. Then the hand was withdrawn, the doctor took off the glove, and put on another one. Perhaps the first had torn? He felt the fingers enter him again, but it felt different, this time, as if there were two places that the doctor's fingers entered, not just one.

He gasped; there was a sharp pain. The doctor apologised and withdrew his hand at once. He said, 'I'm so sorry to have hurt you. I didn't think –' and then he stopped. He stood back, snapped off his glove, and asked him to get up, to dress, and sit on the chair opposite him.

'Have you ever been examined this way before?'

'I don't think so.'

'As a child?'

'Not that I can recall.'

The doctor took off his glasses, rubbed his eyes, put them back again. Patrick's attention was drawn to a small, dark mole on his left ear.

'Well,' said the doctor, 'There are these – congenital conditions. That's why I'm surprised it's not been noticed before.' He paused. 'Have you ever had any – bleeding – from below?'

Patrick felt himself blushing, his cheeks burned hot. A shameful secret had been exposed. It was true; from time to time he had indeed noticed a dull red-brown stain on his underclothes, occasionally blood that was brighter red. He had always assumed it had come from the haemorrhoids that had sometimes troubled him. The boys at school told him that you got them if you sat too long on the hot radiators.

Dr Conti was nodding at him as he explained this. 'And did you notice any pattern to this bleeding? Was it – regular? Occasional?'

'Just now and then.'

'Every few weeks?'

'I don't know – not that often.'

The doctor frowned, then seemed to collect himself, and shuffled the papers on his desk. 'Well,' he said, 'we'll send off those blood tests. And it would be a good idea to have a scan of the abdominal area. We can do that here. Let me just check, Your Holiness. I will be back shortly.'

Patrick waited for some minutes, staring down at the backs of his hands. Then Dr Conti knocked on the door and came in, bowed again briefly.

'If you come with me.'

They walked together along the corridor to a separate room. In it were a machine with a screen on top and another couch on which he was asked to lie down. This time, he did not have to undress; he was given a thin blanket and asked to arrange his clothes so that the abdominal region was exposed. Dr Conti explained that the scan would be done externally, through the abdominal wall; there was nothing to worry about. Patrick closed his eyes again and lay back, trying to relax himself. Could it be a cancer of the prostate? Why else would the doctor want to do a scan, so quickly? He heard a clicking noise and then something cold and hard pressed against his belly. Slowly, carefully, the doctor moved it around. Every now and again Patrick heard the rattling of a keyboard and then a short 'beep'. It seemed to go on for a very long time.

Finally, it was over. Patrick sat up, and Conti passed him a paper towel to wipe the gel away. Dr Conti seemed detached, dismissive. He did not seem to want to look him in the eye.

'Well,' he said, sitting down at his desk and making some notes, 'I want to rule some things out. But please, don't worry. I don't think this is anything sinister, but I just want to be sure – after all, we can't be too careful with your health, Your Holiness.'

He knelt beside his bed and prayed.

Congenital conditions. What did Conti mean, congenital conditions? Though he knew, he had always feared, that there was something not quite right about him. When he was a child, he could tell from the way his mother handled him, the way she looked at him when he was naked – a look of pity, somehow. And he knew that he was smaller than at least many of the other boys. Once he had watched them, behind the bicycle shed at school, competing with each other to see how high they could urinate against the wall. When he saw the size of their penises he was horrified. He fled before they could follow him and ask him to join in with them.

He remembered them chasing him, catching him and trying to undo his trousers, taunting him until the teacher came and mercifully intervened. He had fled into the classroom to take shelter for the rest of the break and been punished by the teacher for disobeying instructions. He was afraid every day for the rest of the week that this episode would be repeated, but the boys seemed to take no further interest in him.

He remembered that it was only his friend, Niall, who had stood up for him. Niall, the neighbour's son he used to play with. He remembered crying in the playground after another unpleasant episode, and Niall putting his arms around him to protect him from the others. It was a long time since he had thought of this. It gave him an uncomfortable feeling, because something had gone wrong between the two of them later and he didn't know why. He had kept up with Niall for a few years after he, Patrick, became a priest, but then Niall had moved to Dublin and suddenly broken off contact.

He supposed it might have been difficult to keep an earthly friendship with someone whose main priority was God.

This incident with the boys at school must have been close to that time when his mother took him to see the doctor. He recalled her embarrassment as she left the room, and the doctor taking him into the corner, where there was a couch behind a screen, and asking him to remove his clothes. The doctor's eyes went to his genitals and looked at them for a long time. He asked permission to touch him and Patrick did not know what else to say, so he nodded his head. The doctor reached out his hand to start to examine him, but as soon as he felt the doctor's hand on his penis, Patrick, to his shame and dismay, found that he was crying, the tears wetting his cheeks and running down his nose so that he had to sniff loudly and wipe them away with the back of his hand. The doctor stopped at once, straightened up and said in a jovial voice, 'Well, nothing too wrong there, then.'

The utter shame of it. The memory made him squirm even now.

He'd dressed hurriedly and the doctor called his mother back in. He heard them talking on the other side of the screen. The doctor was saying that everyone came in different shapes and sizes and that he thought everything would be fine 'once the hormones kicked in' at adolescence.

His mother did not ever mention it again. Not then, not ever.

The Feast of the Ascension of the Lord. The altar and the priests all robed in blue. The incense and the singing rising to the heavens. Solemn prayers. These days, between the departure of the Lord and the coming of the Spirit at Pentecost, would be a time of prayer and reflection for him. He would say a Novena to the Holy Spirit. He resolved to rise early, to meditate before each morning Mass. He would reflect on what Siobhan had told him, on what he should do next.

Nothing had happened about the film footage. Security had been tightened but as Patrick insisted, the Sunday Masses and the Wednesday audiences would go ahead as usual. He felt that he had won a battle. Romano had been put in his place.

Thomas came to sit with him and have lunch together. It was a warm day, overcast and oppressive, and he had left the window open in order to feel a light breeze. All morning, since he had woken, he had felt nervy and nauseous; the fresh air helped him.

'Thomas, the Assembly of the Pontifical Council for the Family is coming up very soon. It is on the "Inviolability of the Human Person". I think this is a perfect opportunity to address the question of the fate of unbaptised babies. This is an issue that concerns me greatly.'

Thomas nodded.

'Of course, it is inconceivable that a loving God would allow the souls of unbaptised babies to perish. And yet this is not clear in doctrine. I think we need to look into this matter, with a view to making clearer guidance. After all, the position of the Church has shifted on suicide, now that we better understand the mental illness that may give rise to it. And we must understand too the pressures in the modern world that women are put under, which means that they feel they must abort their babies. Of course, the fact that so many countries have made this act legal must undermine their moral judgement.'

It was hard to concentrate. They had a simple lunch; salad, some soup, with a piece of bread. The salad leaves were very bitter.

'We must make it clear that abortion is always wrong; that is unchangeable. But we must make sure that we are more merciful to those who have abortions. And to do this, we must also look at those who lose their babies through no fault of their own. We should state more strongly that all these lost babies are full human beings, that they deserve no less dignity when they have died than any other human being.'

'I absolutely accept this,' said Thomas, dipping his bread in the olive oil and wiping it around his plate. 'But this might be difficult, in the case of very early miscarriages.'

'Please, explain.'

'Well, there is the question of how to prove that the woman was pregnant. In many early miscarriages, there is no foetus visible. And it would not be fair to require the mother to somehow collect the remains.' He paused. 'I don't know much about this, though my sister had a miscarriage. I recall that she was very upset because the remains simply went down the toilet.'

Patrick felt violently sick. It came over him without warning, like a great wave rising in him. He stood up from the table, and rushed into his rooms. He threw up violently, before he had time to reach the washbasin. He stood there, retching for a while, till the nausea subsided. In shame at what he had done, he took a towel and cleaned up the vomit from the floor.

It had been a mistake to raise this subject over lunch.

When he went back to the table, he realised he felt ravenous. How could he be sick and yet want to eat, at the same time? He chewed on a piece of plain bread.

Thomas eyed him with deep concern. 'I am sorry, I should not have spoken of this while you were eating. Are you sure you are not ill?'

'Thomas, I have been to see the doctor. They will do some tests.'

'Perhaps you should rest.'

'Come with me for a walk on the terrace. The fresh air will do me good.'

Walking on the roof terrace, high up above the Vatican, he felt better. A slight breeze blew there, stirring his hair, refreshing him.

Passing under the arches, he found a small, abandoned fledgling lying on the hard stones. It was still alive. The pathetic body made little gasping movements as it struggled to breathe, and its feathers quivered. Carefully, he picked it up and held it in the palm of his hand, wondering what he could do with it. Its little beak made gaping movements as if it hoped that he would feed it.

It was like the fledgling bird he had found once on the kitchen step when he went out in the morning to go to school. The little creature must have fallen out of the tree overhanging the wall and injured itself on the concrete slab. He'd picked it up and made a nest for it in a cardboard shoebox and put a shallow dish of water in the corner for the bird to drink. All day long at school he thought of it and he rushed home afterwards to find it still alive. He touched it gently and the bird made pathetic fluttering movements with its half-formed wings.

When his father came home he discovered the bird. He said its wing was broken and it would never fly. He took the bird outside to kill it, saying that it was a kindness, despite Patrick's anguished pleading.

Had it been a kindness? He looked now at the tiny bird. It was suffering, that was certain. He could not help it; he could not imagine himself now taking it back to his rooms and trying to keep it alive. He handed it to Thomas, who took it from him tenderly, and laid it gently on the earth in one of the large pots under the shade of an orange tree, creating a little nest for it out of some dried leaves. At least it was sheltered and no one could tread on it there. Perhaps the mother bird would find it; he could only hope so. If it was God's will, it would survive.

Thomas stood beside him and they stared at the helpless creature in silence, then turned and moved away together, side by side.

Thomas told him that Mary had arrived in Rome and was staying at the Istituto Santissima Bambina.

It was no distance from the Vatican; Patrick said he would go and see her there. He felt an urge to see her outside the Vatican apartments, somewhere away from everyone's prying eyes. The weather had suddenly turned hot, and the air hung heavily in the papal apartments; he had begun to feel suffocated. A car came to take him and they passed by St Peter's Square and then up by the sides of the colonnades, through the metal gate and up the steep road to the courtyard. The nuns had all gathered to see him and he gave them a blessing.

The Mother Superior took him up in the lift to Mary's room. It was a small, plain room with twin beds and a view out over the Vatican. Mary was standing at the far end of the room; he recognised her pale face instantly. When she saw him come in, she did not seem to know how to react, and fell to her knees in front of him.

'Come on, get up, this won't do,' he said.

'Holy Father –'

'Please, don't call me Holy Father now. I am Patrick. We are family. You don't need to stand on ceremony.'

She talked then in a torrent, her accent so familiar to him, seeming to bring with it a breath of fresh Irish air.

'You know, they say you can only be as happy as the least happy of your children. I am in despair about Siobhan. She was difficult from birth; first all the milk was wrong for her, we had to try so many things and she cried and cried for the whole of that first year, we were beside ourselves with worry, and then at school, she was so difficult at school, always in trouble, you remember that, and then there was all this grief with losing her babies. When I heard that she had attacked you –'

'She did me no harm.'

'I have prayed for a miracle. I am taking her to Lourdes. She will never get over the loss of all these babies. And now, with these mental health problems on her record, she will never be able to foster or adopt.'

'I will pray for her, Mary, be assured of that. Let us pray together, now.'

They sat opposite one another, he on the hard chair, she on the edge of the bed. It was silent in the room. She had left the window slightly open and faint sounds came up from the street and the square below. When they had finished and came back to themselves, she rose and stood there silently in front of him, and he could see and feel that she was comforted.

He turned to leave and saw her suitcase lying on the bed, and on top of it, a fine woollen shawl. His fingers reached out and touched it as he passed; the colours were so rich, shades of green, splashed with red flowers.

'It's lovely,' he said. 'These colours remind me of our grandparents' garden near Bantry Bay.'

'Ah!' she said. 'You are homesick. Please take it, as a small gift from me.' And she pressed it into his hands.

On the way out, the Mother Superior came and asked him if he would like to come up on to the roof terrace and see the view. She took him up the staircase and unlocked a heavy door and showed him proudly on to the terrace. The sunlight was so bright that he had to shade his eyes. Orange trees in large terracotta pots surrounded him; he inhaled their scent as he stepped forwards towards the railing. They were so high up that it made him dizzy; from here he could look right out over the colonnades, down into the square and over into the Vatican beyond.

'We keep it closed,' she said, 'During the Wednesday audience and the Sunday Mass. For security reasons.'

He saw exactly what she meant. Below him, he could see the whole of the top part of St Peter's Square, the steps, the great doors and, in front of them, the little dais where he sat and gave his audiences. Why did the sight of it make him feel afraid? The white chair seemed so small and far away beneath him, but the scale of the basilica was so enormous he felt that he could reach out with his hand and touch the dome itself.

He liked to walk in the gardens early in the morning and pray at the little shrine that was a replica of the one at Lourdes. Thomas and Alfonso accompanied him and as they walked they said the rosary together. This morning was cloudy but the air was soft, and he had the feeling that the sun would soon be out. He approached the rocky structure, shrouded with creepers; at the front of the cave an iron fence prevented anyone from entering, but the gate was opened for him and he passed into the cave. In front of him was the altar, and to the right, the white statue of the Virgin above him in a little niche, illuminated by a hidden light. A metal halo around her head proclaimed: 'I am the immaculate conception', the words spoken at Lourdes to Bernadette when she had her vision. A candle had been lit in front of the statue, surrounded by white flowers.

He bowed in front of her and prayed, for the souls of all those unborn children. It was impossible to think of the way these inno-cent lives were being squandered, or that they should suffer after losing their lives in this way. He prayed especially for those who had lost their babies, and for Siobhan. He prayed that through trust in God they might find comfort.

He was standing so still, deep in thought, that a little bird, perhaps not realising that he was a living thing, came down and settled at the foot of the statue, turning its head and fixing its eye on him. It was a goldfinch with a bright crimson head and the gold flash on its wings. It stayed there for a little while, regarding him with curiosity, then ruffled its wings and flew away. He felt a moment of profound connection with this brilliant little creature. It crossed his mind, for a moment, that it was the mother of the little fledgling bird.

His back ached, standing; he carefully lowered himself to kneel on the ground. Thomas knelt to the left of him, close by, and Alfonso to the right, a little further away. Thomas was so close that he could hear the little sound of his lips and tongue moving as he silently said his prayers. He looked at the pale nape of his neck, so vulnerable, beneath the tightly-curled hair.

Siobhan had never been able to bury her babies. In this, they had been of no more importance than the little bird. How could this be right? Before Vatican II, there was no Christian funeral rite for unbaptised infants and they had to be buried in unconsecrated ground. Due to the liturgical reforms after the Council, the *Roman Missal* now had a funeral Mass for a child who died before baptism, if of course their parents intended to present them. Increasingly, this had been extended to those who have suffered a miscarriage, but of course this did not often happen when babies were lost early.

In medieval times, the nature of the foetus had not been understood. It was assumed that the sperm alone carried life and that the mother merely nurtured it. It had been held by Aquinas that infants were 'ensouled' at three months for a male, at five months for a female. No one nowadays thought like this. But the magisterium of the Church had never definitively stated when ensoulment takes place – it had remained an open question. So, to be safe, each human embryo must be treated as if it were already ensouled. In that case, why should not a Christian burial be extended to include the earliest of foetuses, who are also a full human life?

He looked up at the Virgin. Her sweet face looked down at him. His stared back at her for many moments. As he gazed at her, he thought he saw a smile appear on the corners of her mouth. He looked again, but now he could see clearly that the statue did not smile. Had he imagined it? Of course, he knew statues do not really move. He looked again – but he was sure of it – she did smile. He crossed himself and knelt down on the ground in front of her. It was a sign. She intended him to act upon this. She, the blessed mother of God, was in sympathy with his desire.

Romano had asked to see him. As always, he dreaded the meeting. Romano was making more and more difficulties. It was becoming clear that he thought Patrick's election had been a mistake, that he himself should have been the next pope.

Why had they chosen Patrick instead? He had been a complete outsider. He thought back to the election, the conclave within the Sistine chapel, the cardinals walled up and shut out from the outside world. Romano had been on the list of favourites to become pope – it was known how much he wanted this; he had been currying favour with anyone who might support him. It was joked that, in the secret ballot, he would vote only for himself. This, while of course it was not meant to happen, had indeed been allowed for; Pope Paul had called for a two-thirds plus one majority to cover that very possibility. The first two ballots had produced no clear result, but on the third, Romano had been ahead, receiving twenty-seven votes to his own twenty-four. But on the fourth, only two votes separated them. On the fifth vote, Patrick pulled ahead. How ironic it was, that he himself would have preferred not to have had this role thrust upon him, while Romano who had actively sought it had failed.

Yet, did he not in truth believe that he would make a better pope? Did he not at some level secretly revel in the power he had over Romano?

Romano entered, bowed, crossed the room and kissed his ring with the excessive formality he always showed. His face seemed more severe than ever, as if a knife had carved two deep lines down his face on either side of his mouth.

'Your Holiness,' said Romano. 'There is a question I must raise with you.'

'Of course, Your Eminence.' They had already fallen out once over the security arrangements; was this what he wanted to bring up again?

Romano was waving some pieces of paper in front of him.

'I have to say, Your Holiness,' said Romano, 'That there are statements here that, while they may not be heretical in themselves, nonetheless are capable of being interpreted as such.'

Patrick found himself speechless. He looked at Romano, then at the papers. 'What is this, Your Eminence? Please, let me see?'

Romano handed him the papers. They were the rough initial thoughts on his first encyclical, a document he had only begun to work on and had not yet sent out for comment.

'But where did you get this paper? These are merely my thoughts, a very rough draft. I have not shown it to anyone.'

Romano looked confused. 'It was given to me – it was on my desk – I thought –'

'Well, perhaps you should have asked me about it before leaping to conclusions.'

'*Sua Santità*, with respect, these passages cannot stand.'

'Which passages?'

'Here, *Santità* – where you speak of God as our Mother, Christ as our Mother… where you speak of the importance of the divine feminine…'

'But this is from Julian of Norwich! It is backed up by Biblical texts, here, from Hosea… surely you know this? I have made no statement that cannot be considered to be in any way outside the teaching of the Church.'

'But this passage, *Santità*, sounds like something from a, dare I say, New Age publication.' He spat out the words 'New Age' with venom. 'It could be misinterpreted. And why this subject, now? People might think you were leaning towards allowing women priests.'

'Not at all. That question has been settled for all time by his Holiness, John Paul II. I cannot see why you are challenging me. I have had a long theological preparation. I know what I can and cannot say and stay within the bounds of orthodoxy.'

'Exactly so!' Romano pounced on this as if he had won an admission of guilt. 'You stay within the orthodoxy, but you are pushing against it. This is dangerous.'

How dare Romano speak like this, to him? But it was not wise to antagonise Romano further; he took a softer tone. 'As I said, this is simply a rough draft. It was not intended for anyone to read it at this stage. I will of course look at it again, Your Eminence, in the light of your concerns.'

Romano, too, had stepped back a little. 'Of course, *Santità*. But perhaps these little – errors, may I say? – are better left out in case they mislead the faithful who do not have the degree of theological understanding that you have.'

'Your comments will be very useful to me, I am sure. Please mark the passages you mean and return the paper to me. You have not shown it to anyone else?'

Romano admitted reluctantly that he had shared it with Cardinal Wolf, the Prefect for the Congregation of the Doctrine of the Faith.

'And he may have shared it with some others,' he added.

Patrick closed his eyes. There was more to this, he could see.

'This is not all,' said Romano. 'There have been some other statements... the homily you gave that many were deserting the Church due to a lack of feeling welcome, negative experiences, scandals, spiritual mediocrity ... these things may be true, but it is not wise to say them aloud... some have expressed unease... I have received a letter...'

He felt as if Romano's words were coming to him through a fog. He tried to break through it. 'Are you saying that people are not happy with me?'

Romano looked shocked. 'Your Holiness?'

'These... statements aside,' he said, 'I was wondering,' he said, 'If they thought, within the Curia, that on the whole, I am a good pope?'

It sounded crass as soon as he had said it. Why had he asked? Why did he feel the need to abase himself in front of a man he so disliked? Romano's eyes looked straight into his and did not blink.

'Of course,' he answered. 'Why do you think you must ask?'

It was like a game of cat and mouse, he thought, and Romano was the cat. He could almost feel those retracted claws.

A letter came from his mother.

It lay on the table in front of him, in a pale blue airmail envelope. He was surprised that these were still available; perhaps she, who never threw anything away, had some secret stash of them. His mother never used email; she had a fear of anything modern. He hesitated before opening the letter. He knew she tried to be positive, and always began and ended with statements about how proud she was of him and how she prayed for him daily. But in between, in her letters, there was a litany of complaint. About how sore she was and so stiff with her arthritis, and how cold the weather was, and how she seldom saw people these days, and how everything was very dull, as always.

His mother had never been a happy woman. His first clear memory of her, like a faded photograph, was her standing at the window with her back to him. In his memory, he was calling out to her but she did not turn. It was the feeling in this early memory that had stayed with him, the feeling of abandonment. It was raining outside, and the window-pane was wet and streaked with droplets. And then she did turn, and her face was wet with tears, and a drop of water ran down her cheek as if it was reflected in a mirror or the rain had come through the window and splashed her face.

His mother had encouraged him to pray. The house was full of religious pictures and artefacts. The picture of Jesus with the sacred heart hung on the wall above the fireplace, a picture that both repelled and fascinated him. The eyes used to stare at him no matter where he went to stand in the room and seemed to reproach him with their piercing gaze. He knew that everything he did wrong, all his flaws, offended Jesus, and yet he did not know how he could change the way he was – he could not stop his feelings, even if he tried not to act on them. Every night his mother said the rosary and showed him how to say it, too. It was a moment when he felt close to her, sitting next to her on the side of the bed with her attention fully on him as he copied her words and counted the warm beads through his fingers.

He picked up the paper knife and sliced along the top of the envelope, then scanned his eyes rapidly over the page. She was anxious about the assault on him, which she had read about in the papers. Was he really unhurt? It must have been a terrible shock to him. And they said it was Siobhan. Siobhan! She had always been a wayward child. What would they do with her? She hoped they would not keep her in prison; it was her opinion that she was a little touched in the head and that prison would be the worst place for her. Mary had come to Rome to try to bring her back. Had he seen Mary? She had not been in touch, that was thoughtless of her.

His father had not been so well. They had been for tests, it might be his heart. It was difficult for her to cope with him. His father spoke of him often and wished it would be possible for them to come to Rome and see him. Perhaps they could come in the summer.

She signed, 'Your loving mother.'

He put the letter down on the desk in front of him. He thought of how in the evenings she would come to say goodnight but seldom came to sit beside him when he was in bed. Usually she did not stay long, except when he was ill. He used to like those illnesses, when he was excused from school and could stay in bed and feel her maternal care. On one occasion she made him comfortable with the pillows, gave him a hot-water bottle and a spoonful of sticky medicine, and smoothed down his hair, then gave him a little book. On each right-hand page there were coloured pictures, and on the left the words. 'Let me read it to you,' she said. It was called: *Jesus the Helper*.

He could see it now. The first picture showed a man with a brown beard and another man bent on the ground, next to what looked like a stone fountain. The man was ill, his mother said. Jesus was going to make him better.

'Can He make me better, too?' he had asked her.

'I expect He can,' his mother said, 'if you ask Him to.'

'How can I ask Him when He's in the book?'

'He isn't just in the book,' his mother said. 'He can be in our hearts too, if we want Him to be.'

It was strange to think of Jesus being in his heart; he was not sure that he wanted Him there. Was this a bad thought? He imagined the picture of Jesus in the living room downstairs, His hands held out from his chest, which had been torn open to display the red, flaming heart. It was easier for him to think of being in Jesus' heart than to think of Jesus being in his.

'And we can talk to him whenever we like. We just say, "Dear Lord Jesus…"'

He shut his eyes and listened to her prayer. He remembered the softness of her voice, and the feeling of being close to her, closer than he'd felt at any other time.

He folded up her letter and placed it in the drawer. He responded to her with a simple card. 'I am very well. I was not injured at all, and have been to see Siobhan, and Mary when she came. I will pray for Siobhan and hope that the authorities will be merciful towards her, and I will pray for Mary and all the family. Give my love to Father. I hold you both in my thoughts and prayers.'

That night, he lay for many hours between sleep and wakefulness. Fragments of the past came back to him as in a dream. He was an altar boy. Aged ten, he had a black cassock and a white surplice, the ornate over-garment that he remembered his mother pressing with a hot iron in the kitchen, sometimes late on a Saturday night. He remembered how long it took her to iron all the folds and corners, and the steam rising in the cold winter air. It had seemed then such a great responsibility. She told him he must set an example to the congregation by looking alert, making the responses and sitting or standing at all the right times. Sometimes he would carry the cross or the candles, and sometimes he was boat boy, carrying the incense boat so that the thurible could be topped up. He adored the smell of incense and used to open his mouth, like a fish, to gulp in the coils of smoke as they rose up towards heaven. Once the priest had seen him doing this and glared at him fiercely, so he tried to do it surreptitiously, when people's heads were bowed in prayer.

Before the service he rinsed the cruets with clean water before filling them with wine and water and placing everything carefully on the serving table. The bit that he'd liked best was when he rang the bells at communion three times to mark the moment when the bread and wine were mystically transformed into the body and the blood. The sound, thin and clear, used to send shivers up his spine.

He remembered, too, his fear that he would make an error – not just the small mistakes that he did make, that only the priest would notice, but a major error – tripping over the hem of a cassock and going flying, or dropping the paten dish during communion. Mercifully none of these things ever happened, and in time he became less nervous about them. And yet it had happened to him now, as pope, fainting at Mass before the whole world! But this time it was different – no one could now chastise him for it.

He saw the priest's house, the dark entrance and the huge stretch of parquet flooring, the dark mahogany banisters, the study piled high with books and papers and the window looking out over the garden, where it seemed in his memory to be perpetually raining, with drops falling from the big cedar tree. The priest kept a box of sweets on his desk in a tin with a picture of a snow-scene with reindeer and a sleigh, and he used to get it out and offer him one while he talked to his mother. He thought that he too would like to be a priest so that he could live in such a big house.

Then there were the nuns behind the grille in the convent, who kept up the perpetual adoration of the sacred heart. The nuns in their brown habits were white and unwrinkled as if the cares of the world had never touched them. It made them special, holy. He saw the monstrance on the altar and the absolute stillness of the nuns as they gazed upon it, their faces full of peace. The nuns did healings, too. He never doubted for a moment the power of the nuns to cure people. There were other healers, too, in the community, and a holy well with waters that were said to cure eczema, warts and other ailments.

His mother took him there when he was ill in preference to the doctor. He remembered her taking him when he was about thirteen, and he'd had a little bleeding down below. He was too frightened of it to tell his mother, but she must have found some staining on his underpants. She said nothing to him, but took him to the convent where prayers were said. After that, the bleeding stopped.

It was at the same time that all of Ireland was gripped by the Kerry Babies case. Every day he heard the sound of the radio in the kitchen as his mother cooked supper. A baby boy with multiple stab wounds had been found on White Strand in Cahirciveen, and a local girl, Joanne Hayes, who had been pregnant by a married man, confessed to the murder together with her family. But then they withdrew their confession and admitted that Joanne's baby had been born on the farm and died shortly after birth, and had been buried there.

They dug on the farm and found the body of a baby. Tests showed that while this baby had the same blood group as Hayes, the baby on the beach didn't. The only possible way that it could have been hers was if Hayes had become pregnant with twins simultaneously fathered by two different men, and had given birth to both children. Despite the improbability of this happening, rather than admit they had been wrong, the Gardaí insisted that this was the case.

Later, Patrick remembered, the judge threw this out, and the pathologist couldn't prove that Joanne had smothered her baby so she was cleared of its murder. The murder of the first baby was never solved.

People talked about it everywhere, at school, on the streets; his parents discussed it day after day. It was astonishing how many people believed in the story of twins by different fathers. A radio report he heard talked about the strange phenomenon of *heteropaternal superfecundation*. Even after the judge had dismissed this possibility, people still seemed to want to believe it.

One night a row broke out between his parents. He heard their raised voices from the living room below and crept to the top of the stairs, pressing his face against the bannisters.

'You would rather believe anything than that the girl was innocent!' his mother's voice was saying. 'Why does everyone have it in for her? She didn't have an immaculate conception, did she? It was a man that got her pregnant!'

'She was carrying on with a married man, they say,' his father said. 'She was hardly an innocent.'

'But to have had two babies like that, by different men, as they are saying! It's ridiculous. Why should the baby they found on the strand have anything to do with her? I don't understand it.'

'And why are you,' he heard his father say, 'so determined to defend her?'

'I just don't see,' shouted his mother, 'why they cannot just leave the poor girl alone!'

The door downstairs slammed shut and he could no longer hear their words. He sat on the top step and listened to their distant, angry voices, trying to work out his own thoughts. He recalled a vague, uncomfortable feeling of fear, followed by relief that he, as a boy, could never fall pregnant, and would never have to confront the choice the girl had faced.

Chapter Seven

Sunday 15 May. Pentecost. The coming of the Holy Spirit. The altar clothed in flaming red. A solemn Mass at St Peter's. The sun pouring down outside with all the fierce heat of flame.

Dr Conti had told him they would have the results of the tests on Tuesday and had made an appointment for midday. When he arrived at the health centre, a young nun escorted him along the corridor, to a different room, the other side of the building. The door to the doctor's room was open; he hesitated before going in.

The room was large, plain, with little furniture, the tiled floor creating an impression of hardness. The sun shone in through slatted blinds. Above the desk, on the wall, he noticed a carved wooden crucifix, which looked oddly out of place in the functional environment.

There were two doctors sitting behind the desk, Dr Conti, and another, older man, wearing a dark suit. They were looking at a file, his notes perhaps. When he entered, they both rose to their feet and bowed to him. Dr Conti came forward, and introduced the second man as Professor Moretti. He was tall and elegant and middle-aged, with hair so black that Patrick thought it must have been dyed. He did not like the look of him; he seemed like a man who had too much self-regard.

'Professor Moretti is based at the Salvator Mundi International Hospital. He has examined the scans. I trust Your Holiness will not mind him taking part in the consultation? He will be able to explain things more clearly than I can.'

Patrick nodded his head. 'Of course.' The hard floor seemed to shift very slightly beneath him, as if he was on a ship; he knew this could not be good. They had found something wrong. If it was something trivial, they would not need to involve a specialist. He lowered himself carefully into the chair, placed his hands in his lap, and said a short internal prayer as he prepared himself. 'Lord, let it be to thee according to thy will.'

'Well.' Moretti took an audible breath before speaking. 'You have a very unusual condition... it occurs in only something like one in eighty-three thousand births. Let me say straightaway that it is not, in itself, life-threatening. You may be reassured about that. But it is... serious and a little... complicated.'

'I see.' Not life-threatening. He felt his hands, which he now realised had been clenched into tight fists, relax a little. But what could be so serious and yet not life-threatening? And had he not qualified it, 'in itself'? What could that mean?

Moretti continued to explain. 'We have carried out the blood tests and looked at the white blood cells. We found certain... unusual features, and so we decided to examine the chromosomes. We found two types of cells. About half the cells were, as we would expect, XY – that is to say, they are male. But the other half were XX – that is to say, female.'

'I'm sorry. I'm not following you. You mean – I have someone else's blood?' He tried to think back to whether he had ever had a blood transfusion, but he could not remember; he was sure he would remember this, unless he had been very young? His mother had said it was a difficult birth; could he have received one then, as a baby, without him ever having been told of it?

Professor Moretti cleared his throat. 'No, no, the cells are yours. We have the karyotypes here if you want to look at them.'

He felt irritated. What on earth was a karyotype? Why could these doctors not put things into words that could be understood? But he did not like to reveal his ignorance, so he sat still, waiting for the doctor to continue. Probably it would soon become clear. After a brief pause, Moretti carried on. 'Let me explain about the other tests. Here is the scan *Dottore* Conti made of your abdominal region.' The consultant opened his file, and took out a large sheet of photographic paper, which he stared at himself for a few seconds. Then he pushed the blurry, black-and-white image across the desk.

Patrick picked it up and stared at it without being able to make sense of anything at all. It was cloudy, opaque, a mass of vague shadows. He laid the image back down on the desk. The consultant leaned forward and, using his slender silver pen, began to point out various features. 'Here we have, quite clearly, a testis on the right-hand side. You may have been told the testis on the left-hand side was undescended – I cannot understand why nothing was ever done about this in your childhood. We are not quite sure what happened here, because your medical records seem to be incomplete, they do not mention this. But in fact we have discovered that here, on the left-hand side, you do not have a testis at all. Instead, you have an – ovary.'

The blurred shapes seemed to make no sense as they were pointed out to him. And yet he could see, vaguely. But the words did not make any sense. 'An *ovary?*'

'I'm sorry, I realise that this is a shock.' The doctor paused and took a deep breath. 'What it seems to be is this. You are a very rare individual, what we call a genetic chimera. What is most likely is that there were two embryos, fraternal twins, which fused at a very early stage. As I said, it is extremely rare. The resulting cells form a single embryo, which goes on to develop more-or-less normally, but with some cells and organs deriving from one embryo, others from the second.'

Dr Conti spoke. 'There is another possibility. Your mother's egg could have been fertilised by two different sperm at the same time. When the egg is fertilised, a sudden change comes over the surface of the cell membrane, normally preventing a second sperm from entering. But if two were to penetrate at the exact same moment... If we do more tests, perhaps we will be able to determine this.'

He was utterly bewildered. He felt a sense of complete unreality, that this could not be happening to him. What was the doctor implying? He thought at once of the Kerry Babies case, of that strange term they had used then, *heteropaternal superfecundation*. He said, 'You mean I had a twin? You mean – that we have two different fathers?'

'No, no, not at all. There is no twin. As I said, in this circumstance only one embryo would have developed. And the sperm would almost certainly have had to come from the same father. What you are speaking of – well, that is even more rare. There have been perhaps ten or twelve documented cases. For this, it would be necessary for the mother to have had sex with two men very close together, the same day, perhaps. I do not think that we need to even consider this in your case?'

He felt his face blushing red. His mother – it was impossible. He shook his head.

'To continue. Each sperm, like each egg, is unique, with a more-or-less random assortment of the father's genetic material. Had both sperm been male, or both female, possibly no one would ever have known, unless you developed a condition that meant your cells would have been analysed, as we have done now.'

'I still don't understand.' The doctor's words seemed to pass through his mind like a liquid, without him being able to grasp or hold them. He reached wildly around for some kind of understanding. 'Please, can you make this clear. You are saying something went wrong with the embryo, and I have some female cells?'

Professor Moretti twirled his silver pen in his fingers. 'No, it is more than that. You are in fact a mixture of two embryos, one male, one female.'

'Like some kind of – Siamese twin?'

'No, in fact, the opposite. A conjoined twin results when an embryo starts to divide, but does not separate completely. You are probably formed from two embryos which fused.'

He realised his hands were shaking and folded them firmly in his lap. He must try to understand. 'You are telling me I am some kind of – hermaphrodite?'

Professor Moretti made a gesture of dismissal. 'We do not use this term any more. We speak of an intersex condition, a disorder of sexual development.'

The words were shocking, like a blow to his body. Intersex. Disorder. He wanted to reject them, throw them back in the professor's face. How dare they use these words, to him? He struggled to calm himself, to say something reasonable.

'And this condition is somehow making me ill?' He thought perhaps these different cells might be attacking one another in some way, as in some kind of auto-immune condition.

Moretti glanced at Conti, and then looked back at him again. 'Well, not exactly, not in itself. But – look at the scan again. As well as an ovary, you have a womb – here it is. There is the cervix here, and here, the vagina. The fallopian tube on this side, it seems to be intact, though there is none on the other side, the womb is a little misshapen, here... We will need to do more tests. I think that, for today, you have had enough to consider. We suggest we make an appointment for you to come back in a few days, once you have had time to reflect on what we have told you.'

Patrick looked at the scan. Among the blurred shapes, where they had pointed out to him the 'womb', he thought he could see something, a mass in the centre. So, it was as he had feared; a tumour, a cancer, a malignancy.

He could not wait a few days. 'I insist on knowing everything, now. There is something here – I can see quite clearly. Is it cancer?'

They seemed startled by this, and immediately sought to reassure him. 'Your Holiness, please do not trouble yourself about that possibility. We can assure you that it is not cancer.'

'Well, then, if not cancer, what is this?' And he pointed to the scan. The doctors seemed confused, exchanging glances with one another.

An ice-cold feeling of clarity took hold of him. 'I insist, I command you to tell me everything you know. I will not have you keep things from me. It is my body, and I have the right to know.'

Moretti took a deep breath. 'Your Holiness, it is true – there is something in your uterus. It is not a tumour, you don't need to worry about that – instead it is – a foetus.'

Had he heard them properly? 'A what?'

'A developing baby.'

He watched as the two doctors looked at one another, as if not knowing what to say next; it was Dr Conti who then spoke. 'Holy Father, it seems that you are – pregnant.'

What had he said? Pregnant? What did that mean? A baby? Here, in him? It could not be. The words made no sense; it was as if the doctor had addressed him in some foreign language. He stared at them; they must both have taken leave of their senses. Why would they say this? Was it a cruel joke, played perhaps by people who had sympathy with the abortionists? Perhaps he had been set up, taken in completely by them. But he was the pope. Could anyone really play a hoax like this? Could they dare? Perhaps there were abortionists who were so deluded that they could come up with such a scheme to convince him that he was pregnant to see what he would do, how he would react.

He felt the anger rising inside him in a wave of heat. The heat went on rising, lifting him with it, and he felt as if he was no longer in his body, but somewhere else in the room, looking at the scene from outside. He saw himself in his white garment, the two doctors, staring at him, and the top of the wooden desk, on which the scan was laid out at a strange angle. He saw the crucifix on the wall tilting forward in an odd perspective, as in Dali's famous painting, *Christ of St John of the Cross*. The sensation only lasted for a few moments, but he had to put his hand out to grab the edge of the desk to steady himself as he tried to rise to his feet. He could not stand up; his legs would not support him. He realised that he was no longer sitting on the chair, but on the floor, and they were rushing round to come to his aid.

'I am sorry, Your Holiness. This is an immense shock. There was no easy way to tell you this. Would you like me to –'

He felt the hard pressure of the chair against his cheek. He was leaning awkwardly against it, and a sound filled his ears, a buzzing like a swarm of bees.

The two doctors fussed around him; he couldn't stand it. 'Leave me alone!' he shouted. 'Get away from me! I demand to see another doctor! Who sent you here, whose idea was this – it is – insupportable! How could I possibly have become pregnant?'

The doctors backed off at once, and stood, staring at him. With difficultly, he raised himself up and sat back in his chair. His breath was coming in uneven gasps; he made himself take deep breaths, tried to recollect who he was, maintain the dignity of his office.

'This is ridiculous. The scans must have been swapped in error. The blood tests... they could have been mixed up.'

Dr Conti looked alarmed. 'Your Holiness, that's not possible. We have checked. And you must remember – it was me who did the scan.'

'But you said nothing! You must have seen it then, if there was anything to see!'

'At first, like you, I could not take it in, just as you are struggling now, Your Holiness. It seemed absurd, impossible. I wanted to be absolutely sure before I told you; make sure there was no possibility of mistake. I wanted to wait to see the other results.'

Patrick felt calmer now; the shock was abating. He realised at once the need for absolute secrecy while he worked out what to do. 'Does anyone else know of this?'

The two doctors looked at one another. 'No, Your Holiness.'

'But what about the scans – they must be on file somewhere.' He tried to work out what should be done. 'They are my property. They must be destroyed.'

'The scans are here. This has all been kept within the building. Your medical records are confidential, we have them here under your birth name, Patrick O'Sullivan. It is not an uncommon name.'

'It is uncommon in Italy.'

'We have many Irish tourists here in Rome.'

He could not believe that he was having this conversation. Here he was, faced with this devastating news or deception, and they were talking to him about Irish tourists!

He forced himself to keep his temper, to stay silent. He must be very careful. He must let them think that he believed them. 'You must be sworn to absolute secrecy.'

'But this goes without saying, Your Holiness. All doctors must respect medical confidentiality.'

'That does not go far enough for me. Are you both Catholics? Do you have a Bible? You must swear on it at once, to me, now.'

Professor Moretti looked at Dr Conti and nodded. He said, 'I will ask someone to fetch one,' and went out. Dr Conti sat silently and stared out of the window for a few minutes, till the professor returned. They both looked at him with what seemed like pity.

Patrick could not stand it. He thought he knew what they must be thinking. He said, in a sudden outburst, 'Even if this genetic condition is as you say, this is impossible. There is no way that I could have become pregnant. I have never broken my vow of celibacy.'

Dr Conti cleared his throat. 'Well, one thing that was clear when I examined you – there was a hymen, and it was intact. So, this means that technically at least, you are a virgin. This is not absolutely conclusive, of course – there have been examples of women who have got pregnant without full penetration. If sperm are deposited at the entrance to the vagina, it is possible for some to ascend into the womb. I was involved, myself, as an expert witness in a legal case about this, a question of an annulment on grounds of non-consummation in a couple who had a child. A DNA test was done; the child was indisputably his. And yet both husband and wife swore that he had never penetrated her. But, of course, this scenario is most unlikely in your case, and you have said it is not possible, so… we must take into account the possibility of self-insemination.'

'We would like to do more tests,' said Moretti smoothly. 'It is extremely unlikely that both ovary and testis could function at the same time; I would have thought that if you produced enough hormones to ovulate, that would prevent sperm production, but it *may* be possible,' he said. 'We think it wise to do a biopsy of the testis to see if there is any evidence of spermatogenesis.'

Patrick thought that if he heard any more medical terms he would go mad. They were still talking to one another about him as if he wasn't there.

'Could this be possible?' said Dr Conti in a low voice.

'I have searched the medical literature and I don't believe there is any recorded case where this has happened,' said Moretti, equally softly. 'I would doubt very much if it is possible. But we should do a biopsy to be certain.'

Patrick slammed his hand down on the edge of the desk. 'I do not want any biopsies done! I am not an experimental animal!'

Moretti's voice was soothing. 'Of course, Your Holiness, this is up to you. But the results might have a bearing on what you decide.'

'I don't follow.'

'I mean – if it were possible that you have fertilised yourself, it would have implications for the – foetus.'

'Implications? What do you mean?'

Someone knocked at the door and Moretti answered it; he came back in, holding a large black Bible. He carried it in front of him away from his body, as if it was a strange and foreign object. Dr Conti spoke to him briefly in Italian and the consultant sat down beside him again. He leaned forward across the desk.

'Dr Conti has asked me to explain something to you. Every individual carries a number of faulty genes. Usually these are what we call recessive, that is, they do not show if there is only one copy of them. If this is paired with one normal gene, that is enough to prevent the faulty gene being expressed. However, in cases of in-breeding, there is a much stronger likelihood of inheriting two faulty genes. That is perhaps behind the fact that there has always been an incest taboo.'

'So we are very concerned,' Dr Conti said, 'that this might happen here.'

'In these circumstances,' said Moretti, 'many would recommend an abortion. On purely medical grounds, you understand.'

'Indeed,' said Dr Conti. 'And there is your own health to consider. At fifty-five, you are at the very upper limit for natural fertility. At your age – well, a pregnancy is riskier. And even riskier with this condition.'

Patrick felt as if someone had suddenly poured a bucket of cold water over him. It was as if he had been jolted awake. He thought he saw now where this was leading, and why. They were playing some bizarre, elaborate hoax on him, to test him and see how he would react to this news. To see if he would fall into their trap.

Nevertheless he would swear them to secrecy. He put out his hand and reached for the heavy Bible, offering it to each of them in turn. When they had sworn on it, repeating the words after him, pledging total loyalty, Moretti spoke again.

'Your Holiness, we think that, when this news has settled, when you have had time to reflect, you should see us again. In the meantime, take this.' He handed him the scan. 'You can take this away and consider it in private. It may help to clarify your thoughts.'

He could not reply. He took the grainy black-and-white image and stood up, walking to the window so the light fell on it, hoping the image would become sharper. But he could make out nothing clearly. Was it only because he expected to see it that he could make out what might be a head, body, limbs? He stared out of the window, along the red-tiled rooftops.

'You don't have to decide on anything at once, Your Holiness. You can take a few days and then come back and discuss it with me. You can call me whenever you like.'

'This is enough,' said Patrick, wishing only to be out of there, overwhelmed now with an immense weariness. 'This has taken up enough time. I have urgent things to do.'

'But you can't wait too long,' said Conti, 'if you want to act. This is important. We think that you should also seek some counselling. You can then talk over your options, in complete confidentiality. And then there are the tests that should be done.'

'What tests?'

Moretti spoke as if he was addressing an inattentive child. 'As I said before, to see if there is anything wrong with the baby. We have analysed your blood tests, and everything looks normal in those. We can do some scans. At eleven to fourteen weeks, we can do a test where we take cells from the placenta, which is made from the same tissue as the embryo. This will show if there is any genetic abnormality.' He paused. 'I should inform you that there is a small risk of it causing a termination, something in the order of one to two per cent.' He paused. 'We can arrange everything for you.'

The shock was fading now, to be replaced with a cold, clear anger. 'You may spare yourselves the trouble. I don't want these tests.'

'I'm sorry?'

'You may spare yourselves the trouble. If what you say is true, I would in any case continue with the pregnancy.'

'Of course, Your Holiness. But many people who wish to do this still want the tests, so that they can prepare themselves.'

'Not if there is any risk to the baby.'

'We highly recommend them.'

'Well, I am sorry. I will not take your recommendation.' He stood up and walked, a little unsteadily, to the door.

Dr Conti rushed to assist him, but he pushed his hand away. Conti hovered, awkward, at his side.

He turned to Conti. 'Leave me! You are forgetting who I am.'

'But with respect, Your Holiness, that is not the case. Believe me, we have thought of almost nothing else.'

Chapter Eight

He stood at the window in his bedchamber. He had no recollection of getting back to his rooms; he knew that he must have left the medical centre, walked across the Vatican streets and back to his apartments, but it was as if this had happened to him in a dream. He was not sure whether what had happened was real or a strange delusion of some sort. A strange chill seemed to have come over him; he was shivering and could not keep his hands still.

He went into the bathroom, ran warm water and splashed his face with it. He stared at his wet, dripping face in the mirror. The eyes stared back at him, one hazel-brown, the other blue. Of course, he had always known it. There was a reason why his eyes were different colours. There was something profoundly and fundamentally wrong with him. He was a freak of nature. He knew that these things happened, of course. There was always a scientific explanation for them. Once, when he was a young priest, he had been asked to visit conjoined twins who had been born some years before in the neighbourhood. They were joined at the skull, the tops of their heads fused in such a way that they had to bend over like an arch facing one another, looking down at the floor. It was not possible medically to separate them. And these two boys fought with one another! Their mother was in despair. He remembered the revulsion, the nausea he had felt when he saw them, like some hideous image in a fairground distorting mirror. What use was a God who allowed this?

At least, in the order of freaks of nature, his own condition was not so bad. He was not disabled. It was not clear to others that there was something wrong. His mind was not affected.

He tried to calm himself, to work out exactly what they had said to him. He knew little about medicine or science. They could have completely bamboozled him. Of course, he knew that there were intersex conditions. He had never wanted to know too much about them; there was something deeply distasteful about the whole issue. He had felt nothing but pity for such people, and understood that they needed surgery and sometimes hormones to correct their gender, to make them either male or female. But then there were the people who had decided that they had the wrong gender, the transsexuals. While he felt pity for their psychological problems, he had always thought that people should accept who they are, not want to disfigure their bodies and mutilate themselves with sex-change operations. The Church was clear that this went against the will of God.

But he was one of these people. He, who had always believed himself to be a man, was not a man. Or not a proper man. How could he live with himself? How could he continue as he was? Only a man could be a priest, only a man could be pope.

But even this was not the main problem. He was celibate, he did not want to have sex; if he had this intersex condition it might be bizarre, but it was of no real consequence to him. The problem was if it was true that he was pregnant. Pregnant and a virgin, as they had said.

If this is true, he thought, my life as I knew it is over. I am now responsible for another life. Nothing else matters. How could this have come about?

He went back into his office, stood in front of the icon of the Virgin and Child.

It must be a miracle. He had been chosen for a miracle.

But what could it mean? And why, then, was he not filled with joy? Why did he instead feel this terror? Was it possible that it was not a miracle, but a dreadful mistake? Was Romano right, that all along he had been the wrong choice? Though had they not been guided by the Holy Spirit?

Perhaps it was not true; perhaps it was indeed a hoax. He would have to be sure, to get some independent verification. He could do nothing until he was sure. But how to do this?

He'd told Thomas to cancel all his appointments and now there was nothing for him to do. He knelt in prayer, but could find no peace. Instead, another thought had come to him. What could it mean for him to be both male and female? He had argued many times from Scripture that: 'God created man in his own image... male and female he created them' and that 'Man and woman bear the image and likeness of God not only as individuals, but also together.' This was the true meaning of marriage. In giving of themselves one to another, the husband and wife reflected and embodied the self-giving of God within the Holy Trinity.

In the modern world – he had spoken in his homily only the other day – there are many who aim to annul sexual differences. But he had argued that removing this difference created a great problem for contemporary society, a problem that went against God's plan for humanity.

But if *he* was a mixture of man and woman, in one body, how did this fit in with God's plan? Did it annul every statement, everything that he had said? This was more than a crisis. What could it mean? He was a theologian. He must make theological sense of what this meant. But – he must not let his mind run away from him. He was upset, this was not the time to think about this matter. He must not just assume this was a miracle, he must first explore all of the more rational possibilities.

He returned to his bedchamber, went into the bathroom, and locked the door. He leaned against it for a moment, feeling the hard wood against his cheek, bringing him back to reality. He pulled up his robes, removed his underwear and bent over, trying to examine his genitals. It was hard to see; his back hurt with bending. On the shelf above the basin was a little shaving mirror; he took it down and angled it between his legs, trying to see more clearly.

He had never looked at himself before; the thought of it was shameful. To look at his genitals, he had always thought, might lead to sinful thoughts. It might lead to the erections or wet dreams which the other boys had spoken of at school. Well, he must look at himself now, to ascertain the truth.

On the underside of his penis, which was perfectly formed and as neat as that on a Greek statue, there was a strange line on the skin. It ran down to the bulging scrotum on the right-hand side, and then into a deep crevice that ran back towards the anus. On the left-hand side, under the fuzz of pubic hair, he could see a raised lip that ran along the side of the crack. The two sides were not symmetrical; that was clear. But was there a hole? It was hard to tell.

He put his hands to the crack and pulled apart the skin. There was a gap between the folds of skin, but he could not see into it. A faint musky smell came from it; he was aware of his disgust, even as he tried to rationalise it away. The body was the temple of the spirit; so how could it be so messy, so malodorous? He put out his forefinger and tentatively pushed it into the warm, damp flesh. There was resistance; he tried another angle. Yes, there was an opening. His finger slid in easily; it did not hurt, but he was afraid to explore further. How could he know from touch whether it led into a blind alley or went on into the – he could not even bear to name it.

So, it was true, he could see it with his own eyes. He was as they said, half-man, half-woman.

He thought of the words of St Paul in Galatians 3:28, 'There is no longer male and female; for all of you are one in Christ Jesus.'

He got to his feet, arranged his clothes, and washed his hands. Even after he had washed them, he thought he could still detect that strange, pungent scent on his finger.

He went to the chapel, took a candle from the rack, and stood before the statue of the Virgin. When he put the match to the red wick, the wax melted and formed a little stain like blood on the white surface. He watched the flame flutter and hiss before starting to burn steadily; he placed the candle carefully on the metal stand. Usually it was a comfort, to hand over his worries and his prayers to the Virgin and release himself from them, but today he could not calm himself. He went over and over the conversation with the doctors, trying to make sense of it. They had said it was not possible for him to fertilise himself, that there had been no recorded case in the medical literature. He knew that he had not had sex with anyone. His pregnancy must be, therefore, a miracle.

It would not be easy to declare a miracle. He could not just declare it himself. If a miracle was to be recognised by the Church, careful research had to be undertaken to make sure that every natural explanation had been dismissed. This was what happened when a Vatican-appointed Miracle Commission sifted through the hundreds of miraculous claims that were received. Theologians and scientific experts examined all the evidence. Nearly all these miracles were examples of spontaneous, instantaneous and complete healing. Doctors and medical experts would have to conclude that there was no natural explanation for what had happened. A woman, for instance, whose breast cancer was suddenly cured wouldn't qualify if she had been given a small percentage chance of survival – she would need to have been told there was no chance of survival at all before any divine intervention could be accepted.

He thought of what declaring a miracle in this instance would involve. First, they would want to be sure that he had been celibate. They would be interviewing everyone who knew him, members of the papal household. He felt humiliated at the thought. They would ultimately have to take his word on this. But still, they had said he was a virgin. That was only a technical matter; you could have sexual relations and still retain the hymen, that was clear from what they had said. No, even though he knew he had nothing to hide, he could not bear the thought of people prying into this with other members of the papal household.

And they would, of course, want to find out whether he might have been able to inseminate himself. It might be possible – just because it had not happened before did not mean that it could not happen now. He remembered the nights when he'd had those erotic dreams. It was shameful. He could not bear to think about it, let alone discuss it with others.

He determined to look coldly at the evidence, to do the work that they would do. Firstly, he needed to be sure that he really was with child, that they were not mistaken or lying to him. That would be easy enough to do. Yes, he had seen the scans. But the scans could have been faked. They could be someone else's. This was a more likely explanation than a miracle of this order. What the doctors said was surely impossible; it could not happen. He would find another doctor, someone he chose on his own who could not be part of this plot.

He could not risk letting anyone else know. He would ring another hospital, one outside the Vatican. But how could he do this, without someone realising who he was? He could not think straight.

He would ask Thomas, in confidence, to find him another specialist.

But what would the specialist be? A gynaecologist? That was unthinkable, he was not a woman. A geneticist, perhaps?

He left the chapel and returned to his rooms. Everything now seemed strange and unreal to him. He sat at his desk and felt the hard surface of the wood. This at least was solid. He walked across the floor, felt his feet press against the wooden surface, heard the wood, faintly, creak. How could this condition not have been discovered before? Someone must have known something. His mother must have known, his doctor, back in County Cork. That he had a rare genetic condition, yes, that he could accept. But this other thing – no, that had to be a lie, a deliberate plan to undermine him.

He knew that you could get a pregnancy test. You could buy one at a chemist. That should be simple. But how to get one, without the whole Vatican knowing?

He thought of his dream, the dream where someone came into his bed, the feel of naked flesh against his flesh, the exquisite feeling that had rushed through him, but pushed this aside as he dismissed inappropriate thoughts in prayer. He did not want to remember.

He woke to the now familiar sense of nausea. Could this be what they called morning sickness? It was true, then, he was indeed pregnant. It was not a dream. He rose and dressed hastily, his hands trembling and fumbling with the heavy cloth.

He said Mass as usual. He managed to control the nausea and when he returned and had breakfast the weak tea and toast settled his stomach. He wondered if there was any way the doctors could be wrong.

Thomas was there with the papers and some correspondence, cheerful and attentive as always. He poured black coffee from the pot, even though Patrick now hardly touched it.

Siobhan had written to him. He took the letter and looked at the neat, carefully composed handwriting.

Holy Father, cousin Patrick, I write to unreservedly apologise for my attack on you. I realise now that it is only by my own good fortune that I did not injure you or cause any permanent damage to you. I pray for forgiveness, though I know I do not deserve it – but perhaps none of us deserve it, truly. Thank you for coming to see me in the hospital. It appears that I will not be charged, but be referred for psychiatric treatment. I do not want to be treated with drugs but I am not sure I will have any choice in the matter. I do not know if you can say anything to them. It is my belief that I was out of my mind with grief for the losses of my babies and my fears that, as St Augustine said, that they would suffer eternal damnation. I do not know if you can understand that, even though I am not sure I believe any more; it is hard to overcome what I have been told all my life. I know you tried to reassure me that this was not the case but I am not convinced. I would rather be in hell with the souls of my dead babies than be in heaven and be eternally separated from them.

I still hold to everything I said to you in Rome, except one thing. I told you that I would become an enemy of religion, but that is not strictly true. I wish that religion would cease to be an enemy to itself so that I could believe again. I find it hard to believe in any God who would damn these half-formed babies. If I am to come back to the Church, I need to know that my children will be saved. I pray that you will forgive me for my action and bear these words in mind.

He handed the letter to Thomas, who read it and handed it back again.

'It is well put.'

'It is, however, foolish. We can never have certainty about the fate of another. All we can do is trust in God's goodness. I will continue to pray for her.'

There was a letter from his mother; Thomas passed him the blue envelope. He read it quickly; she had concerns for his father's health, there was an appointment at the hospital, she hoped it was not serious. Patrick laid it down on his desk.

Did she know? Surely she must know. He would have to ask her. But how?

Thomas cleared his throat. 'Holy Father. Shall we look at the other correspondence?'

He realised he was not concentrating.

'Are you feeling unwell, Holy Father? If there is something wrong, please let me know so that I can help you.'

Thomas's eyes were on him, watchful. Thomas, of course, knew something was wrong. It would be impossible to spend time with Thomas, every day, without making some explanation for his distress. What could he tell him?

He smelled the bitter coffee, and put the cup back on the table. Thomas looked away, then reached for the newspapers.

'Thomas.' He put out his arm and touched Thomas's sleeve. Thomas started, almost recoiled, he was sure, at his touch; then he recovered himself.

'There is something I need to tell you.'

'You are ill?' An expression of concern, of deep sympathy, marked Thomas's face.

'You are the only one I can trust. Will you promise me that you will keep this to yourself?'

Thomas seemed injured by this appeal. 'You don't need to ask me that, Holy Father.'

'I'm sorry.' They sat in silence. Thomas said nothing, simply waiting for him to speak. His presence in the room was consoling; Patrick wanted this moment to last a long time. It was very quiet. In the corridor outside he heard, distantly, voices talking, then the sound of fading footsteps. Thomas raised his head at last, with a questioning look.

He knew he must speak.

'I have been to the Vatican Health Service, as you know, for a check-up. It seems I have a rare genetic condition. I have always been in good health so it was not picked up before.'

Thomas hesitated. His hand nervously fingered the silver pectoral cross that hung over his black robes. 'Is it – serious? Will it have severe effects?'

'That's hard to know. They tell me it is not, should not be, life-threatening.' Should he say more? No, he couldn't. It was enough for now. 'I need more tests. But I want to see a specialist, a geneticist, someone outside the Vatican. I don't trust the man they brought in to see me. I want an entirely independent opinion, from someone who does not know that I am the pope. I will need your help with this.'

Thomas looked alarmed. 'Of course, Holy Father. I will do anything I can to assist.'

But now that he had asked Thomas, he was paralysed with indecision. How could he get a scan, when he was not a woman? How could he keep it confidential? He would have to think about this.

'It is imperative that news of this does not leak out. It must be done with the utmost confidentiality. I will need to go to a private clinic, under an assumed name.' He paused. 'I will need to pay. It would be most discreet to use cash. Would it be possible for you to arrange this for me?' He paused; he must not alarm Thomas unduly. 'There is no huge rush,' he added.

Thomas looked surprised, but he nodded. 'Of course. But would it not be better –'

'Thomas. Do not argue with me, please. I have my reasons. I will explain everything to you later.'

Thursday 26 May. The Feast of Corpus Christi, the Most Holy Body and Blood of Christ. He led the procession with candles at dusk from the Archbasilica of St John Lateran to the Basilica of Santa Maria Maggiore, concluding with Benediction of the Blessed Sacrament. Enormous crowds had gathered. He was warned that this would be a security headache but it all passed off without any incident.

Thomas told him that he had made an appointment at a private clinic in the evening, at a time when he would normally be in his rooms. He had made all the arrangements to transport him there, found out how much the scan had cost and withdrawn enough cash to cover it. Recently, there had been rumours circulating that Pope Patrick sometimes went out from the Vatican at night, on errands of mercy, dressed as an ordinary priest, and Patrick had done nothing to suppress them. He supposed that if anyone saw him leave they would think that this was what he was doing.

He asked Thomas to find some clothes to change into and bring them to him, ones that would fit – loose, casual trousers, a baggy sweater that he privately hoped would be loose enough to disguise the fact that he had no breasts. He had the headscarf Mary had given him, but he would not wear that now. He put the clothes on and covered them up with a black cassock, and put on a black clerical hat with a broad brim. He took out his sunglasses from the drawer – his eyes were too unusual; he did not want anyone to recognise them.

The nuns were busy preparing his dinner; he could hear them talking in the kitchen as Thomas ushered him along the corridor; he had already sent Alfonso on some errand. No one seemed interested in who he was, leaving the building. When he stepped outside, it was time for the Angelus and all the bells were ringing, their sound carrying far in the mellow air. The car was waiting for him; the driver was standing attentively by the car, opening the door for him. Patrick assumed that he would think he was visiting a sick person at the clinic.

The car drove swiftly through the streets. The traffic, travelling uphill, was heavy; the journey seemed to go on interminably. He worried that he would be late. He thought how it would feel, in an hour or so, to be driving back again, but this time knowing for certain. It made him think of that moment when, walking home from school, he had first become aware of the mystery of time. He must have been about nine or ten years old. He had been walking along the path by the hedge, when the thought had come to him: how could it be that he was here, walking along in the sunshine, and in half an hour he would be at home, reading a book, and looking back at this moment as something that had happened, a moment that was gone and would never return? He thought about the book he had read, and how it had once been written, step by step, but now existed complete for all to experience it again, unfolding in time, as they read it. He remembered thinking then, was that how it was for God? That he had created the world in all its fullness, past, present and future, and for Him it all existed all at once, as a book?

The clinic was in the Gianiculo, just south of the Vatican, beautiful in the evening sunlight with elegant houses half-hidden by parasol pines and Lombardy poplars. The taxi pulled up outside a large, modern building with a forecourt where the driver left him. To go into the building alone with no one accompanying him was unnerving. He felt that everyone would be looking at him, that one of them would inevitably spot that there was something wrong, and then there would be a dreadful scene. But no one paid him the slightest attention.

He walked along the corridor and found a men's toilet, and went into one of the cubicles. He quickly pulled off the cassock to reveal the clothes that Thomas had brought him. He stuffed the cassock and the hat into a small cloth bag containing an envelope with the cash that Thomas had provided. He heard someone come in and decided to wait while he used the urinal and splashed his hands at the sink. As soon as he heard the door close, he came out of the cubicle and stepped out into the corridor. He reached in the bottom of the bag and pulled out Mary's scarf, put it over his head and tied it roughly under his chin.

At the desk, he asked where to go, trying to keep his voice as light as possible. The receptionist told him to go up to the first floor. One side of the lift was a large mirror. He went up to the top of the building to give him time to adjust his clothing so that it looked right. The scarf, with its red flowers on a green background, was the only thing that he was wearing that was clearly feminine.

He looked strange in the mirror, not like himself at all. He adjusted his hair so a small fringe poked out from below the scarf. He tied it round the back of his neck like a movie star, not like – he did not want to look like – a Muslim woman. Could he really pass as a woman? It was so hard to know. Perhaps people did not really look, not going further than their first assumptions. And wouldn't he look too old to be a mother? This was absurd. He hadn't really thought it all through – there was bound to be an embarrassing situation. But he was committed now. The doors opened at the top of the building, and a woman in a white coat stepped in, staring at some notes. She nodded at him as she entered and showed no sign that there was anything odd about him.

When he reached the first floor, a handful of women were sitting in the waiting room, browsing magazines, or looking nervously around them, some alone, others with men, their husbands no doubt, or perhaps, in this modern world, lovers. He could see that they were restless and uneasy; a young woman flipped the pages of the magazines mechanically, without reading them. It was not long before he was called.

In the doctor's office he explained that he wanted to confirm that he was pregnant. The doctor, an attractive woman with short, dark hair, looked astonished.

'But this is the wrong clinic,' she said. 'I –'

'I have come here because I have been told that there is a strong possibility of there being a genetic abnormality,' he said. 'But before I go any further, for tests and so on, I would like it to be confirmed that I am definitely pregnant.'

'Well, we can take a urine sample and you can come back tomorrow, or –'

'It has to be today.'

The doctor looked irritated. 'We need to send it down to the lab, and they are not there right now. Did you do a test at home?'

He wondered why on earth he had not just found a way to get this done. But would it be definitive, in any case? 'What about an ultrasound scan?'

She sighed, then she picked up the phone. She spoke for a while in Italian, so rapidly that he found it hard to follow. She hung up, and turned to look at him.

'You need to complete this form,' she said. 'At the bottom here you need to put your payment method. Just sit down over there and fill it out.'

He completed the form with Mary's name and address in Rome, and for payment method he wrote 'cash'. He handed the form back to the receptionist.

'I will need your payment first.'

'Of course.' He took the money from his bag and counted it out before sliding it awkwardly across the desk. The receptionist checked it and printed out a receipt.

'Well, there is a radiographer ready and you can go straight down. It's the third door on the right.'

He walked down the corridor. His heart was beating very rapidly and his mouth felt dry. He felt as he had always felt in the minutes before an important school exam, a mixture of fear and anticipation. In a few minutes, he would know the truth. He tried not to think about it. He found the room. He was terrified that the radiographer would make him get undressed but she told him this wasn't necessary, she only needed to expose his abdomen. She asked him simply to lie down on the couch as he had done before, and pull up his sweater and top. He rested his arm on top of his chest, on top of the rucked-up sweater, relieved that she would notice nothing unusual about his lack of breasts.

'Would you like to take off your sunglasses?'

It would seem strange to leave them on, so he nodded and removed them. He narrowed his eyes to conceal the iris and lay back on the couch.

'May I see the screen?'

'Yes, of course, I'll angle it towards you.' She took a bottle and squeezed some cold liquid on to his belly. Then she took the hard probe and began to press it down on his skin, moving it around, tapping buttons on the scanning machine, which bleeped in response.

On the screen, dark shapes emerged from the greyness and blurred back again as she moved the probe.

'Here,' she said, pointing to the indistinct image. 'Here is the baby – you can just see the outline.'

He caught his breath. He could see the screen, but nothing on it made any sense. 'Are you sure? I can't see clearly.'

'Look, I can see the heart beating. Here.' And she pointed. He could see something throbbing, rhythmically contracting and releasing. Another life buried deep inside him.

It was true, then. They were not testing him.

He lay back and closed his eyes. Was it possible to feel two opposite things at once? To feel a sense both of terror and of wonder? He felt hot, and then cold. The radiographer continued to move the probe around his belly; he wished that she would stop.

He opened his eyes. An image came into view for a moment, something round, like a baby's head, and she stopped the scan again, freezing the image on the screen.

He listened to her tapping on the keyboard, to some more bleeps. She said, 'I can measure the baby's head, that will give us a good idea of the due date.'

'And the baby… does it look normal?'

'Oh, yes. Everything looks fine to me. You can see here… the arms, the legs. All the fingers and toes.' She paused. 'It's a little early to tell the sex. Would you like to know?'

'I think so… yes.' This was becoming too real. There was a heartbeat. She was talking about a due date, about the baby's gender.

'As I say, it's too early to be certain. You should ask again, at the twenty-week scan. But it does look to me like it might be a boy. You see, there?'

He looked at the moving image; he could see the head, the arms, quite clearly, but nothing more distinct than that. But there was no denying it; this was, then, real. He was going to have a child, a son. He felt the strangest sensation take hold of him. Lying here, in ordinary clothes, no longer feeling like the pope, he had a moment of true privacy. He was like any other woman, discovering that she was pregnant. Some, of course, would be thrilled; some had no doubt been longing for this moment. But others would not be so happy. Some might even be terrified, as he was. Was that what he felt? Terror? Or something else?

The sense he had was more revulsion than fear. It felt as if he had woken in another body, one that did not have anything to do with him, and one which had been invaded by an alien being which he did not want.

The radiographer took more measurements, then removed the probe. She gave him a cloth to wipe up the gel and told him to get off the couch.

'When is it due?' He could not bring himself to say, the baby.

'You are about eleven weeks. It's a bit early, for the scan. You should come back and we can be more accurate next time. Do you want to take the report and scan with you now, or shall I send it on to your doctor?'

'Thank you, I will take it now.'

She handed him an envelope and disc and smiled at him. 'Congratulations,' she said. 'I hope everything goes well for you.'

In the taxi, going back, he realised that he was shaking; he hoped the driver wouldn't notice. He tried to still the tremors but he could not. He felt faint, and dreadfully tired; he wanted to sleep, to lie down, to forget everything. The bright lights in the shops outside shone into the cab and lit up the interior, flickering light and dark as they drove through the busy streets.

Back in his room, he could not settle. Outside, it was dark and the lights of the city outshone the stars; the sky looked black, a darkness that pressed down on him and did not allow him to look beyond. Although in the cab he had felt so weary he thought he could sleep for ever, but now that he could rest, he was wide awake. The full horror of his position was now becoming clear to him. He was pregnant. This thing, this creature, this child was growing inside him.

But it was not possible for him to be pregnant. It was unthinkable. How could he, the pope, be pregnant? He would become a laughing stock. The Church would be held up to ridicule and scorn. Think what the world would do to him, what the papers would say. It would be the end of the Vatican, of Catholicism as he knew it. No, it was a nightmare, He was asleep, he had been tired, he would wake up. He slapped his face. He was hallucinating, he was under stress. This would not happen. It would go away.

He must carry on as usual. No one must suspect anything was wrong.

He tried to eat his supper, but it was hard to force each mouthful down. Afterwards, he sat as usual with Thomas and Father Alfonso to pray. While he saw nothing different in Alfonso's manner, Thomas looked nervous and watchful. He would be wondering, of course, about the results of the tests.

'Is everything all right?' he asked when Alfonso had gone to make some tea.

'I think so. I am very tired, Thomas. The worry of it all has taken it out of me. I think I will go to bed now.'

'You look very pale. Would you like a glass of brandy?'

He nodded; perhaps that was just what he did need. Thomas went to the cabinet and took out a bottle and poured him a small glass. The drink gave him an instant feeling of relief, but as soon as he had swallowed it, he felt guilt. You were not, of course, meant to drink alcohol in pregnancy. Why had he not thought of this before? Was it that at some level, he wanted to harm the baby?

Chapter Nine

A sound jolted him awake. He sat up; Thomas was standing in the room, by the door, looking towards him, his face in shadow.

'What is it?' He could not keep the anger from his voice; why had Thomas felt he could disturb him? Once he had been woken in the night it was almost impossible for him to get back to sleep.

'Holy Father, you called for me.'

'Me? Call? I most certainly did not.'

'Forgive me, Holy Father. I was sure I heard – I thought perhaps you were in danger.'

'Why?'

'Holy Father, it was clearly a mistake. Perhaps you called out in your sleep? I am so sorry to have disturbed you.'

'Please, go now.'

The door closed. Patrick felt a strange, disturbed sensation. He had indeed been dreaming. He was in a garden at night, a formal garden with tall Lombardy poplars which cast long shadows in the moonlight. He had been looking for Thomas, following him through a maze. Had he called for him? Could Thomas have heard, down the corridor, round a corner and behind two heavy doors? Or had they become so close that there was some kind of psychic connection between them?

He rose and went to the window. The great dome of St Peter's, brightly lit, loomed over the square.

He knelt on his prie-dieu and calmed his mind. He waited patiently, and after a long time – there – just a moment's touch – he felt that sense of presence. It reminded him of when he was a boy and one night his father had woken him from sleep and taken him out into the countryside to see the shooting stars. It was in summer, but the night was cold, and the stars were very clear. Above them hung the Milky Way, a starry path across the heavens. They looked out to the north-east and he saw the whole sky in front of him in all its immensity. For a long time nothing happened and then – whoosh! – a meteor streaked overhead, trailing golden fire. Again he waited, and just as he thought there would be no more, there was another – and another; ephemeral streaks of burning light. It was exactly like waiting on God in prayer. You could not make the meteors come or speed up their presence, but if you watched and waited long enough, they would appear and their beauty pierced your heart.

The moment passed. There was nothing else. Instead, his thoughts intruded and he could not stop them. What was the meaning of what had happened to him? What was he to do? If it were to prove to be a miracle, what would be the point of it? The Messiah had been born, once and for all time. There could not be any need of another. And God had not spoken to him; he could not assume this was a divine birth. No, he must think of this, as the doctors did, in human terms. They did not seem to think it was impossible.

He tried to consider what he should do. Clearly, it was impossible for him to keep the baby. He could go away, go on retreat, give birth to the baby, and hand it over to someone else, a young Catholic couple perhaps who would adopt it and bring the child up as their own. Perhaps it could all be kept a secret. But today, with the mass media, when scandal after scandal was revealed, would it not eventually come out? And then what? But there was another thought that kept coming into his mind, insistent, which he tried to push away and yet it kept coming back to him. He did have the power to make all this go away. He thought of what Professor Moretti had said, that if it was a case of self-insemination there was a high risk that the baby would be abnormal. Professor Moretti, of course, did not know that it was truly impossible for him to have become pregnant in any other way. Perhaps a doctor like Moretti would always believe in the most likely biological explanation, that he had been fertilised by someone else. But *he* knew that this could not be true.

He could have the tests, to see if there was any possibility that – he shuddered – he had fertilised himself. But then if this was not so, he would be under even more suspicion than he was now. And if the baby were abnormal? The scan had shown nothing wrong. That was a relief, but it did not have to be something visible, it could be some other disorder. Perhaps the child would be blighted by some genetic disease or even born dead, unable to survive outside the womb. Was there anything wrong in his family? Not that he knew of.

He knew it was allowed, under the law, to have a termination. How simple it would all be. He would go to a clinic somewhere, near at hand, in disguise as he had done before, and it would all be over in an hour or two. No one need ever know anything about it. And if he took this step – everything would go on, then, as it was before. The outside world – the papers, the cardinals, the faithful everywhere – they would never know. An immense, an enormous weight would be lifted from him.

How could he even think of this? That he – he, the head of the Church – would have committed this unspeakable sin.

But would it be a sin if he sacrificed his child for the good of the Church? He thought of Abraham and Isaac. Abraham proved his faithfulness to God by being prepared to sacrifice his beloved son. And the sacrifice of Christ himself, the only Son of God. Though of course, he had always struggled with this point. God after all did not sacrifice his Son directly. Rather, it was human beings who killed him, killed him because he would not compromise or be other than he was. Humankind cannot bear such witness to the truth. But – and this he knew came perilously close to heresy – was it in fact God's will that his Son be killed then, and in this manner? Was everything preordained? Or had there been, in fact, choices? He could not know; this was one of the great mysteries. Perhaps God had other plans for his Messiah, plans that were destroyed by human actions. The chilling words of the high priest Caiaphas in John 11: 49-50 echoed in his mind: 'You do not understand that it is better for you to have one man die for the people, than to have the whole nation destroyed.'

No, it could not be God's will; it could never be his will to take a human life. If he did this, would God forgive him? Would he not, afterwards, repent? But could he embark on such a terrible crime with the intention of repenting afterwards? No, this added to the mortal sin of murder the sin of presumption, which could only deepen his offence against God. But what if he sacrificed himself and his immortal soul to damnation to save the Church, so that through it, others could be saved?

He went again to confession.

'I have despaired of God's mercy. I have not always told the truth. I have wished harm to another.'

'Blessed are those whose sins have been forgiven. Rejoice in the Lord, and go in peace.'

Sister Veronica brought him his infusion in the morning. Uncharacteristically, she lingered in the room.

'Is there anything else I can bring you? Something to eat, perhaps, a biscuit, a piece of toast?'

'No, thank you. Nothing else.'

'I have been thinking you are looking very pale, Holy Father. We think that you have lost weight. Is everything all right?'

'Yes, yes, I am fine, thank you.'

She hovered, awkwardly. He didn't want to talk about his health, lest he be drawn into a further falsehood; he must change the conversation to some other topic.

'Sister Veronica, you never found that cross and chain I asked you about?'

She shook her head. 'No, Holy Father. I looked everywhere, in all the drawers and under the furniture.'

'Perhaps you could check with the laundry, to see if it could have got caught up somehow in my robes?'

'I have already done so, Holy Father. They have not found it.'

'Thank you, Sister. Don't trouble yourself any further. It is of no importance.'

'But it belonged to your grandmother, you must be sad to lose it. I will keep looking, Holy Father.'

He nodded, and she turned and left. He sipped the hot tea; it calmed him. It was a mystery about the cross. Perhaps he had not left it on the bedside table after all. Perhaps he had been wearing it and the chain had broken and it had fallen somewhere, perhaps even outside the Vatican. Well, it did not matter. He must not get attached to material things, not even such a personal possession as this.

Patrick had a meeting with the Secretary of the Pontifical Council for the Family, Cardinal Paul Lebrun, in preparation for its annual assembly. He had arranged to see him in the library. They sat on the pale cream chairs on an oriental carpet at the far end of the room, under Perugino's *Resurrection of Christ*.

Lebrun was a plump, jolly man who did not seem at all awed in the presence of the pope. In their previous meetings he had seemed genial and likeable and Patrick sensed that he would be an ally. After Patrick had outlined his thoughts on the need for clarity over the fate of unbaptised infants and the fate of embryos in storage, Lebrun frowned and looked down at his lap for some long moments.

'I am rather in agreement with you,' he said, 'but this is an issue that has been discussed many times in many different forums and we have never been able to clarify it. Many will not be on your side. I think particularly of Cardinal Wolf, the Prefect of the Congregation of the Doctrine of the Faith, and also I think, Rubio Gonzales, the President of the Council.'

'Exactly. But can I look to you for support?'

Lebrun nodded. 'Of course, Your Holiness. But this may not be enough.'

'What others might support me?'

'Many of the laity will, of course. But there will not be many among the cardinals.' He hesitated. 'You are new, and you are young, with many years ahead of you. Perhaps it would be wise to go more slowly.'

'God is calling me to act. I cannot ignore this call.'

Lebrun inclined his head. 'I will do my best to support you. I will speak to others. At least we can once more open up the debate.'

'Our strongest argument in the case of aborted foetuses may be the idea of the baptism of blood, where martyrs who have died for their faith before being baptised may be saved. There is the example of the Holy Innocents.' Patrick did not need to explain to Lebrun that he referred to those babies killed by Herod who were considered martyrs even though they could have had no knowledge of Christ. 'Perhaps all these babies who die unborn as a result of violence might be compared with them.'

'This is a robust argument, I agree, Your Holiness. You will be able to put this forward with passion and vigour.'

He nodded. He did not, at this moment, feel capable of either. He thought of his moment of weakness last night. This debate had now taken on another, a personal dimension, as if a resolution of the question was necessary for his own salvation.

'And then there is the question of the baptism of desire. Those who desire baptism but die before they can receive it can still be cleansed of sin. If the parents had wished for baptism of their children –'

'Exactly so, Your Holiness.' Lebrun nodded. 'All these things must be taken into account. Well, we will see. I look forward to it.'

Lebrun did not help him; he merely agreed with everything he said. Patrick could hardly contain his irritation. It was a relief when Lebrun left.

He had to go back to see the doctors. It would be, they said, a 'high-risk' pregnancy. They said he needed monitoring and help.

When he arrived at the health centre, the specialist was there again, Professor Moretti, and another, introduced as Dr De Luca. He was a small, untidy-looking man with unkempt grey hair, but an air of authority nonetheless, as if he was too important to care about his own appearance. So now he had to confide in another doctor. How many others would they expect him to allow into the secret? How long before something leaked?

He told Moretti that he did not want to talk to anyone else.

'Dr De Luca is an obstetrician,' Moretti said. 'You must talk to him and seek his advice. It is essential for the health of the baby.'

Every time they said that word, 'baby', he felt anger rising in him. It seemed demeaning, patronising. It filled him with shame, that there was a part of him, something inside him, that he couldn't control, something whose well-being seemed more important to them than his own. He thought for a moment of the Irish woman, Aisling, who had died because they would not perform an abortion.

Dr De Luca was smiling and started to chatter somewhat nervously. 'Your Holiness, this is not the first time I have come across such a case,' he said. 'Last year I saw a woman who was pregnant with her third child who came to have an amniocentesis, to see if the baby was normal. But it revealed something astonishing – that she was, like you, a genetic chimera, and many of the cells in her body were male.'

How could he not be angry? He was a 'case'. A medical anomaly.

Professor Moretti broke in and said that he had consulted, in complete confidence of course, about his condition. He leaned forward across the desk, resting his hands flat on the table. 'First, we must spell out the risks. We must warn you that there is an increased risk of developing a cancer in the ovary or testis, about a ten per cent chance in a case like yours. So we must strongly recommend that after the pregnancy ends you have these tissues removed.'

'Tissues.'

'Yes, the ovary and testis.' He paused. 'Of course this would mean you would not be able to have any more children. But I am sure that would not be an issue for you.'

Were they mocking at him? They could not be serious. He stared at their solemn faces; they seemed serious enough. There was too much information for him to absorb. With every word they spoke his situation seemed more impossible.

De Luca ran a hand through his untidy hair, hoping perhaps to straighten it. If so, he did not succeed. He said, 'There may be some changes that you witness, due to the increased levels of oestrogen and progesterone that will be circulating in your body. Your breasts may grow larger. We have not been able to investigate to see if they contain sufficient mammary tissue for you to feed your baby.'

What was this? He, breastfeed a baby? What seemed so right and natural for a woman seemed abominable to him. And whatever happened, he was unlikely to be the one who brought up this baby. What was De Luca saying now?

'Second, we are very concerned that there may be a risk as you approach the end of the pregnancy.' De Luca seemed less nervous now. 'The baby can double or treble in weight in the last two months of the pregnancy. Your womb may not be fully formed, there was evidence of this from the scan, and there may be some problems. I have looked up the literature. It seems that in such patients, the rate of caesarean section is very high. It may be that the womb is elastic enough to accommodate the baby, but it may lack the capacity to respond fully in labour by dilating appropriately. We must make sure that you give birth where there are adequate facilities.'

'I see.' Gone, then, was his idea that he might give birth secretly somewhere, hidden away from the world. How could he keep this secret in a hospital? He supposed that it would be possible to go under another identity, as he had done for the scan. He closed his eyes again.

'There have been eleven documented births to anatomically male people with your condition,' said De Luca. 'I have looked up the literature. All of them, curiously, were male. There must be some genetic basis for this, but we don't know what it is. It could relate to the pairing of chromosomes at fertilisation.'

'How fascinating,' said Moretti. 'Well worth investigating.'

Again, that sharp prick of anger at being, to them, so interesting.

'The good thing is,' De Luca said, 'that if you make it past twenty-eight weeks, the baby has a very good chance of survival, even if delivered prematurely.'

He saw in his mind a premature baby, one of those bird-like scraps he had seen in incubators in the hospital in Dublin. How could he abandon such a creature? And who but him would want it?

Dr De Luca came round and sat on the edge of the desk. 'May I examine you, Your Holiness?'

'No.' He could not do it – could not consent to more prying hands in his most intimate places. It was as if his body no longer belonged to him but had become the property of others. He said, 'Not now. Another time, perhaps.'

'Very well. We should do blood tests and take a urine sample. And I would like to see another scan.'

'I already had one done. I wanted a second opinion.' Patrick took out the letter and the disc from the private clinic and handed it over. Conti looked at the name on the notes, and raised his eyebrows.

'This is yours?'

'I used another name, to keep it confidential.'

'Of course, Your Holiness.' Conti loaded the scan on to the computer and the three doctors gathered round the screen, talking to one another in Italian. Then Moretti apologised and swivelled the screen around to face Patrick.

'If you look at this, here' – and he pointed to the lower part of the scan – 'you can see that the placenta is rather low, right by the cervix. This can rectify itself as the pregnancy continues; it is very early days, but we do need to watch it.'

'Why?'

'If the placenta covers the entrance to the womb, there is a higher risk of miscarriage. And when you go into labour, you can bleed uncontrollably. This is very dangerous. Don't worry, we will be monitoring you. But you must, as the pregnancy goes on, report any vaginal bleeding to us.'

De Luca paused and looked up from the scan. He took a deep breath and hesitated, as if he was trying to decide whether to speak or not. 'I understand your position, Your Holiness, but as your clinician I must point out to you that if you did not want to go ahead, abortion is legal in Italy. You are approaching the end of the period of ninety days when it can be done on request. All that is needed is for me to issue a certificate of consent, and then seven days need to pass before the procedure can be done, to allow you a period of reflection. We can arrange for some counselling, by telephone of course so that you can remain anonymous, if that would help you. But what I am saying is, if you do choose to act, it is best to do so now.'

'Are you mocking me?' His anger was overwhelming. He felt like striking De Luca, knocking him to the floor.

De Luca looked down and shook his head. 'Not at all, Your Holiness. It is important that I explain your options. We have tried to explain all the reasons why this pregnancy is dangerous – the risk of abnormalities in the foetus, the risk of premature birth, the risk of your... intersex condition, and your age. Of course, if it should become clear that your health or life is in danger, or if the foetus has a severe abnormality, or would be unable to survive outside the womb, a termination can still be carried out later.'

Again, that voice of temptation, murmuring in his ear. Perhaps that was the way out; perhaps such an act could be justified. But no, even that violated the Church's position. 'This is, of course, unthinkable.'

'Of course, Your Holiness, I understand. I hope you will not hold it against me but I must, as a doctor, give you my best advice.'

'So you would advise me to – abort.'

'No, Your Holiness, I would never say that, but I must advise you that this pregnancy is full of risk, for you and for the baby. It is important that you have the full facts but the choice, of course, must be yours.'

He sat in the darkness of his office, in front of the icon of the Virgin. The light from the candles flickered over her face, casting shadows that moved around her eyes and nose and mouth. And then, as before, he saw the Virgin smile at him. He knew at one level that this was simply an effect of the light and shadows playing on her face, but at a deeper level, in his heart, he felt it was a sign. It was as if some special understanding had passed between them. He felt a closeness, an identity as if they were both, after all, in the same situation. For what must have passed through Mary's mind when she came to see Joseph and give him the news? That she, a young maiden, was carrying a child. In Matthew, Joseph considered quietly divorcing her. He tried to visualise the scene. Joseph, the carpenter, in his workshop, surrounded by shavings of wood. The harsh Middle Eastern light outside. Mary, dressed in drab clothes, a veil over her head, entering and standing in the doorway, the light forming a halo around her slight form. A woman clothed in modesty, as far as was possible to imagine from the Queen of Heaven who would later be clothed by the sun.

He imagined her stepping forward, bowing meekly in front of the man who was to be her husband, begging him in advance to believe what she was going to tell him.

And Joseph did believe – but only after an angel had visited him. Why, then, had he not been so visited? Why did he, the pope, have so little faith?

There had been a girl at school, her name was Marie. She had long, dark hair and a sweet face and was much fancied by the boys. At sixteen she had confessed to him and others in the class (they were gathered at the back of the classroom in the lunch break while the other children were playing outside; he could still see that worn, graffiti-covered desk) that she had slept with her boyfriend. They were to be married that year with their parents' consent. Her great regret, she said, at being no longer a virgin, was that she could never be chosen by God to bear a divine child. Patrick recalled his shock that she might ever have presumed to fill so great a role. For Mary, immaculately conceived, was no ordinary woman.

Mary had been given a choice. Gabriel had come to her and told her what was to happen, and she had accepted; 'Be it to thee according to thy will.' Patrick had been given no choice at all. It had happened to him without his consent. How was he to think of this, then? Could it be – a divine rape?

He started physically at the thought, shocked out of his meditation. Had he gone mad? These thoughts would not do. He went back to his bedchamber but he could not sleep, could not sit still. He rose and walked backwards and forwards, prowling like a wild animal. It was intolerable; he had to speak to someone. But who could he speak to? Not the doctors. There was no one he could take in to his confidence. Thomas? No, not even Thomas. He dreaded to think how Thomas would react. He thought of what it would be like to explain to him; his face flushed red and hot. He would become an object of mockery to the person he cared about most. No, he couldn't do this. It would remain a secret between him and God. Unless he spoke to the counsellor De Luca had recommended for him.

Dr Conti sent him a mobile phone, a pay-as-you-go, he said, which was untraceable, which he could use in his own rooms. Dr Conti had already spoken with the counsellor and explained that someone would contact her, someone who did not wish to give a name. Now, Patrick sat at his desk, fiddled with the slip of paper on which the woman's name and number had been written. Would it help him to talk to someone about this, anonymously?

His fingers shook on the small buttons as he dialled the counsellor's number. The ringtone sounded loudly and the woman's voice, soft and well-spoken, was unexpectedly clear.

'Ah, Dr Conti told me you would phone. Please, how can I help you?'

'I find myself – unexpectedly pregnant and considering a termination.' Why did he say this? He was not considering it at all. It was as if some other part of himself had taken over and was speaking instead of him.

'Of course. Perhaps it would be helpful if you tell me a little about the situation.' Her voice was soothing. 'Remember that this space is for you; I am here help you to decide what is best for you, not to try to persuade you or to judge you in any way.'

He fell silent. He tried to think of something to say that would make sense. 'My circumstances are very – particular,' he said, 'I can't explain everything, but there are so many factors to consider.'

'Yes,' she said, simply and sympathetically, 'there always are.'

He felt a dizzying sensation, as if he was falling, realising for a moment that his situation was perhaps no different to that of many others this counsellor had spoken to. No woman *wanted* an abortion. Their circumstances pushed them towards it. And yet, of course, they could resist.

The counsellor's voice came again, quiet, seductive. 'Perhaps you could tell me a little more.'

He felt then as if he was playing a game; well, he would play the role that was expected of him. 'I don't know who the father is.'

'Ah, yes, that is difficult.'

'And there is the question of my job. I would lose it, if people knew about the baby.'

'There is legal protection for women in your situation. It is illegal to fire a woman because she is pregnant.'

'But I have only just taken up my post.'

'I see.' There was a long pause. 'Do you have other children?'

How strange these questions seemed, how divorced from his reality. 'No, this is my first.'

'If the situation was ideal, would you want this baby?'

'I don't know how to answer that question. There are some – special circumstances.'

'Ah, yes.'

He felt angry then. How could he possibly have this conversation? How could she possibly help him when she didn't know the whole truth?

'I am a Catholic.'

'Ah; that is hard. But I have counselled many Catholics. Many do choose to have a termination.'

'Even though it is a mortal sin.'

She was silent for a long time.

'I cannot tell you how many times women have told me this. They don't want an abortion, they know it is wrong. But.'

'But?'

'They will do it anyway. They hope that they can be forgiven. They would do it even if they went to hell. In my experience, most woman do not feel they have a choice. They simply do not feel it is possible for them to have a baby at that time. They know they cannot do it.'

Again, that echo of recognition within him. He did not feel that he could do it either. He did not think he had the strength. Yet surely, God would give it to him?

'I have always spoken out strongly against abortion.'

She laughed, then, not out loud, but he could hear it in her voice. 'Well, that is very common too. Only last week, I counselled the daughter of a woman who was a pro-life campaigner. The daughter was only sixteen. She was threatening suicide. The mother made the appointment and agreed that the termination should be done. It was, she said, a special case.'

Did such hypocrisy exist? Of course, it did. He had seen it himself. And could he be guilty of such hypocrisy himself?

Suddenly he was nauseated by the conversation.

'Thank you for your time,' he said, 'It has been helpful. But I have decided not to have an abortion.'

Her voice was gentle. 'In case you change your mind, you have my number. If you do want to call me, you can do so any time between 9am and 9pm. If you leave a message, I will call you back.'

'Please, wait – wait.' He did not want her to hang up.

'Yes?'

He sat, staring at the desk. He felt the connection between them over the silent airwaves and did not want to sever it, even though he had nothing to say.

He said, 'Thank you for your help. It has clarified my mind.' He hung up and went to the window and looked out over the square. But the conversation had not helped him; it had made him even more aware of the impossibility of his position. He was no further on from knowing what to do than he had been before.

In the evenings he spent time in the living room with Father Alfonso and with Thomas, watching the news so that he was up to date with current affairs, and listening to Thomas playing the piano. The small upright had been put there for the former pope, who had liked to play, but Thomas played with almost a professional standard. He sat there now, his back to the room, playing one of the Schubert impromptus, Patrick's favourite one in A-flat minor with its cascading arpeggios and quiet chords. The music filled him with an aching longing. This evening, he could not stay and listen to it. His nerves were jangled.

Patrick could not help noticing as well that an awkward atmosphere had sprung up between the two private secretaries. Either they were excessively polite to one another or they bickered over tiny things. This evening, Alfonso was annoyed because he said he did not like Schubert. He was too emotional, he said – he preferred the intellectualism of Bach. Thomas disagreed. Bach, he said, was passionate. Think of some of the cantatas and chorales, pleading love for the bridegroom, Christ. As Thomas said this, a brief expression of bliss passed over his face, as if he had personally known this intense longing. It was deeply moving.

Patrick ended the argument by saying he would like the Schubert. Thomas smiled and nodded gratefully, turned his back and continued to play.

Perhaps he should not have taken Thomas's side. It would have been impossible for Father Alfonso not to notice his increased intimacy with Thomas. He was not meant to be partial; all men were his brothers, he must treat them equally. Rising suddenly from his chair, he sought the solitude of his room.

As he knelt to pray, he tried to hollow out his own heart, to leave nothing there but a bare, empty space which God would fill. His only wish, his desire, was to do the will of God. What would he wish if he was this baby? Could it ever be the will of any creature not to be born? Did he wish that he, a freak of nature, had never been born? It was a temptation, that was sure. But whatever pain and anguish he had suffered and was suffering now, he could not find it in himself to wish himself unborn.

It would have been better if he had been diagnosed with cancer. At least then it would be comprehensible, at least people would feel sympathy for him. He would go quietly, would resign, for reasons of health. But no, this would be a disaster for the Church. They could not have two popes resign in quick succession. How could he think this? There must be another way.

What was it the doctor had said? Ninety days. It would be so simple. You went to a clinic, and they inserted a tube and sucked everything out. The whole thing would take just a couple of hours. Everything would go back to how it had been before. He would not have to tell anyone. The doctors would understand, they had practically recommended it. His body felt a shock at the intensity of his relief when he imagined it all over. But again, he dismissed the temptation. How could he even think this? Because he was weak, because he was isolated and cut off from anyone he could discuss it with or who could help and support him.

He thought again of the counsellor. She said he could call at any time. He still had the mobile phone in the drawer of his desk. It was not too late – before 9pm. His hand shaking a little, he dialled the number.

The phone rang. Her voice answered; she sounded a little startled. '*Pronto?*'

'Is this a good time to talk?'

She shifted to English at once. 'Of course.'

'When I spoke to you before, I did not tell you everything. The doctors have told me there is a high risk for this pregnancy. There is, apparently, some abnormality in my womb. And, I am fifty-five.'

She hesitated for a moment. 'That is very unusual,' she said. 'It is a natural pregnancy?'

Again it came to him, in a hot stab of shame, the thought that he might have conceived this child himself, in a moment of impurity, of sinfulness. Was it natural? How could he say?

'I have not had any medical intervention, if that's what you mean. Otherwise I would not be considering a termination.'

'Have you been told there is a high risk of abnormality in the baby?'

'Indeed, I have.'

'You've had scans? Blood tests?'

'Yes, it all seemed to be normal, but it is still an early stage.'

'But you've been warned?'

'Yes, I've been warned that there is a high risk of abnormality, a high risk of problems in pregnancy, a high risk of stillbirth.' Only now that he was telling her this did the risk he was taking strike home; only now did it seem real. He realised that he was frightened. He realised how much of a relief it would be to end the pregnancy.

She spoke to him calmly. 'This is something you should discuss with your doctors.'

'I have. They have advised me that a – termination – would be wise.'

'But I suppose this means – at your age – that you feel this is a last chance for you. To have a baby, I mean.'

'It is the only chance.' He thought – it was surprising to him that he hadn't thought before – how many women in the Bible had conceived at a late age. It was a sign of God's special favour.

'That must be very hard for you.' She waited for a long time, and then she said, 'I have a feeling that you may want me to say something that will take the decision away from you. That I should say, I think you should have the abortion. That is what many women want me to say. All I can say is, no one could blame you for choosing to end this pregnancy. But you are the only one who has to live with this choice.

I wish there was something I could say, to make it easier for you. But only you can decide.'

'Thank you.' He hung up, abruptly. He was angry. He had not wanted her to decide for him. Even he could not make the choice. Only God could decide.

He threw the mobile back into the drawer and slammed it shut. However it had been conceived, it was not the child's fault. Killing the baby would be as bad, or worse, than killing himself. It was the great sin of despair. He remembered someone telling him that most people who attempted or succeeded in committing suicide did not really want to die. They simply did not want to have the life that they were living. They could not see the possibility that things would get better and that the pain they were suffering now might pass. Mental pain, he knew, was just as terrible as physical pain. Just as someone who was being tortured beyond their capacity to bear it might beg to die, so those in mental agony felt that they must end their lives rather than endure a moment longer.

But his agony was not – yet – of that pitch. And he knew that if he truly prayed, he could hand his pain over to God. God would take it from him, could wipe out his suffering in the radiant intensity of His presence. There was no need to torment himself with these thoughts. For had not Paul said in 1 Corinthians, Chapter 6 verses 19-20, that his body was not his own, but a temple of the Holy Spirit, which he had from God? It had been bought with a price. Why did he not believe that what had happened was God's will? Why should he not use his body to bear witness to his faith? It could be for him a martyrdom, not the white martyrdom of penitence and prayer, but perhaps for him a martyrdom of blood.

Chapter Ten

The weather had become unseasonably hot, with heavy clouds and humid air. The oppressive atmosphere seemed to make his morning sickness worse. The only thing that helped was to walk in the Vatican gardens under the trees, past the cool fountains which splashed down the hill and over the stone watercourses.

He could only walk here in the early morning and the evening, now that groups of tourists were allowed access to the gardens. This evening, as he stepped outside, he saw the last group leaving, following their guide with her little flag and walking in procession with their earpieces in their ears. Mass tourism had become a terrible thing, throttling and overwhelming the city; he had seen the crowds of tourists in the Vatican museum staring at the paintings, which had been ripped from their devotional contexts and held up as mere objects for their glazed and often uncomprehending eyes. Perhaps, he thought, the whole place should be closed and the artworks should be returned to the churches where they came from so that they could act again as windows into the divine reality.

He stopped to pray in the olive grove, behind the shrine of the Virgin of Fatima. Here, he could imagine himself together with Christ in the garden, under the shade of the olive trees. As he knelt in silence, the sound of the morning traffic rose up from behind the walls below; the growl of engines, the clanking of a heavy lorry, the throaty roar of a motorcycle.

Thomas knelt to the right of him, Alfonso on the left. They all prayed, silently, together, but he did not feel comforted. Somewhere in the distance, a funeral bell tolled, the sound coming to him on the gentle breeze. And here he was, struggling in his own Gethsemane, asking that this burden be taken away from him.

He was walking back down the uneven steps by the fountains when his leg somehow became caught in his robes. He could not stop himself – he was flying downwards, bumping hard against the ground, his body awkward, twisting. He tried to spin over so his belly was protected and he skidded downwards on his side and came to an abrupt stop at the bottom of the steps, his hand wedged awkwardly against a stone. He lay there, stunned. Was anything broken? Tentatively he moved his arms and legs. His hand was bleeding; his ribs hurt. Thomas and Alfonso were leaning over him. They said, 'Don't move, don't move, don't get up yet, we need to make sure that nothing is broken.' He obeyed them. He realised that his only thought was for the baby. He concentrated on his belly. Was there any pain there?

Alfonso said, 'I'll go and get a doctor.' Patrick heard his feet crunch rapidly away across the gravel. He rested on the ground, looking up at the trees, seeing the wind blow through them and the leaves tremble; grey clouds were passing slowly overhead. Thomas sat by his side. The noisy splashing of the fountain drowned out all other sounds.

Thomas did not say anything; he reached out and took his hand. Patrick did not now feel much pain; perhaps he should sit up, but it was so peaceful lying here in quiet companionship under the swaying trees. Then he heard voices, further down the path. Thomas stood up and moved away and he pushed himself up into a sitting position. He said as they approached, 'It is nothing. I am fine.'

Dr Conti knelt down beside him. 'Any pain? Let me feel your ribs.' Patrick then held out his bruised wrist and twisted ankle. Conti examined him carefully. 'There is nothing broken, Your Holiness. Some bruises, but that is all. It is best that you rest.'

Patrick asked, 'Can I speak to you in private?'

'Of course.'

Thomas and the doctor helped him to his feet and walked with him slowly back to the apostolic palace. In the privacy of his chambers he asked the doctor the only question that was troubling him – would it have harmed the baby?

'Well, if it was that easy to end a pregnancy –' Dr Conti broke off. Then he continued, 'Your Holiness, I do not think there is any danger. All the same, I suggest you rest for the remainder of today.'

In his rooms, he pondered Conti's seemingly casual remark. Did Conti think that he had fallen deliberately? Did he think that he had tried to end the pregnancy? He could not rest. The Council was starting next week. He felt that he had lost too much time already, and there was so much to be done.

The day of the meeting dawned. The sky was milky-white; it was the kind of day he had called a plain day as a child, when the sky through his bedroom window was a uniform white or lightest grey with no feature in it. From his window he saw no breath of wind, and a kind of pale haze hung over the city, not enough to be perceptible as a mist, but enough to merge the outlines of anything in the distance. The air felt cool, expectant.

As he dressed, he noticed there were some tiny red smears of blood on his underwear. He felt a disturbing sense of both familiarity and shock. He understood, now, from everything they told him, that on the few occasions when this had happened in the past it was likely to have been him menstruating. But surely, when he was pregnant, he should not bleed? Was it normal, to have a little loss of blood? The doctors had told him to report any bleeding, but they had not said how much. Did they mean heavy bleeding? He did not want to go to them. A feeling of shame overcame him, an instinct to deny what was happening.

He sat down heavily on the side of the bed. Any minute now they would come to fetch him. What could this mean? Was he going to miscarry? Was it all to be over, before it had even begun? Had his prayers been answered, that he would not have to bear this burden? Or was this a punishment for what he had thought? Perhaps it was his own fault. He had wished to get rid of the baby, and had been deliberately careless with himself. Perhaps, unconsciously, he had caused himself to slip. Or was it simply what they had said – what was it? – the low-lying placenta.

But what if he bled again, more heavily? He put on extra layers of undergarments to absorb any further flow. He regretted, for a moment, that he was wearing these white robes, symbolic of course of purity. It would be terrible if they were visibly stained by blood.

He called for Thomas and said that he felt unwell. He had planned to greet each one of the bishops personally – this was an opportunity for him to find out what they thought, to see who was on his side and who might oppose him. But now, he could not face it. Instead, he would simply address the meeting with the speech he had prepared for the Committee – those fifteen cardinals, twelve archbishops and bishops, nineteen carefully selected married couples from all over the world, and thirty-nine consultors who included both theologians and lay people.

At ten o'clock he was ready; he checked and there was no more bleeding. Perhaps it had been nothing after all.

He heard an expectant murmur of voices through the great doors that led into the Consistory Hall. When he came in, with Thomas walking just behind him holding his papers, they all rose and a hush fell. The silence was so intense that he could hear his shoes tap loudly on the marble floors. He glanced up at the ornate painted ceilings, trying not to look at the cardinals and bishops and the members of the Council gathered at one end of the enormous space. Why could the meeting not take place in smaller, intimate, more human surroundings? Perhaps more would be accomplished that way.

He went to the lectern, placed in front of the large white throne. He felt unready, unprepared, and his hands were shaky; he was afraid that he would drop the papers Thomas handed to him. Thomas stood there beside him and put out his hand to steady him.

He looked up at the faces in front of him. The cardinals sat at the front, and behind them were the consultors and the families, dressed in bright costumes from every continent. They looked back at him, expectant. Why did he feel so nervous? It was because he felt they judged him, were all waiting for him to make an error. He did not like the way the cardinals looked at him. It reminded him uncomfortably of the way the children had all stared at him on the first day of secondary school, as if the boys already recognised him as different from them. And he had been different; he had been put up a year because of his academic prowess, which only served to separate him from the others. He recalled how they had laughed at his high-pitched voice and his short stature. Well, now, no one would laugh.

He started; he was not concentrating. He took the microphone, waited as one by one they withdrew their gaze, shuffled their papers, coughed and cleared their throats. He looked out among them for those that would support him and those who might oppose; Gonzales, and Cardinal Wolf, the Prefect of the Congregation of the Doctrine of the Faith.

He opened with a simple prayer, then turned to the first page of his statement.

'There are two issues that preoccupy me, which are becoming critical in today's world, on which I feel the Church must give an unequivocal guidance. The first is the fate of the unbaptised babies who are lost through abortion, whether natural or induced. The second is the fate of unborn children who have been created by IVF and frozen in deep storage, to be ultimately destroyed when their parents have no use for them.

'We must address the question of whether we are treating such babies as full human beings. What should we do in the funerals of unbaptised babies, and should we conduct such ceremonies for miscarried and aborted babies? And is it right to rescue those frozen embryos in storage, to implant them into a mother who wants to but is unable to bear a child?

'The Church has no official position on these matters. All we can say is that we "hope" for the salvation of such babies, and that "there is no solution" to the fate of frozen embryos. Further, the great majority of these babies never have a proper funeral. This is not good enough.

'I hope that with prayer and with the guidance of the Holy Spirit, this meeting will produce the answers so that we can respond adequately to the communities we serve.'

As he spoke, he was aware of an uncomfortable feeling in his abdomen, as if a pigeon's claw was contracting and squeezing his insides. Was he imagining it, or was there a feeling of dampness down there, between his legs? He tried to dismiss the sensation, to concentrate on what he was saying, but again thought he felt something warm and wet trickling down the inside of his leg. He could do nothing about it, could not hold it in; that was what disturbed him, that he could not control his body. It was shameful.

Perhaps he was miscarrying. It could not happen now, not at this moment.

Cardinal Wolf stood up. With a little flourish he took out his glasses and perched them on the end of his nose. With a thick German accent, he read from a statement in front of him. 'The position is clear. The Congregation of the Doctrine of the Faith has expressed it clearly: the embryo demands the unconditional respect that is morally due to the human being in his bodily and spiritual totality. The human being is to be respected and treated as a person from the moment of conception. Let us examine the full implications of this undisputed truth.'

He felt relief, now. Cardinal Wolf would surely back him.

Now one of the consultors, president of a Catholic university in Spain, quoted from *Donum Vitae*, the Gift of Life, the *Instruction from the Congregation of the Doctrine of the Faith on Respect for Human Life in its Origin and on the Dignity of Procreation*, which, Patrick recalled, had been issued in 1987. 'By virtue of its substantial union with a spiritual soul, the human body cannot be considered as a mere complex of tissues, organs and functions, nor can it be evaluated in the same way as the body of animals; rather it is a constitutive part of the person who manifests and expresses himself through it. Of course, the presence of the spiritual soul cannot be ascertained experimentally.'

Patrick, distracted, fastened on to these words. He thought for a moment of those experiments he had read about, in which someone had tried to weigh the body just before and after death, to see if the soul could be weighed. What nonsense was this? He struggled to keep up. Someone was quoting scripture, he heard the familiar references. 'By becoming one of us, the Son makes it possible for us to become "children of God" (John 1:12), "participants of the divine nature" (2 Peter 1:4).'

The President of the Council, Archbishop Gonzales, took the floor. He paused dramatically before speaking, looking around at everyone in the room before finally resting his gaze on Patrick. 'Human life,' he said, 'is a manifestation of God in the world, a sign of his presence, a trace of his glory.' This, Patrick knew, was from Pope John Paul II's encyclical, *Evangelium Vitae*. 'Thus to attack a human embryo is to attack God. In every human being, above all in the least among us, one meets Christ himself. And,' he went on: '"What you do to one of the least of my brethren, you do unto me" (Matthew 25:40). So too with the unborn child. When we kill a helpless baby, we are killing Christ.'

Patrick was impatient; this was taking up too much time, they only had two days. They were simply stating what was already accepted, not debating anything new. After several people had spoken in similar vein, he stood up.

'It is clear that we do not in practice treat embryos and infants in the same way. *Donum Vitae* says, "The corpses of human embryos and foetuses, whether they have been deliberately aborted or not, must be respected just as the remains of other human beings." Yet we are not doing this.'

Many of the cardinals agreed with him; he could see their heads nodding. His eye caught Lebrun's and he saw him smile. No, it was the lay people, the mothers, who made most objection to this argument. A woman asked, how were they to know if what they experienced was a late period or an early miscarriage? Would they have to have this checked? Would they need to have a pregnancy test every month? Where would they go to be sure? Would it be incumbent on them to collect the remains? Should they collect the blood from every menstrual period to be examined by doctors in case it contained a fertilised egg?

And what about the funeral? Was not its main purpose to comfort the bereaved? How could you mourn for someone you didn't even know, who you didn't even know existed?

'Do you not realise what this would mean?' said one of the consultors. 'In biological terms, it is known that only about half of fertilised eggs implant successfully. If they do, they do not all develop – many are then miscarried. In many cases the woman will not know that she has even become pregnant.'

'We must allow common sense to prevail,' said Gonzales. 'The Church never has considered such early embryos to count in the same way as a child that has been born. Even though we know they have the potential to become a full human being, they are not yet a full human person. We accept that something like one in four or five pregnancies miscarries. If we include those that the mother does not even know about, it could be even more, perhaps one in every two or three pregnancies.'

He found it harder and harder to listen to the debate. It was strange, as Siobhan had said, that God allowed such a massacre of innocents.

Why had God made human reproduction such an uncertain matter? It was not enough to say that it was simply part of the fallen nature of the world. And what if he were to lose his own child? How would he feel? Could God have made him conceive and go through all this mental torment just for him to lose it? What purpose or meaning could there be in this?

He began to feel the strangest sensation. They were discussing 'the embryo' as he had done a thousand times, but now, for him, the embryo was not an abstract thing at all. It was something very real inside of him, something whose presence preoccupied him at every moment. He was acutely aware of every tiny sensation in his body. He heard the arguments come over him like waves in between the new and uncomfortable awareness of his situation. He left the room to go to the toilets down the corridor and checked his underwear, which was stained red with blood. He cleaned himself up as well as he could, padded himself with paper towels and went back into the Council.

The debate had moved on. They were now discussing what to do with the large number of frozen embryos already in existence. Gonzales again stood up; his loud voice boomed around the hall. 'Of course, I commend the sentiments that have been expressed,' he said, 'but all solutions continue the separation of the act of marital love from conception. This means there can be no morally licit solution regarding the human destiny of these thousands and thousands of "frozen" embryos.'

One of the laywomen stood up and spoke with a heavy Polish accent, arguing against him. She said that putting an already existing embryo into the womb of a married woman was simply to adopt a child before it was born. How could this be wrong? It served a double need – to give an infertile woman a child and enable her to fulfil her role, and to save and nurture a human life.

Wolf stood up again, quoting the Congregation for the Doctrine of the Faith's 2008 instruction *Dignitas Personae*; Patrick recognised the text. 'It has also been proposed, solely in order to allow human beings to be born who are otherwise condemned to destruction, that there could be a form of "prenatal adoption". This proposal, praiseworthy with regard to the intention of respecting and defending human life, presents however various problems... All things considered, it needs to be recognised that the thousands of abandoned embryos represent a situation of injustice which in fact cannot be resolved.' Wolf's position was simple; it should not have happened, therefore nothing could be done about it.

Now one of the bishops had raised the issue of what he called 'technological adultery'. 'As St Paul said, "The wife's body does not belong to her alone but to her husband. In the same way, the husband's body does not belong to him alone but to his wife."' He said that to place someone else's child into the body of the wife would violate the integrity of the marital union unique to that husband and wife.

Thankfully, there were some ordinary Catholic couples to join the debate, not just theologians. A married couple at the back of the room stood up; a tall African and his wife, who was splendidly dressed in a bright red garment which outshone the cardinals' robes. The husband's deep voice was calm and dignified. 'Those who say that embryo adoption violates the conjugal act, or that it achieves procreation apart from the marital union, are forgetting the fact that the child *already exists*. The child has already been procreated and simply awaits a loving couple who will come forward to save him or her. Please tell me, how is this different from adoption?'

An image came in to Patrick's mind, of an embryo in a jar in front of them, a real human soul whose fate they had to decide. Would they then decide differently? An embryo could not be kept in vitro forever; sooner or later it had to be either implanted, or destroyed. Would any of them present have the capacity to do the latter? He rose to speak; everyone fell silent, as if waiting for his words to solve the problem. What could he say, without inflaming things further?

Yet perhaps now was the time to say what he thought, to speak freely. 'The solution, that we leave these embryos frozen indefinitely, cannot be satisfactory. This issue has been causing problems and uncertainty among us for too long. We are not treating these embryos as if they are fully human. If there were hundreds of thousands of frozen three-year-olds in storage tanks throughout the world, wouldn't the tone of our theological and ethical discussion be a little different?'

He saw Gonzales, across the hall, shaking his head, and Cardinal Wolf's face turn hard as stone.

At the end of the first day, he called for Thomas and asked him to call Dr Conti to his rooms.

'Are you feeling ill again, Holy Father?'

'No – yes, a little. I am just tired. I think I will lie down for a while.'

'Can I help in any way?'

'No, Thomas, thank you, but you can't help.'

Again he thought he saw the pain of rejection in Thomas's eyes. He moved to say something, but Thomas had turned to leave the room.

He went into his bedchamber and lay down on the bed. It was an instinct. He found that he could not bear to walk up and down, that he wanted to lie still, to try to protect the life inside him, even though he didn't want it.

The doctor came. He examined him, pressing very gently on the abdominal region. 'Is there pain?'

'No – no, not really.'

'Any tenderness?'

'I don't think so.'

The doctor straightened up and then sat down on a chair which he pulled up close to the bed. He said, 'There is little we can do. Bleeding like this is not uncommon in pregnancy, even in people who go on to have a healthy baby. There is bleeding in about one in four pregnancies, and half of these will go on to develop normally. However, there is evidence that miscarriages tend to occur around the twelfth week – it may be because at this time, the hormones that support the pregnancy switch over from the ovaries to the placenta. If the bleeding gets heavier, if you experience pain or cramping, then it is very likely that you will lose the baby, and then you will need medical help.' He paused. 'We don't even think that bed rest helps – the thinking is that if you are going to lose the baby, it will happen anyway. But some people prefer to rest, to feel that they have done everything they can, and not to take part in any strenuous activities.'

'I have the Pontifical Council again tomorrow.'

'Well, Your Holiness, I think I would advise against attending it.'

'But I must be there. At least for the summing up at the end.' Without his presence there, he knew nothing would be achieved.

'Your Holiness, it is up to you. Perhaps, in a day or two, if the bleeding persists, we can do a scan. Sometimes that will tell us if the pregnancy is viable.'

'Let me think about it.' Something held him back – a desire not to know. The scan would not actually do anything to help. He would prefer to wait and see what happened.

'In the meantime,' said Dr Conti, 'I will get some sanitary towels for you, to absorb the bleeding. I will put them in an unmarked bag so no one need know.'

The doctor seemed only too aware of his sense of shame.

Conti bowed and left him. Patrick could not get to sleep. He still had a few of the sleeping pills, but he did not dare take them in case they might be harmful to the baby. He was tormented in the night with the thought that he wanted this pregnancy to end, that he had not done enough to safeguard it, that his actions in insisting on continuing with the Council had prejudiced the pregnancy. Was failing to stop an abortion as bad as actively seeking one? Jesus had said, he who looks on a woman to lust after her has already committed adultery in his heart. Had he not also committed an abortion in his heart?

Throughout the night he got up and examined the sanitary towel. Sometimes there was a streak of blood, sometimes not. He felt fear and relief alternating within him, but he was not always sure which was which.

He thought of Siobhan, of how she must have gone through this time and again. He prayed, 'Not my will, but Thine, be done.'

He fell asleep heavily just before dawn and woke to find Sister Veronica at his bedside, offering him a cup of tea.

'You will be late for Mass, Holy Father,' she said.

He dressed hurriedly. There was no more bleeding this morning.

After Mass, Thomas told him that a large group of people had gathered outside the Vatican to protest about the Church's teaching on abortion. It was no doubt connected with the Council meeting. He went to the window where he delivered his Angelus prayers every Sunday and looked out; a large group of women had gathered below him, waving flags and banners. He saw the familiar slogans: 'Not the Church and not the State, Women must decide their fate.' Why had the police not cleared the demonstration straight away, and how had they hidden these enormous banners from the police who patrolled the entrance to the square? He could hear the voices rising up from below, an angry, jarring sound of shouts and curses. Some of them had drums and horns and other instruments which they blasted into the air.

Below him, as if they had read his mind, the black-clothed police started to move in on the protesters. They moved in a line, truncheons ready, helmets down. He saw the protesters fight back and there were scuffles, people shouting out loudly in anger. He wanted to open the window and ask them to stop, but Thomas grabbed his arm and prevented him. He said they would ignore him, or shout abuse at him; he would seem powerless and impotent and that would reduce his authority.

'Someone may be armed. It is not safe.'

'I'm sorry.' He looked down at Thomas's arm, holding tightly to his wrist, and Thomas abruptly let go and turned away.

He looked out from behind the net curtain. He saw a woman suddenly break out from the crowd and start to run towards the palace. Somehow she had got through the police lines and she was running, running, her dark hair flying behind her. He watched in horror as a policeman darted forward, hit her with a truncheon, grabbed her arm and pulled her hand behind her back, forcing her down on to the ground. She struggled helplessly against his bulk, making little fluttering attempts to rise like a wounded bird.

He thought of Siobhan, of her white face, her anger, and the way she had shouted 'Murderer!' at him.

In the morning, as he walked back to the Consistory Hall along the corridor, he felt again the sensation of wet warmth between his legs. He stopped for a moment, and squeezed his legs together. Should he go back to his room? He felt an urge to lie down on the floor, to make supplication. Why had he not taken the doctor's advice and rested? Was it too late even now to go back to his bed? Was it stubbornness that made him persist? Did he really want to save the baby?

He continued down the corridor, walking slowly, trying to calm himself.

In the hall, they all bowed to him as he made his way to the throne-like chair. All day, the debate continued. It did not seem to be getting anywhere. Every couple of hours he went to check if he was still bleeding. He could see that people were beginning to look at him, to murmur, wondering no doubt if there was something wrong. Sometimes there was just a brownish smear, sometimes a larger red patch; it made him feel ill. He was ashamed of this blood. He did not know how to dispose of the stained sanitary towels in the men's lavatories; perhaps they would block the Vatican's plumbing and he would be found out, but what could he do? He shredded them into small pieces and flushed them away. Back in the Council, he realised he did not have the energy to try to steer the debate in the direction that he wanted.

He was called on to sum up. As he stood, he felt another flow of blood. He had to hold on to the lectern to steady himself. Perhaps he was bleeding too much; perhaps it was dangerous. But it would not be long. Fortunately he had prepared his speech. He looked beyond the cardinals to the ordinary families, their faces eager, expectant; it was for them he spoke.

'We have listened to one another; we have examined the issues with a sense of mutual respect and openness. We will continue to seek to deepen the theology of the family and discern the pastoral practices that our present situation requires, and to do so thoughtfully and without falling into casuistry.' He looked up at this point, to see the reaction. He knew it would annoy the cardinals; well, let them be annoyed. 'We are called to acknowledge how indispensable the family is for the life of the world and for the future of humanity, to make known God's magnificent plan for the family and provide pastoral care that is sound, courageous and full of love.'

He ended with a prayer. Finally, it was over. He knew it was a failure. Lebrun was right; he could not make too many enemies. In time a statement would be issued, but it would say nothing new. In any event it seemed nothing to him in the light of the extraordinary events that were taking place within him.

Thomas was there in his rooms, waiting for him when he got back.

'Well,' said Patrick, 'I have tried. I am exhausted. I will go and rest for a while.'

'You have not failed,' said Thomas. 'It is important that these views are heard and debated. This in itself is an achievement. You have opened the debate.'

Patrick shook his head. He felt profoundly depressed at the out-come. He had not achieved what he had hoped and he had not tried to save the pregnancy, either.

He took to his bed. Dr Conti came to see him and told him again that all he could do was rest and wait.

When he had gone, Sister Veronica came to him with some herbal tea and paracetamol.

'Would you like me to sit with you for a while, Holy Father? We are all praying that you feel better soon.'

'No – I would rather sleep. But I am grateful for your prayers.' He was worried that if she stayed with him she might realise what was wrong. Then he said, 'Just stay for a few moments.'

She sat on the chair by the bed. It was comforting to have someone there with him, a calming womanly presence.

'Sister Veronica, did you never want children?'

'Holy Father, I do not think I would have been a suitable person to be a mother,' she said. 'Ever since I was fourteen, and had my vision, I have had thoughts only of God. Children would have been a distraction.'

She was so certain. How could she be so certain about everything, and he was not?

After the Council, the bleeding went on for several days. He told Thomas he was unwell and to cancel his appointments. He was afraid above all that he would haemorrhage suddenly and then the secret would be out. He could not stay in bed all the time, but walked gently around the apartments. He continued with some desk-work, but all the time he was aware of his body, waiting for the slightest symptom, a twinge in his side that might develop into something worse, or a worsening of the bleeding. Was it like this, he thought, for women, waiting for their period? This extraordinary awareness of the body, so foreign to him who had never really thought about his body at all?

After four days, the bleeding stopped. He did not know whether he felt relief or disappointment.

So, that was how it was. He was not going to lose the baby. And it was too late now to abort, even had he wanted to. He needed another plan.

After evening prayer, he and Thomas ate a light supper together, a chicken salad and a fruit salad. He did not feel as nauseous as he had done before.

'Many of the cardinals do not see the problem,' Patrick said, still preoccupied with the Council. 'They do not see why we cannot continue as we are. They do not see that the position of the Church on these matters has changed in the past and that it should continue to evolve and change today, in the light of new circumstances and scientific understanding.'

He was aware of Thomas watching him, his face very still. 'Science is indeed presenting us with new problems,' he said. 'It is sometimes difficult to reconcile new information with what we have always believed.'

'What were you thinking?'

For the first time, he felt there was a reluctance in Thomas to speak – a barrier between them. He went on, 'You are thinking of something specific?'

'I am thinking,' said Thomas, 'about how scientific knowledge might ultimately change our perspective on some issues. For example, this question of homosexuality. If science is genuinely showing us – as some people are arguing – that a homosexual orientation is not a matter of an individual's choice, but is genetically determined… well, we cannot take quite the same view on it.'

Why had Thomas raised this, suddenly? 'You know that we must always make a distinction between homosexual orientation, and acts.'

'Of course.' Thomas fell silent, looking at the floor. Patrick felt that he had somehow offended Thomas and was surprised at how upset this made him.

He was reminded of the anonymous letters that he'd given Thomas to deal with. He had heard no more about them. 'Thomas, did any more happen about those letters?'

'Letters?' Then Thomas seemed to recall. 'Oh, I don't think so. In any event, nothing has ever appeared in the papers.' He seemed to want to say no more on the subject.

'But you gave them to Cardinal Romano?'

'I think he was too busy to look at them.'

'Well, perhaps better to forget it, then.'

'Indeed. That's what I thought, Holy Father.'

Well, it was of no real importance. Patrick rose from the table and went into the living room and Thomas sat down at the piano. He ran his hands down his thighs over the silk robe, then sat, his head bowed, collecting himself, as he always did before he began playing. His right hand felt out the chords, then he began; the slow movement from the *Moonlight Sonata*. Patrick sat and watched his hands move over the keys. The movements were simple, quiet, understated. He did not seem to be touching many notes, the piece did not look difficult, and yet the music which came from the instrument tore at his heart.

A memory came back to him. He was in Cork one afternoon, after school, wandering the streets on his own. Outside the cornmarket, a man had set up a piano and was playing. The wooden front had been taken off so that the sound sung out clearly and he could see the hammers moving, striking the strings. The plaintive notes rang out; he could hear their timbre, the deep plangent bass and the high ringing tones. As he stood opposite, two priests walked past, their waists tight, their black skirts blowing out in the wind, deep in conversation, seeming to float over the ground, swaying slightly as if in time to the music. Was that the moment that had made him want to become a priest? He could see those two men in his mind's eye as if they were in front of him now; he was not sure why, but he thought it was the way they walked in step, the intentness of their conversation, as though nothing in the outside world had any importance for them. Had that been the moment? But perhaps there was no one moment of choice. It had been a gradual thing, growing on him throughout his teenage years. He had told his mother of his wish, several times, but she did not take it seriously. 'When you get older, you may change your mind and decide to do something else,' she said. But he could tell she was pleased.

When he finally told her he was certain of it, he remembered her delight. She had clasped her hands, then opened them wide and wrapped them around him, about the only time he had ever known her do that. And he, so unused to it, instead of responding to her, had stood wooden and aloof so that she let go of him at once and rushed to tell his father.

His father had been standing by the fireplace, his hands behind his back, warming himself in front of the flames. With his tall, thin frame he always felt the cold. He was not pleased at the news.

'You are sure?'

'Completely sure.'

'There is no point in trying to persuade you any differently?'

'No point.'

His father looked down at him stiffly. 'Then I had better, as it were, give you my blessing.'

He did not refer to it again.

Friday 24 June. The Nativity of St John the Baptist. A baptism in the Sistine Chapel. There, at the stone font in front of *The Last Judgement* and under the frescoes of the Creation, the mother held the baby out to him. He poured the water from the little silver cup over the baby's forehead; in the Name of the Father, Son and Holy Spirit. He rested his hand for a moment on the baby's bald head; it did not cry, but gave a kind of startled gurgle.

He had performed this act so many times, handling the child automatically, but now he stared at this baby with a new curiosity. It seemed almost like a marine life-form, the way it opened and closed its tiny mouth like a fish, blowing tiny bubbles from its pouting lips, and opening and closing its tiny starfish hands.

For the first time, what was happening to him seemed real. He too would have one of these strange creatures. He was becoming used to the idea. Now that he no longer felt so sick, he did not experience the baby as something foreign, something hostile, inside him. Instead, he began to feel almost a tenderness towards it.

But he had done nothing to sort out what would happen to the child.

It seemed to him more and more when he prayed that God was not listening to him. In his prayers he no longer felt any warmth or solace, only a hollow emptiness. Perhaps this was indeed the Dark Night. He knew what to do in such times of spiritual desolation; he should wait patiently for God to find him. He must seek no reward, only give himself completely to God. Yet how hard it was, when God was silent.

It seemed to him clear that just when he was beginning to feel a love for this child, that he must give him up, for his sake, for the sake of the Church. To grow up as his child, even if he were not the pope, even if he resigned and gave up the priesthood, would not be natural. The child could not grow as it should, in a loving family, with a mother and a father and other children. He must put the child's needs first. That much was clear. And yet it pained him to think that he would be forever separated from him. Could he visit from time to time, as a kind of godfather? Would he be able to still love the child from afar?

He asked again and again, why, why me? And the only answer that came back was, 'Why not?' He knew that Jesus himself received no answer when he felt himself forsaken, neither in the garden of Gethsemane nor on the cross.

He rose from his knees and took the diary from its shelf. A thought came to him, that he was addressing the diary to the wrong person. It was not God that he should be writing to, for God, it seemed, had withdrawn from him. He thought of another who he should address, the child who might never know him. It was difficult to begin. He thought at first that he would be unable to commit a single thought to paper. The page, so white and clean, dazzled him. He did not want to sully it with any mark or imperfection. He took up his pen. He had thought of confessing everything that was on his mind, but he was afraid to share it with another human being. Yet he wanted to record it. If he did not, he was afraid his memory would distort everything.

It could be something that could be kept for his child to read when he was adult, a record of the truth, a token of his love. As long as it would never fall into the wrong hands.

He closed the diary, took a piece of paper from his desk and wrote:

My son,

If you ever read this it will be because you have never known me. I will have given you up to someone who will care for you far better than I will ever be able to. I have done this for your sake. You will never know how much it has troubled me to do this, though as I write this I do not know if you will even live. Perhaps I will not live, either. Perhaps I should not write to you at all, should never burden you with my hopes and fears. For by the time you read this, you will be eighteen. You will be a man. You will have no need of me.

All life is a gift from God, even if it does not always appear like that to us. You were a gift to me, and I have gifted you to someone else. I hope that you will not think unkindly of me. Of course, I hope, like all parents, that you will have something in you of myself. I hope you will find a place for yourself in the world and I hope you will be happy.

Something wet splashed on to the paper in front of him, smearing the fresh ink. He realised that he was weeping. It was a shock; it was the first time since he was a young child that he had shed tears. He blotted the page, put the letter in an unmarked envelope and hid it in the drawer in his desk. He wiped the tears from his eyes with his sleeve, but they kept on coming. It was strange, because he did not feel upset; there was nothing in the letter that should have caused such a torrent. Where were the tears coming from? Was he crying for his child, for himself, for Siobhan, for every mother who had lost her child, or for the whole suffering mass of humanity? It was as if the whole world had suddenly become personalised, made flesh in this one small unborn child whom he might never know. It was too much to bear. He realised that, once he had started, the tears would not stop. He found himself washed over by a tide of grief, as if the very act of weeping had caused the emotion. He walked up and down in his room, unable to calm himself, sobbing, stifling the moans that rose up in his throat, trying to calm his ragged breathing, letting the storm of feeling pass by, hoping that no one in the papal household was near enough to hear him.

There was a sudden change in him. A luxurious feeling of ease filled his whole body; the aching, the nausea, the tiredness had all gone. He thought that perhaps something had happened inside him, a reverse creation, a second miracle which would relieve him of his burden. Was he no longer pregnant? As soon as he had this thought, he realised with a start that he did not want the child not to exist.

He would ring Dr Conti and go and see him, to check that all was well.

It was morning. The sun was already fierce, blazing into the room. His coffee was not there by the door; he had failed to drink it for so long that they must have decided not to bring it. Now he instinctively knew that the smell of coffee would no longer nauseate him.

When he said Mass, he felt at peace. His mind felt sharp again, and it was easier to attend to all the paperwork. His appetite returned. Food was no longer repellent to him. At lunchtime, they brought him a salad, of delicate green leaves and thinly sliced cucumber, tomatoes, and a few basil leaves, dressed with the lightest oil and vinegar. Then a mushroom risotto, cooked to just the consistency that he liked. A small glass of good Chianti, in a thin-stemmed goblet; he would take just a few sips, not enough to cause any harm to the baby. A single rose-blossom stood in a vase on the table-top and trembled slightly in the breeze that came in through the open window. He and Thomas sat in a deep, companionable silence. He ate slowly, savouring each mouthful, and after the meal he had a very small espresso with two squares of darkest chocolate.

In the afternoon, he decided to have a nap instead of reading his papers. He took off his shoes and lay on his back, staring up at the ceiling, at the ornate cornices and the narrow crack that ran across the centre of the room. For once, his mind was still. He deliberately relaxed his limbs, tightening the muscles and then letting go, from his feet all the way up to his eyebrows. A heavy tranquillity filled his body, and his limbs sank into the softness of the bed.

Sister Veronica brought a herbal tea and smiled at him. He had never before slept in the afternoon; now he would insist on it. Her look was so intent and knowing that he wondered if she had guessed at something.

Then, in the depths of his body, he felt a weird sensation. It felt like bubbles rising and falling in his belly, something stirring deep inside him.

Chapter Eleven

Thomas came running towards him down the corridor. Patrick could see from his face that there was something wrong.

'Your mother,' Thomas said, breathless. 'On the phone.'

He rushed to the office. His mother's voice sounded different, very old and frail.

'How can I say this?' There came a short pause. 'Your father has died,' she said. 'It was a stroke.' She paused. 'I'm so sorry to bring you this bad news.' She sounded apologetic, as if it was her fault.

'When?' How little he had thought of his parents in all this time – he had forgotten even to mention them in his prayers! And his mother had written to say his father had been unwell, and he had not even found time to reply to her.

'This morning. It was very sudden. He was walking in the garden, and I saw him fall –' he heard the catch in her voice – 'and I ran to him, and he was lying on the ground, with his eyes wide open, and I knew at once, even though of course I called an ambulance –'

There was a disconnection between what he felt and what he knew he should feel. The overwhelming emotion was of relief – that he would never now have to fear that his father would find out what was happening to him.

'I am so sorry,' he said. 'What a terrible thing for you. But for him –'

'No, he didn't suffer. And we were in church on Sunday. I don't know when he last made confession –'

He knew what she was thinking. That there was not time for the last rites.

'I need to arrange the funeral,' she said. 'I need to know when you can come.'

'I will look at my schedule and will let you know,' he said. 'Of course this takes precedence over everything else.'

He said a prayer with her then, and hung up the phone. He stood for a long moment in silence. Thomas was standing looking at him, his face very close. Patrick had not noticed before how long his eyelashes were.

'My father,' he said. 'A stroke. He is – dead. I will need to attend the funeral.'

Thomas nodded, and hesitated for a moment as if uncertain what to say. When he spoke, his words seemed strangely formal. 'I am so sorry for your loss... Holy Father, accept my deepest condolences. Of course I will make all the arrangements for you.'

So, he would go to Ireland. How strange that was. He could stay at the bishop's house in Cork. It need only be a short trip. Or perhaps, if he wanted, he could stay longer. He had a longing now to see his country, to get away from the atmosphere in Rome, to walk by the sea and to go perhaps to his grandfather's house, their holiday place, and pray in his old room with the view of the bay and the islands stretching out into the west.

As he sat in prayer, he thought of his father. A severe, stern presence in the household, a man of few words, and strict conduct. He remembered his father sitting at his desk over his engineering drawings, with his set square and compasses, intent, methodical. He, to his father's frustration, did not do so well at maths; there were tormenting hours when his father insisted on going through his maths problems with him, and the longer it went on, the stupider he felt. The questions were so pointless, filled as they were with impossible scenarios. Assume the balls are of equal weight. Assume the train is moving at a steady speed of fifty miles per hour. Assume the surface is frictionless. What was the point of it? The world was not like that.

His father had always seemed so distant, hidden behind the crinkling pages of his newspaper or shut away in his study with the door firmly closed. He recalled how his father did not like to make conversation in the car because it put him off driving, so that they sat in silence, even when they were going on holiday to the west coast and he wanted nothing more than to chatter about what he planned to do when they were there, and a feeling of melancholy would come over him that killed the holiday mood. He looked out of the car window as they drove down the wild Atlantic way and saw the hedgerows full of red fuchsia flowers that fell on the roadway like drops of blood.

Meals were not much better; his father said grace and then conversation was stilted – the dreaded question about how he was getting on at school, which he answered as shortly as possible; his father made dutiful enquiries into his mother's charitable works and an enquiry or two about their friends' health. His mother answered politely, she smiled at him cheerfully, but she never seemed to say anything that was interesting. Those meals were almost monastic, the only sounds the chip and scrape of cutlery on the plates, the suppressed munching, the occasional swish of a car going past or voices outside the window.

He'd always felt his father was ashamed of him in some way. Even when his school reports praised his intelligence and application, his father did not reward him. He tried even harder to excel, but his father did not seem interested. When he received the school prize his father framed it and hung it on the wall of the dining area, but he didn't mention it. Patrick had stared at it during meal times and, for some reason that he couldn't understand, it made him feel ashamed.

Now the memories were coming back to him, flooding into his mind in quick succession. His first experience of death. His grandfather had passed away when he was eight years old. He remembered the oppressive atmosphere in his uncle's house, the growing tension as his grandfather's end grew near. The old man's bed had been brought downstairs into the drawing room, and he lay there in the dark room in the light of an open fire, the clutter of pills and medical paraphernalia on the table next to him, a strange smell of various ointments and potions, his grandfather's hands trembling and pulling at the old quilt.

Over the fireplace hung a large, ornate mirror. It leaned out slightly from the wall and seemed to reflect the room at a strange angle. When he was younger he would sit and look in the mirror and sometimes had an odd feeling that the mirror, with its strange reversed topography, might be the real world, and the world in which he sat only an imitation of it. He sometimes wondered whether there was any way you could get into the world beyond the frame, as Alice did in *Through the Looking-Glass*. In the days leading up to his grandfather's death he could not look at him directly; he just glimpsed in the mirror the edge of the bed and his grandfather's strange shrunken form on the pillow.

He did not like sitting in that room. The next day, while his mother visited, he waited in the kitchen, sipping orange squash, hearing his grandfather's voice from the other room, raving, calling for his other brother who had died in France in the war. Then came the morning when they did not go to the house. His mother told him over breakfast that his grandfather had died in the night. In the end he had been very peaceful, she said. Death was not a thing to be afraid of. It happened to everyone, and if they had been a good Catholic they would be going to God. She did not sound sad or upset; on the contrary, she seemed to be relieved that it was all over. He, too, was pleased that he would not have to sit in that kitchen and listen to any more of his grandfather's raving.

His mother sat and said a prayer with him. He wondered why, when death was not a bad thing, he felt so terribly, dreadfully scared of it.

They went to pay their last respects to his grandfather. It was a cold day, and there was still some frost on the lawn under the shadow of the big trees, but the bright golden daffodils were opening in the front garden. It seemed to him strange that the spring was coming and his grandfather would not see it. They went into the living room. His grandfather was laid out on the bed and his uncle had pinned photographs of his life around the room, times when he had been happy. Patrick stared at the photo of the young, vigorous man on his wedding day, at family gatherings. He, too, one day, would grow old and die. He would be laid out on the bed, and people would come to look at him. He knew it was so, and yet he couldn't quite believe it.

He approached his grandfather's bed and looked down at the pale, translucent skin. He looked as empty as a shell. He had been anxious beforehand, but now the sight did not frighten him. This was not his grandfather; his grandfather was gone. At his mother's prompting, he reached out his hand and gently touched his grandfather's forehead. The skin felt cool and damp and odd, like a piece of uncooked meat.

'There,' said his mother. 'Now you'll never see a ghost.'

The funeral was to be on Friday. 'The flight is arranged,' said Thomas. 'It will leave from Ciampino tomorrow. The helicopter will come to collect you at nine o'clock. I have cleared all your appointments from the diary for the next three days.'

'Thank you, Thomas.' Patrick had checked with Dr Conti and been told that it was not too dangerous to travel, but he was nervous all the same.

'You do not want me to accompany you, Holy Father?'

'No, that is a kind thought, but it will not be necessary.'

Thomas nodded and looked down. Patrick could see that he was disappointed, and felt a pang himself at leaving him behind. They had hardly been apart in all these months; he would miss his support and his company. But he knew it would be a mistake to travel with him. It had not occurred to him till now, but he realised that he would have an opportunity to talk to his mother, to discover what she knew. Thomas's presence at this time could only be an obstacle to him. This was something he had to do alone.

The bishop's house had been his home for some nine years. The dark brick mansion stood high on the hill surrounded by an untidy garden full of sombre evergreens. As his car swept in, he saw a small crowd of people at the gates; the Gardaí in their dark blue uniforms stood on duty and closed the gates behind him. When he had lived there, they had always been open, and people were free to walk in and out.

They opened the car door for him and he stepped out into the fresh, damp air. The house looked down over the strange neo-Gothic cathedral below, the Shandon bell-tower where he remembered as a child climbing up to pull the ropes and sound a simple hymn tune on the bells, and the city lying in the valley below him. It was all just as he remembered.

Bishop Murphy came out to greet him. Patrick had known him quite well, but now the bishop seemed awkward and overawed by his presence. He bowed his tall, thin frame and kissed his ring, then took him inside, into the familiar study.

Patrick crossed the room, stopped and stroked the surface of the old oak desk which stood in front of the window, and looked out over the lawn. Now, he wished that he had never left. If his pregnancy had happened when he was Bishop of Cork, he could have resigned, and passed into quiet obscurity. He shut his eyes and breathed in the familiar fusty smell of the room; the faint smell of furniture polish, the hint of wood smoke.

'We have arranged everything as you wish,' said the bishop.

'Thank you, that's good, that's very good.' He paused. 'I wanted to see my mother, that is the first thing I need.'

'We have told her you have arrived. Should she come over?'

'That would be grand.'

'We will call her at once.'

There was an awkward silence.

'I would like to be alone for a while. It has been a tiring journey. May I stay here?"

'Of course.' The bishop seemed relieved to be able to leave. Once the door had closed, Patrick sat at the desk and stared at the small crucifix in front of him. Somehow, he never became inured to that image. The twisted body and the grave and dignified expression of the face still moved him.

After half an hour, there was a knock on the door. His mother came in; she was dressed in a smart tweed suit with a brooch on the lapel, clearly trying to make a good impression, to look her best, but she looked smaller to him, thinner, older. Her hair had turned whiter and was wispy at the front. It was a shock to him; it was never pleasant to see someone age.

She came over, put her hands in his, then bowed before him.

'I can't get used to it, indeed I can't,' she said. 'My son, the pope! How should I address you? Holy Father?'

'No, this is not necessary, now,' he said. He detected a tiny tremor in her hand. Was it nerves, or perhaps the frailty of age, or something more, the first signs of Parkinson's?

'I am so sorry, mother. Let us sit and pray together.' He indicated a chair near the desk, and she sank into it. He prayed, and she made the responses. It felt mechanical to him, as if neither of them really had their heart in what they were saying.

'And how are you coping?' he asked her afterwards. 'Are you missing him?'

'It is very strange being alone in the house; I can't get used to it yet.'

'Of course not, that will take a long time. It has only been a few days.'

There was a long silence. He thought he should wait till after the funeral to ask her the questions that he longed for, but he knew he could not wait that long. It was too important to him. He forced himself to listen to her talking, reciting to him the content of the letters and the phone calls she had received; then she made some comments about the plans for the Requiem Mass, the readings that she had chosen, and whether he wanted to make any changes. He said that it was all perfect.

'And there is something I wanted to ask you,' she said. 'The little cross I gave you, which was my mother's – you still have it? You keep it safe, I hope?'

He hesitated. How could he tell her that he had lost it? He knew he should not lie, but he could not tell her the truth without hurting her deeply. He knew how much that cross had meant to her. He nodded. 'Such a precious gift,' he said. There, he had not lied directly; she was satisfied. At the same time he felt angry with himself, and that anger suddenly turned against his mother. He had so little time; he could not spare her feelings.

'Mother, I wanted to ask you something. Something important.'

She fiddled with the hem of her jacket, which he noticed, now, was slightly frayed.

'About what, Patrick?'

'About me, Mother.'

'You?'

'When I was a child. You knew there was something not quite right with me, didn't you? Why did you never say?'

'I don't know what you mean, Patrick. And why must we have this conversation now? It is hardly the time for it, just when your father is dead and lying in his coffin.'

He knew that she was right and that he should not intrude, but something almost cruel in him made him persist. 'Mother, there may never be another time for it. The funeral is tomorrow, and in the evening I must return to Rome. I wanted to spend more time here, but it was not possible.'

'I can't talk about anything now, Patrick, what are you thinking of.' It was strange; all the awe she had seemed to feel when she entered the room had fallen away, and it was as if he was a child again, trying to get his mother to respond to him in the way that he had always wanted, while she stubbornly resisted him.

Anger flashed in him; he had to know the truth. 'Well, if you will not talk to me about it now, as your son, then I must command you as your pope.'

He watched, detached, as she twisted her hands in her lap, and turned her head slightly from side to side as if hoping she could somehow get away from him. 'There is nothing I can say to you about it. I took you to the doctor once and he told me there was nothing wrong.'

'Well, Mother, I think you know this – there *is* something wrong. I had to see a doctor in Rome because of certain... symptoms. It seems I have what they call an *intersex* condition.' He could hardly bring himself to say that word – intersex. 'What they call a disorder of sexual development.'

She looked at him with wide eyes, like a rabbit caught in the headlights. 'I don't know anything about this, to be sure, I don't.'

'But you didn't think to take me to another doctor. You didn't think to take me to a specialist.'

'The doctor said that it might right itself at adolescence, with the hormones, he said it wasn't anything to worry about. I prayed for you, that everything would work out all right. And then, of course, it was not right for me to see you naked. I never saw you naked, after you were a little boy. So I didn't know anything about it then. I trusted what the doctor said, I trusted God that he would make all well.'

She was staring out of the window; she could not look at him. She took a tissue out of her bag, and as she spoke she folded and refolded it with her shaking fingers. 'The truth is, I didn't want the doctors to interfere with you. I loved you, Patrick, as you were. And I thought there would be time enough to do something, when you were older and knew what you wanted. And then you were set to become a priest. And I thought, it will not matter if he becomes a priest. You know I believe that God has given us our bodies and that is a precious thing and if he gave you a body that was a little different there must be some purpose in it.'

'Well,' he said, 'I am grateful for that at least. That you decided not to have me – operated on.'

She looked at him longingly, like a distressed animal.

'Well, you are right, Mother, perhaps if you had taken me back they would have operated on me. Who knows what they might have done. I could have been – mutilated. They might have given me hormones, they might have turned me into someone else.' He thought for a moment what his life might have been like if he had been turned into and raised as a woman; nothing would have been the same. 'I wanted in fact to thank you for leaving me as I am.'

She turned to him, but did not move. He knew she would not come and embrace him. He remembered all the times when he was a teenager when he longed for her to embrace him but she never did. At a certain point, she had stopped touching him entirely. He remembered sitting on her lap when he was small, of her kissing him and hugging him before he went to bed, but then it had all stopped.

'Did you tell Father?'

'Never.'

'And he didn't see?'

'Your father would never have noticed anything like that. He would not have looked. And he did very little with you, when you were small. That was all my business.'

He thought back to when he was small, how he had always felt such a sense of… shame. But that was how it was for all of them, shame of their bodies, shame about their sexuality. It was all mixed up for him with the feeling that he'd had at the time, of cold, wet winters, endless rain, damp Sunday afternoons in his bedroom. He had avoided playing with the other boys and girls, so he had nothing to do but read and wait for the clock to tick away the hours till supper-time, the bored procrastinations until he started his homework, sometimes far too late, so that after wasting a whole afternoon he would have to sit up late struggling with maths problems until his eyes ached with tiredness. Why had he never felt any desire to escape? It was as if he had been paralysed.

His mother was talking to him again. 'Anyway, I can't imagine why you would want to talk about it, now. It hardly matters to you, does it?'

Could he tell her? No, not now. It was the wrong time. The shock of his father's death was enough for her to take. He would have to wait.

Then she said, 'I was worried for you, mind, when you were to become pope. I remembered those stories about Pope Joan. And how afterwards, there was a special chair so they could inspect the pope to check that he was a man –'

'That is nonsense, Mother. There is no such thing. And the story about Pope Joan... that is also nonsense. It has been completely discredited.'

'I remember how I liked that story,' she said. 'About how she disguised herself, and rose up through the ranks of the clergy, and it was only discovered when she gave birth after she fell off her horse during a procession and... are you all right?'

He felt dizzy for a moment; yet again, a sense of complete unreality came over him. 'Let us end this conversation, Mother. I did not call you here to speak about such inanities as Pope Joan.'

'There was a reason,' she said, suddenly, looking down at the floor. 'A reason?'

'Why I wanted to do nothing. There was a neighbour of ours, she'd had a baby boy. But the boy had something wrong with his – his thing – the hole was in the wrong place. And they said they would operate on it, and they tried several times. But something went wrong, and in the end they had to remove it. And then they said the best thing would be to turn him into a girl and bring him up as a girl so that he wouldn't know there was something wrong with him.' She sighed. 'Except that he never was right as a girl, poor thing. He was always interested in the boy's games. He followed them around. And then of course, when he was older, someone had to explain to him. Because he couldn't have children, of course, he couldn't have a – normal life.'

'And you knew this boy?'

'His mother wrote to me for years. I didn't want something like that to happen to you. And praise be that it didn't, or you could never have become our Holy Father.' She searched around for her handbag, found it wedged behind her on the chair, and got to her feet. 'Let us not talk about this any more. You will be going to the funeral parlour to see your father, won't you, before everyone arrives tomorrow? The house… it's too small, we couldn't fit the crowds in there, and then, won't there be your bodyguards? Everyone will be wanting to come, of course, because of you. Well, what could I say, I couldn't stop them, could I?'

Chapter Twelve

His father's body had lain in the funeral parlour for two days. It was strange to be going to that place driven in a large car with police and bodyguards, and step out into the familiar street to see people staring at him. Word must have got out and a small crowd was gathering; the Gardaí kept them back, but they waved and called to him. He wondered whether he should cross the road and speak to them, but the bodyguards steered him into the parlour. Inside, the place was tastefully decorated, with pale carpet and the walls a creamy white, and the staff were standing by to greet him. They showed him up the steps leading into the room where the coffin could be viewed, and then stepped back, tactfully giving him space.

He went up to the coffin and, crossing himself, looked in. His father lay, his face pale and austere, in a dark suit, his hands clasping a crystal rosary.

He was used to death. It had been so much a part of his life as a priest – it was a time when people needed God the most, during their sorrow and affliction, when they hoped desperately that this death was not the end. His father did not look quite dead at first; his face had been touched up, no doubt with rouge, to give a faint hue of colour to his cheeks. But as he looked, it was the absolute immobility of his features that gave away the truth.

He sat by his father's body. The curtains were drawn and a narrow strip of sunlight came through the gap between them and fell on to the coffin. He watched it move slowly across his father's body, till it illuminated his face. He felt for an instant that the sun might animate him, bring the cold face back to life. How little he had known his father. It hurt him, more than he had thought, that he now never could.

The words from Luke 16:26 came into his mind with astonishing force: 'Between you and us a great chasm has been fixed, so that those who might want to pass from here to you cannot do so, and no one can cross from there to us.' How harsh he had always found these words; but perhaps they were no more than a statement of simple truth. The chasm was perhaps not, as in the parable, that between heaven and hell, but between the living and the dead, the chasm of time itself. He felt an unbearable desire to go back into the past and try to reach his father's heart.

He heard voices outside. It was time, then; soon people would be coming in. It was nearly an hour before he was due to say the rosary, but they would come early. He stayed where he was. The women came in, and sat in the chairs which had been set out for them; the men stood around, talking. They looked at him, but no one approached him. When his mother came, she too came up to the coffin and then they withdrew to sit on the chairs alongside.

One by one, in turn, the people who had gathered went up to sympathise with his father in the coffin. He heard the women whisper to one another, 'How wonderful he looks, how peaceful, doesn't he look beautiful.' He realised that he was angry with them; to him, his father did not look beautiful. His father looked as cold in death as he had been in life.

More people came. They crammed into the room, talking and greeting one another. He saw faces he knew – cousins and uncles and aunts. And who was this? – Mary Connelly. She alone of all of them came up to him, bowed and said, 'Thank you, Holy Father, for intervening with Siobhan.'

'I did nothing, truly.'

'She is still receiving treatment for her illness… she wanted to come here to thank you in person, but she was not well enough. She is hoping to come to the service tomorrow.'

'I am sorry to hear that she is ill. I will continue to pray for her.'

At four o'clock he said the rosary. He used his mother's rosary – the plain wooden beads, smooth and worn with use, slipped through his fingers automatically as he quietly recited the prayers. He began by holding the crucifix, saying, 'In the Name of the Father and of the Son and of the Holy Spirit,' making the sign of the cross, and then he said the Apostles' Creed.

He saw his mother bowing her head, her lips moving as she silently said the prayers with him.

On the single bead just above the cross, he prayed the 'Our Father.' Then on to the next cluster of three beads, reciting the 'Hail Mary'. He did not have to think about the prayers any more; they rose in his heart and were sounded on his lips without thought, as a meditation.

On the chain after the three beads, he said the 'Glory be…'

When he had ended, people came to him to thank him, to ask for a blessing, to touch him, to say, no doubt, that they had touched the pope. Then someone different stood in front of him; someone who did not bow. He looked up. It was his old friend, Niall, smiling down at him. How extraordinary! He looked almost the same, with the warm brown eyes and lopsided smile – he would have recognised him anywhere.

Niall said, 'I am so sorry about your father. I remember him as a fine man.'

'Thank you. It was very sudden. At least he did not suffer.' He paused. 'It's good to see you.'

Niall hesitated, then he said, 'I thought of writing – to congratulate you. But I felt guilty that I never replied to your letters. I was – going through a difficult time.' He paused. 'May I… is it possible to see you, speak to you in private? I mean, not here, not at the funeral.'

'Of course. How can I contact you?'

Niall handed him a card and turned away.

The coffin was closed and taken to the cathedral where it would rest overnight before the Requiem Mass the following day.

How strange, that he should see Niall again.

Niall had been his only childhood friend. They walked to school together and on the way home they sometimes went to the playground and spent an hour or so there, playing on the climbing frame and swings. They avoided the other boys; if the playground was crowded they preferred to go back to Niall's house and play with his soldiers or to his own place, where they would play Trojan Wars with a pack of playing cards, black suits for the Trojans, red for the Greeks. Achilles, he remembered, was the Ace of Hearts, Patrocles the Ace of Diamonds.

It had been a friendship mainly of convenience. As they grew older, it became clear that he and Niall had little in common. Niall was much more interested in sport than in study. He became less interested in their games and it was Patrick who had to persuade him to continue with them – after all, you needed two people to play pirates or Trojan Wars. And being together did preserve them both from the playground bullies, and kept his parents from constantly asking him who he was with and where he was going.

Niall came to his house far more often than he went there. He knew that something had happened in Niall's house that made it feel cold and strange. Niall had hinted at something but when he tried to find out more, Niall wouldn't say. Niall's mother was a sad-looking woman. Occasionally, when he came down into the kitchen for a glass of water, he would see that she had been crying. A kind of heaviness, almost a darkness, seemed to emanate from her. Once, when Patrick went downstairs to the toilet, he heard Niall's mother crying from behind the closed kitchen door.

Eventually Patrick's mother told him what had happened. Niall had not been an only child; there had been a brother who had been born sickly and had died after a long illness. The baby had been so ill that it had never left the hospital; no one had ever seen him. Niall's mother had never got over the grief and guilt.

This sense of tragedy was something Patrick had not felt before. At home, he had always felt safe. And his mother had always reassured him that if he prayed, God wouldn't let bad things happen to him. But this was his first real test of faith. Why had God not helped Niall's mother? She was very religious. She was always in church, she wore a silver cross around her neck, she had a picture of Our Lady over the fireplace. Hadn't she prayed for her baby? How she would have prayed and prayed and prayed for her baby to be healed. But he hadn't been healed; he had got worse, and died. Jesus, who had healed the sick and raised Lazarus, had done nothing for Niall's baby brother.

How long ago it seemed. And then there had been that mysterious silence after Niall moved to Dublin, when he had not replied to Patrick's letters. Perhaps he would finally find out what had happened.

In the evening, he rang the number Niall had given him.

'Can you come tomorrow, in the morning, to the bishop's house? I will have half an hour or so to have coffee.'

Niall said that would be his pleasure.

He waited for Niall in the living room, sombre in the daytime because of all the surrounding trees which at this time of year were heavy with leaves. The housekeeper came to bring coffee on a tray. In the distance he could hear the clattering plates in the kitchen as someone helped with the washing-up. Niall was already five minutes late. He was irritated; he was not used to waiting for people – on the contrary, people always had to wait for him.

The door opened, and Niall was ushered in. There was a moment's awkwardness. Should they embrace? Shake hands? In the event they did neither. Patrick sat down at the table and poured him a coffee.

'A biscuit?'

'No, thanks. Trying to keep the weight off.'

Patrick wondered if Niall thought his own expansion round the waist was caused by laziness or indulgence.

'Well,' said Niall, 'This is very strange. Should I address you as Holy Father?'

'No, of course not. You can call me Patrick, as before. Please, let us talk, just think that I am your old schoolfriend.' He stirred his coffee. There was a silence, then they both spoke at once.

'I wondered –'

'Do you think –'

They broke off and then laughed, Niall a little tensely.

Patrick tried to start the conversation. 'Tell me about yourself, first. What you're doing. How you are. If you have a family.'

'A family? No – no family.'

'And you teach?'

'Yes, I am a PE teacher.'

'That was your favourite subject.'

'It's hard work sometimes, but with a good class, I enjoy it.'

'And your parents?'

'Still doing well. In the same house. I don't see them much. They disapprove of – my lifestyle.'

There was a pause. He was not sure what Niall meant. Did he mean, because he had not settled down and had a family? Should he probe further? He thought that he should not. But Niall didn't say any more, so he found himself echoing, 'Your lifestyle?'

'Yes. I may as well say it. You are probably wondering why I broke off contact with you. I think I always had an idea about it, but I didn't say anything to anyone. Then I fell for someone and I couldn't conceal it any longer. I'm gay, you see.'

'I see.' A little shock went through him.

'There didn't seem to be any point in contacting you. I'm not religious. I know what you think, it's "intrinsically evil and disordered", but I can't think that. It's just me. It's how I am. And if you don't want to accept this, then please say so and we can just part now, without saying any more, without arguing or offending each other.'

'I am not offended,' he said. But perhaps he was.

Niall raised his cup of coffee to his lips. 'Then may I be frank?'

'Of course.'

'Well, I often thought we were friends, as teenagers, because neither of us had the slightest interest in girls. Me, because – well, now you know why – and you, because you seemed to have no interest in sex at all.'

'No interest?' He found he did not know what to say and so kept reflecting back the words he had just heard, like an idiot. And he began to have an uncomfortable feeling. All his life he had thought that his lack of sexual feelings was the result of his will-power and desire for holiness. He had thought it was possible for everyone to control their sexuality as he had done. He had prayed each day not to be led into temptation, and he had not been led. It had never occurred to him to imagine what it would have been like to experience real temptation, to be overwhelmed, driven mad by it. Now he realised that his holiness in this regard might have been illusory. It might not have been to do with his strength of mind, rather to his physical condition. He was not, after all, better than other people.

Niall was still talking. 'And then you found God.'

'Or God found me.'

'Whichever.' Niall hesitated, as though there was something else he wanted to say but did not have the courage. 'May I mention something – about our maths teacher, at school, Father Walsh. Did anything happen to you, with him?'

Patrick felt dismayed. So this was what Niall wanted to talk to him about – another sordid tale of sexual abuse. He had heard of so many such cases. He shook his head.

'Well, he kept me back after class, once –' He paused. 'You recall I was not very good at maths.'

'Yes, I remember that.'

'Well, he was explaining something to me, but I could not listen, I could not take it in. He had me there, at the desk, right next to him, and then I realised as he was talking, that his breath had started to sound peculiar. And then I realised that he was stroking himself, down below, and that he had taken his thing out and – I remember being horrified at the sight of it. Even now, the shame makes the skin burn on my face and I remember the terrible feeling of being trapped there, of being involved in something dirty and shameful. And then he asked me to hold it, and I don't know how, but I just jumped up and ran out of the classroom and left my books behind.' He paused. 'The next morning, he gave me the books back and said no more about it. But I wondered – he never gave any sign of this to you?'

Patrick again shook his head. 'As a matter of fact, he did not.' He could not have imagined something this shocking of the gentle and rather ineffectual Father Walsh. He had known nothing of it, not even a rumour. Was it possible? Was this corruption everywhere? But Niall wouldn't lie, not about something like this.

Niall continued. 'The second time it happened, I shouted loudly, "Fire! Fire!" and someone who was walking past the classroom came in. I don't know if they knew what was happening, but anyway, I was sent to the headmaster and punished for raising a false alarm. But the next day I was passing Father Walsh in the corridor. And I said, 'If you do that again I will tell the headmaster. I don't care if he doesn't believe me, I will do it anyway.'

'And he never tried again?'

'No.'

'And you never told anyone?'

'No – I was too ashamed. And… there was part of me that wanted to know that other people were attracted to the same sex.'

He began to see where this conversation was going. 'As you were?'

'Yes, as I was.'

He took a deep breath. 'You know, it is not a sin in itself to have this orientation, you must know that. People are subject to a wide variety of desires over which they have little direct control, but these only become sinful if you act upon them.'

Niall laughed. 'Well, certainly I have acted upon them,' he said. 'And I am not ashamed.'

Patrick could not help a sudden flash of anger. He did not know what to say to Niall. He didn't think he had ever before been in this position, of someone he had known, a friend, standing before him like this without fear or shame, openly challenging him. How could Niall think it was appropriate to come and speak to him in this way? And just now, before his father's funeral? Why had he agreed to see Niall, when he should have been praying and thinking of his father? This was no time and place to have an argument of this kind.

'We cannot go on with this conversation. I thought you had come here because of our friendship. I see now that you have come here because of this, to challenge me. Well, you can spare yourself the trouble. You know what the position of the Church is on this. The Catechism clearly says, "Sexuality is realised in a truly human way only if it is an integral part of the love by which men and women commit themselves totally to one another unto death."'

'The Church's position is so impossibly idealised,' said Niall. 'No human being could live up to it. I'm not sure any human being should even try. Perfection is possible only for God, if he even exists, which I now doubt. I knew you as a boy. You were not perfect then. You are not perfect now. And yet you are the pope, God's representative on earth. If you are not perfect, what hope is there for the rest of us?'

'With God's help,' he said, 'we can resist temptation to sin. We must all strive to do so.'

'So, you believe I sin.'

'We all sin.'

'Some sins are worse than others.'

'Of course.'

'And my sin?'

'To have the feelings you have is not in itself a sin. Only, as I have said, to act upon them.'

'And you do not care that you are condemning so many to misery, to cutting themselves off from any fulfilment or happiness? How can one fully love another human being, if not physically?'

'One can love in other ways.'

'But a mother, for instance, a mother would not be loving her child if she refused to touch it. The child would become disturbed. He or she must be loved physically.'

Patrick thought of his own mother's coldness and his sense of shame and isolation. 'In that case, yes, physically, but not sexually.'

'But among husbands and wives, the marriage is no marriage if it is not consummated. That is the very essence of married love. So you see, you are denying to those like me the very thing that is central to the relations between heterosexual partners in marriage. We all need to touch other human beings to stay sane.'

He shut his eyes. He felt, for a moment, as if they were back in those days when, after they had walked home from school with their satchels heavy on their backs, they had sat in one another's room and argued, sometimes so intent on winning an argument that it spilled over into hostility and they fought with one another.

'And yet,' said Niall, pressing on, 'You condemn me and others like me, you say we are "intrinsically disordered". You say that, let me get this right, that this inclination is "a strong tendency toward an intrinsic moral evil".'

Patrick flinched, acknowledging how harsh these words sounded. 'But it is only a tendency,' he said, weakly. 'We do not condemn anyone –'

Niall made a gesture of impatience and despair. 'No, I am wasting my breath. I am sorry to have even mentioned it. I just thought that if you realised that I, who you knew, and were friends with, and were once close to, was a homosexual and proud to be one –'

'Please. Do not say that. Each male should accept his sexual identity as a man, and each female her sexual identity as a woman; that is all.'

Even as he said this, he realised what he was saying. What identity did he have, to embrace? What if he were to find himself attracted to someone? If a female, that might be the male part of himself; if a male, then what? What answer was there to fit his position? How could he speak to Niall without hypocrisy?

Niall was continuing to talk, almost as if he had read his thoughts. 'I don't accept that. Aren't there many different ways of being male or female? What about those people who feel they are the wrong sex? What about them?'

This was enough. 'I am sorry, Niall. I would like to talk to you further on this matter, that is certain, but I have no more time. I shall pray for you.'

Niall opened his mouth to speak, but then he closed it again, and got to his feet. He seemed uncertain what to do. He, Patrick, could see that he did not want to bow to him or kiss his ring or give him the respect due to his office; when he held out his hand Niall looked at the ring and seemed to flinch. Then he took his hand and shook it; his hand was warm and dry and his grip was warm. Patrick could not help imagining, for a moment, where that hand had been, and to his discomfort found that it made him feel, for an instant, slightly sick.

When he entered the cathedral, a hush fell. It was crowded to capacity; extra seats had been put in around the walls but even these were all taken. Security men in plain clothes stood discreetly in the background, but he noticed them, watchful, patrolling the aisles. He and his mother were taken to the front row where they sat near the coffin, turned so that his father's feet faced the altar. His bodyguards sat directly behind him. He could not help it; their presence annoyed him. Could he not even grieve his father in peace? He had suggested to his mother a small private funeral, but she said there were too many relatives and connections, everyone would want to pay their respects. Patrick suspected that his mother also wanted everyone to see her with her son, the pope.

He glanced around him. The cathedral was not old and had always felt austere to him with its pale, waxed wooden floor and light cream walls with white ribs and vaulting, the plain wooden pillars. The only colour came from the bright blue stained-glass window behind the altar, with vivid green grass and a blood-red cross on which Christ hung. On either side, narrow windows of blue and green let in the sunlight.

Ahead of him, a square concrete altar stood under a round corona which was lit up for the Mass. On the left was a white-robed Virgin on a golden cloud, clutching a rosary, a filigree crown on her head topped with a tiny cross. When he turned to look behind him at the rear of the cathedral, he saw, above the organ loft, another round window, a dove sitting in the centre of a sun, its rays streaming down in a blue sky.

The bishop sat on his chair behind the altar.

The cathedral was full. Not everyone was there for his father, he knew. Many of them would have come because they knew the pope was there. Many of them would be expecting him to speak, but he had chosen not to. He had asked the bishop to give the eulogy.

He looked at the coffin standing before the altar, plain, unadorned. The organ played quiet, sombre music. He heard the shuffling of people's feet, the gentle murmuring of voices.

He thought again of his father, a man who seldom smiled or expressed any joy about anything. A man dissatisfied with life, who tried to do his duty but failed to extract any pleasure from any of his actions. Who was now lying in that coffin, utterly and irretrievably dead. It seemed a terrible waste.

The bishop rose. 'I am the Resurrection and the Life.'

The choir sung the Introit, 'Eternal rest, give to them, O Lord; and let perpetual light shine upon them.' The sound, for a moment, lifted him out of himself. His mother, sitting beside him, stifled a sob. He took her hand and squeezed it, but this did not seem to comfort her, only make her weep the more, so he withdrew it.

At the end of the Mass, the bishop sprinkled the coffin with holy water and it was censed, and then the bearers lifted the coffin and the choir sang the *In Paradiso*.

Why could he not concentrate? What would his father have thought, if he knew?

There was a heavy shower when they left the cathedral. One of his bodyguards held an umbrella over him as he waited for the car and he watched the raindrops jumping on the surface of the road. He heard his mother say, 'Mary!' and looked up to see Mary at her side. Siobhan was there with her. Her face seemed even paler than the last time he had seen her and a strand of damp hair straggled down her cheek.

She seemed oblivious to the rain which was drenching her. She said, 'You did not reply to my letter.' Her words seemed slightly slurred, as if she was drugged.

'Siobhan, that is no way to address the Holy Father!'

'He is my cousin, I can address him as I like.'

'She is right, I should have replied,' he said. 'Perhaps I did not have the courage.'

'But, Patrick, you are grieving,' Siobhan said. 'We will not argue now.' And she put her hand affectionately on his arm. The gesture made him feel a sudden warmth for her; he wanted for a moment to embrace her, to say that he understood her. But what would she think if she knew of his situation? He would like to stay for a moment, to talk to her, but his bodyguard stepped forward and ushered him towards the car. The rain came down more heavily and as he slid onto the back seat he saw Mary take hold of Siobhan's arm and drag her away.

The sun came out as they arrived at the cemetery and suddenly it was very warm. His mother took off her coat and hung it awkwardly over her arm as they walked up the path behind the coffin. The bodyguards fell back to a discreet distance. They stood with their backs to the sun, and their shadows fell over the grave. Those old words, stark yet comforting: 'Remember, O Lord, that we are dust, like grass, like the flower of the field.' The earth breaking on the coffin. 'To You, O Lord, we commend the soul of Oisín, your servant; in the sight of the world he is now dead; in Your sight may he live forever.' A bird sang. Then a butterfly – a red admiral, he saw it was – came fluttering up from behind the grave, hovered over the coffin, and then flew towards them, landing on the lapel of his mother's jacket. Everyone saw it; everyone was thinking the same thing. It was his father's spirit, come to say goodbye to her.

She said afterwards that this sign was the only thing that had brought true comfort.

After the wake he was exhausted. There were too many people, and they all wanted to be with him or shake his hand and ask him for a blessing. He had looked round for Siobhan, but she was not there. He asked the bodyguards to take him to his mother's house. It was the strangest feeling to be back there, in the mean rooms which had changed very little since his childhood, with the cheap religious paintings on the walls and the dowdy sofa and armchairs. Jesus with the sacred heart still hung on the wall above the fireplace, though the formerly bright colours were faded now with age.

He went into his father's study. The books, all carefully arranged by theme on the shelves. His engineering books, his gardening books. The novels, what there were of them, a preponderance of Irish writers, and many of the novels of Graham Greene and Brian Moore.

He wondered what his father had been working on all those years, in this small study with the window that looked out on to walls and a small glimpse into the garden. He had always had a fantasy that his father was working on some massive project, but there were no signs of any personal papers or manuscripts. He opened the drawers to the desk, and searched the neatly-ordered contents. He knew what he was looking for; any letters, a diary, anything personal that would give him an insight into his father's character. He straightened up; his mother had returned from the wake and was standing in the doorway watching him.

'He did have a diary,' she said, as if reading his thoughts. 'But he burned it a few months ago, when he was feeling unwell.'

'Did he say why?'

'He said there were some things in there that it was better for people not to know. I think he felt, because of you, that people might pry into them, might be interested in what they contained. So he destroyed them.'

'I see.' He thought, uncomfortably, for a moment, of his own diary, hidden in his bookshelf in Rome. That, too, might have to be destroyed. Well, there was nothing in this office to interest him, no hidden stacks of paper, no photographs, no mementos. His father would remain an enigma. He left the room and closed the door behind him with a firm thud.

He went upstairs, to look at his old room. It was the same, shut up as if he had never left it. The iron-framed bed, pushed against the wall. The flowery curtains through which the sun had shone and which he had gazed at so intently when he lay ill in bed, now faded and dingy.

And then a memory came back, of his father, standing beside him on the hard floorboards by the bed.

'This is how you pray,' his father said. 'First, get on your knees, like this.'

He remembered the awkwardness of the posture, the hardness of the wooden floorboards on his bare knees, the way it hurt and made him feel vulnerable.

'Then put your hands together, like this.' And his father pressed his palms together, fingers up, so his hands looked a bit like the steeple on the church.

'Why?' Patrick asked him. He expected him to give that reason, so that they looked like a church. But he didn't. He looked irritated, and said, 'Because people have always prayed this way, for centuries.'

He was silent, kneeling there, his knees hurting, his hands pressed together hard, waiting.

'Now close your eyes.'

He squeezed them shut. He became aware of the sounds all around him, the leaves rustling outside the open window, a bird chattering, distant voices, a passing car. He felt his eyelids soften and he let his fingers relax a little, and a softness come over him as if he was lying in bed and getting ready to drift off to sleep.

'Now, speak after me. Our Father.'

'Our Father.'

'In heaven.'

As he repeated the words, Patrick thought of the sky as he had seen it in paintings, pale blue and scattered with fluffy white clouds, pink-tinged and fading away into the distance.

'Hallowed be your name.'

Hallowed. What did that mean, hallowed? It sounded like hollow, it had an empty, ringing sound to it, but also a grand, distant feeling, of something mysterious and remote and far away.

'Your Kingdom come.'

He had felt close to his father, then. Was it the only time? He had felt his father's comforting presence, the faint scent of tobacco on his clothes, the strength of his body as he held himself in the posture of prayer. He realised that he had always associated something of the mysterious nature of his Father in heaven with his earthly father. Something cold and forbidding, something distant, judging.

He looked around him. How strange it was, to think that this room had belonged to a child who was now a pope.

His mother was standing in the hallway. She was wearing the old brooch that he remembered from his childhood, a square Perspex thing with three white roses in it. As a boy he'd been fascinated by it, how the fragile flowers had got inside the hard plastic. He'd wondered what they were made of, too; paper and wood, or real flowers. Only later when she'd taken it off and put it on her dressing-table did he realise that it was an illusion. The Perspex was etched out on the back and the flowers were not real.

They sat in front of the fire in the living room and he watched the flames, recalling how in childhood he used to stare at the fire, heaped high with coals and sometimes a log of wood, and watch the shooting flames which flickered and leapt as he imagined the Holy Spirit moved above the heads of the disciples in the Upper Room.

His mother turned to him. 'Must you go in the morning?'

'Yes, I must leave early. I will go back to the bishop's house in an hour or so.'

'Before you go, I want to talk to you,' she said. 'There's a lot you don't know. I didn't want to speak of it while your father was still alive, I was afraid that perhaps he would know, even if I asked you not to tell him. It seemed disrespectful somehow, for you to know and not him. But now, he is gone, and I want to confess to you.'

So now, finally, she was going to tell him what he wanted to know. They went and sat in the living room. His mother was so familiar, and yet a stranger. He felt he didn't know her at all. Now, he felt a softness about her, which he didn't remember from before.

'I suffered a lot,' she said. And then she fell into silence, as if what she wanted to tell him was too difficult to speak of.

'You want to tell me,' he said, 'I can see.'

'Before I married your father,' she said, folding her hands in her lap first one way, then another, and then turning her head to look out of the window, 'I had a relationship with a boy, a boy from school, that I was in love with. Oh, how I was in love with that boy Seamus. I was so much in love that I allowed him to do what he wanted to me. I was so much in love with him that I wanted it, too.'

Her face flickered for a moment, with an expression that was something between joy and tearfulness. 'I don't know if he loved me and anyway, afterwards he was sent away. I was sent away too. I was sent to London to have an abortion.'

So it was not about him that she wanted to speak, it was her own, private tragedy. The shock of it was absolute. He never would have guessed – his mother – after all the things that she had said to him over the years, in front of his father, in front of his friends, about the sanctity of life – when she herself –

'I had no choice, really, I was so young. I always regretted it. Of course it was impossible in that time to have the baby, but I still regretted it. I cried for that baby every night. I wanted it so much. I was mad to have a child until I had you.'

'Have you confessed? Have you sought absolution?'

'I have indeed, many times I have confessed it and have been absolved by the bishop, but I have never felt forgiven in my heart. Perhaps it is because I knew, that even though I know it is a terrible sin and even though I wept for that child, I would have done the same again. I was not ready for a child. I was not ready to care for it. That sounds terrible, I know... but it is the truth.'

She turned to him. 'Would you absolve me? I feel that perhaps if you, my son, who I have robbed most – of a sibling, perhaps nephews and nieces – and as head of the Church, if you were to absolve me?'

'Are you willing, now, to forgive yourself? Otherwise I cannot give you absolution.'

'But do *you* forgive me, Patrick?'

'Of course.'

She hesitated and then said softly, 'Then, Patrick. I am ready.'

He felt a great tenderness for her now, a forgiveness that he perhaps could never have fully granted in his heart if he had not also suffered the same temptation. And that she had wanted the child, and been forced to give it up, while he, who did not want it, had to carry on! And was he not also going to rob her of the knowledge of something she would have wanted more than anything – a grandson? Perhaps he, too, should ask her for forgiveness. Should he confess everything to her? He found he could not. She knelt before him, her slight frame almost trembling with the effort, and he saw that her white hair was thinning so that he could see the pink skin beneath. He said the words of absolution and laid his hands over her head, and there they stayed, mother and son, in silence for a long, long time.

Chapter Thirteen

After the cool and dampness of an Irish summer, the heat in Rome was a shock. As he stepped out of the helicopter into the Vatican Gardens, the sun stood directly overhead. The light was blinding and the dry heat seemed to sap all the energy from his limbs. Back in the apostolic palace, they were waiting for him, lined up in the apartments, welcoming him back. Everywhere people had words of sympathy.

When he finally reached the office and sat down at his desk, Thomas came in and hesitated in the doorway, bowed and then smiled. Patrick was so pleased to see him that he wanted to get up and embrace him, but something held him back, perhaps a fear that Thomas might think it not appropriate.

Thomas hesitated a moment longer, as if he too was uncertain about something; then he crossed the room and handed Patrick his schedule.

'Did everything go well, Your Holiness?' he asked.

'The funeral was beautiful, thank you.'

Piles of letters and papers awaited him. He had forgotten how much there was to do. Thomas stood at his elbow.

'If you are too tired I am sure most of it can wait till tomorrow.'

'No, I am not too tired.'

'Holy Father, the Cardinal Secretary of State has asked to see you in private.'

'When?'

'Whenever you are ready.'

Why did he feel such uneasiness? 'Did he say what it was for?'

'No, Holy Father, only that it was urgent.'

'Well, then, can I see him later today?' He might as well get it over with, he would only worry all night about what Romano had to say.

'He could come at six, Holy Father.'

It was strange how, while he had been in Ireland, his pregnancy had seemed more natural. He had felt safe. It had not occupied every moment of his waking thoughts. Now that he was back here, he sensed the danger. What could Romano want? When six o'clock came, he shuffled papers around his desk. He wanted it to look as if he was working. Was that because it would act as a kind of shield, give him something to look at, a pen to wield in his hand? Perhaps it was nothing. It was not so surprising that Romano had asked to see him now, after several days' absence. It did not necessarily mean that something was wrong.

He waited for the knock at the door, but it didn't come. He looked at the clock. Already, he was ten minutes late. He felt, even though he did not want to see Romano, and had hoped he would not come, a touch of irritation. People did not keep him waiting. What was the Cardinal Secretary of State thinking of? He thought of Niall, how he had also kept him waiting, making some kind of point, no doubt.

The Secretary of State came to his office. He apologised for being late, but clearly did not mean it. He seemed thinner than ever, bird-like, sharp as a razor. He bowed deeply and then went to stand over by the bookcase. As Patrick watched him, the archbishop's eyes were sliding along the bookshelves, reading the titles, his hands clasped behind his back. Patrick saw at once that his diary stood slightly proud from the other titles, not pushed back as it had been earlier.

Romano's eyes were cold and grey, his voice precise and measured. Patrick was so preoccupied with the diary that he did not take in what he was saying. He wasn't sure if he imagined it, or whether several times during the conversation, Romano's gaze slipped down towards his belly.

'I have heard some rumours,' said Romano. 'I wish you to reassure me that they are not true.'

'Rumours? What rumours?' Patrick felt unsteady on his feet. Was this it, then?

'That you are ill. That you have been seen repeatedly visiting the Vatican Health Service. That it is something serious. I understand of course, Your Holiness, your right to medical confidentiality. But this is too important. I have visits to arrange, with heads of state, there is the planned visit to China – I need to know if you can meet this schedule. It would be best not to have to cancel these at the last moment.'

'Of course.' Thank heaven; he did not know the truth. 'It is true, I have been out of sorts lately,' he said. 'A little unwell. I have had some tests. And the shock of my father's death. I was concerned that people may have noticed.'

'People understand what a hard job it is, *Santità*, how you have so much to attend to. It is not surprising that you should feel tired at times. But what I speak of is more than this. You must tell us if something is wrong.'

He was sick of the way that they danced around him, hid their real thoughts and feelings. He felt he was surrounded by enemies. The only people he trusted were Thomas and Veronica. Everyone else was suspect.

He could not lie, but he could equivocate. He must speak as close to the truth as he could without giving himself away. 'Well, I will admit that the tests have shown that there is an issue, but let me reassure you that this is not life-threatening. I may need to be out of action for a few weeks, towards the end of the year, for – elective surgery. But then, this might not be necessary after all. I do not wish to release the details, it is far too premature.'

'Of course, *Santità*. I understand your desire for privacy. And we do not wish to cause alarm. But, people will talk. They will notice any absence. If you are ill, the press office must say something. It is much better to be open about such things. Otherwise rumours will simply spread and cause concern and suffering among the faithful.'

Patrick nodded. 'I will be seeing the doctors tomorrow,' he said. 'I will see what they have to say. That is all for now.'

'There is one other thing.'

'Yes?'

'There is a tape circulating, it seems, *Santità*. From the day of that – unfortunate incident. I have seen it. The tape shows you striking that woman, hard. It is quite ugly.'

'I have seen it.'

'If this should come into the public realm –'

Patrick could not contain his anger. 'Eminence, are you threatening me?'

'*Santità!*' Romano's face assumed an expression of outrage. 'This is unworthy of you.'

'I was threatened with this tape before, weeks ago. Nothing has happened. I forbid you to talk about it, to discuss it with anyone.'

'I wished simply to prepare –'

'I will not discuss it. The whole incident is over, finished. No one is interested.'

'Of course, *Santità*.' Romano bowed deeply, and left the room.

After he had gone, Patrick pulled the diary out and opened it. The ribbon which had marked the pages was no longer in the same place, on his last entry; instead it had been moved to the back of the book. He was sure that he had left the ribbon in place; he was most particular about it. There was no doubt; someone had read it. But who? And who would have been careless enough not to replace the ribbon? Or had whoever read it done so deliberately, to let him know? He counted all the people who had access to his study. The nuns, Thomas – surely it could not have been Thomas? But he kept seeing in his mind the figure of the Secretary of State, standing a little too composedly in front of the bookshelves, his arms held behind his back as if to show he had not touched anything.

If Romano had read his diary, could he work out what had happened? How clear had he been? How stupid he had been to commit his thoughts to paper, to think it could be kept private in a place like this. The letter to his son. Well, would they think that he had got a woman pregnant? That at least would be a scandal they might control. But how could he tell? If they did not confront him with it, how best to proceed? Romano was working against him, he was sure. He must try to find out what Romano knew.

He must ask Thomas if he had moved the diary. Thomas was the only person who knew where it was; perhaps he had checked it was there, as he had told him. If Thomas had read it, then that was bad enough, but at least he trusted Thomas to tell no one. If there was one person he could confide in, it was Thomas. He would ascertain the whole truth now.

Thomas arrived, slightly breathless, alarmed. 'Holy Father, you wanted me?'

'Yes, I –' As soon as he saw Thomas, he realised that he couldn't accuse him of anything. He didn't have the words. It would sound ridiculous, absurd. He did not believe that Thomas would have read the diary. If he said anything he might lose Thomas's support and that was the one thing he could not risk. He said, 'Never mind; not now. There is something on my mind, but perhaps it will become clearer with time. I will pray about it.'

Thomas's eyes rested on him.

'I would hope you would feel able to confide in me, Holy Father,' he said. 'But of course, when you feel ready.'

He breathed in, slowly. 'You have not seen my diary, Thomas?'

'Your diary?' He looked puzzled. 'The one that is on your office desk?'

'My personal diary. The one I asked you to destroy if anything happened to me.'

'It is there, isn't it? Where you told me it would be.' He cast his eyes towards the bookcase.

'You haven't moved it?'

'You have not asked me to, Holy Father.'

It was quite impossible that Thomas was lying to him. If he thought that, then everything he trusted would be overturned. 'Well, that is of no matter. Perhaps I am ready to tell you my news, after all. Come, let us pray together.'

He had to confide in someone. He would need help, of a practical sort as well as emotional support. He could not go on alone without anyone knowing, and if he was to tell anyone, surely it must be Thomas.

The late afternoon sunshine filtered through the gauze curtains and fell across the faded carpet. A little breeze from the open window grazed his face and tickled the hair on the back of his neck. A great lassitude came over him. He felt an intense sense of Thomas's presence. He was tired of thinking, of feeling. He let go of his thoughts, his anxieties, and let himself fall open like a book. It was not up to him to do anything; it was for God to guide him. He was waiting, expecting nothing, doing nothing, simply resting in that moment.

He heard a clock in the distance chime and knew that in a few moments, he would have to tell Thomas the truth.

They stood side by side in the warmth of the sunlight. When they had finished praying, said 'Amen' and come slowly back to themselves, Patrick sat down next to Thomas on the two chairs by the window. He cleared his throat.

'Thomas.'

'Yes, Holy Father?'

'This is a very difficult thing to tell you. I am not sure if I should. Well, eventually you will have to know. And I need someone to talk to, someone who can guard this knowledge with the utmost secrecy.'

Thomas leant forward, almost eager. 'Holy Father, I am listening.'

'You know that I have this genetic condition – I told you this.'

'Of course, Holy Father. I was hoping, since you had said nothing more, that it was nothing serious. Those last few days, before your father's funeral, you seemed much better.'

'Well, it is a very rare condition. It is not dangerous in itself but it means, Thomas, that I…' how could he say this? 'I have a mixture of male and female cells in my body. I have, as well as male, some female organs. That is, internally.'

Thomas did not speak; he looked bewildered. Then he said, 'I am sorry, Holy Father, but I don't understand.'

Patrick tried to explain, but Thomas's horrified expression stopped him. A silence fell.

'Is this some kind of a joke, Holy Father?' Thomas said, finally. 'I'm sorry, but if so I cannot see the point of it.'

'It is not a joke.'

'Then – you are seriously telling me that you are some kind of – hermaphrodite?'

'That is not the term they use nowadays, Thomas, but yes, that is what I am saying.'

Thomas's face was blank for a few moments. Then he made a strange, explosive sound, like a sneeze. He doubled up, pressed his hand in front of his mouth as if to silence himself, but did not succeed. He was, astonishingly, laughing. It was not a normal kind of laughter; it burst out loudly, hysterically. Thomas walked up and down in front of the window, clutching his sides; tears poured down his cheeks and his breath came in great, shuddering gasps.

Patrick leaped to his feet, alarmed. 'Stop!' he shouted. 'Thomas! Stop this at once!'

'I am sorry – Holy Father – I can't help it,' Thomas gasped, between more outbursts of manic, helpless laughter. Patrick could only stand and watch until they died away.

As soon as the laughter stopped, Thomas looked mortified. 'I am so sorry, Holy Father. It was the shock. I could not help myself.'

Patrick could not carry on with this conversation, not now. His full confession would have to wait till another time. 'Come, we must leave this. I will need your help, Thomas, but it must wait until you have composed yourself. Now, I need to rest and sleep.'

'Holy Father...'

'Please. We can continue, if you are able, in the morning.'

Thomas, reluctant, nodded, turned and left the room. Patrick was not sure whether he could hear suppressed laughter retreating in the corridor outside.

He sat in silence. Thomas's reaction had disturbed him more than he could say.

22 July. The Feast of St Mary Magdalene. The black Vatican car took him to the church of Santa Maria della Vittoria in the Rione Sallustiano, where he was to say Mass. This little church contained Bernini's masterpiece, the sculpture of the Ecstasy of St Teresa of Avila, and he had asked to go early to the chapel to pray. Thomas was not with him; after his outburst the day before, he had pleaded illness. A severe migraine, he said.

It had rained, just a shower, and the steps were wet and slippery as Patrick entered the church. A few people stood outside to greet him, but the crowds had not yet arrived. His bodyguards directed him down the aisle.

To the left at the end of the ornate church he found the statue. He had seen images of the sculpture before, but the reality of it astonished him. Above the white marble was a stained-glass window with a gold sun in which a white dove hovered. Because it was cloudy outside they turned the light on so that the statue was illuminated from above. Gilded sunbeams shone down on to the saint's face which, in an expression of utter ecstasy, was turned up towards heaven. Her hands, her feet, were limp with delight, and the roundness of her body contrasted with the angular, almost postmodern forms of her robes. The angel stood beside and above her, holding the flaming spear, one hand holding the robe as if uncovering her breast to aid the passage of its tip into her white flesh.

It was undeniably erotic. But people who found that shocking did not understand that the erotic metaphor had long been used by the Christian mystics to refer to the soul's union with God, a union in which, like lovers, the soul and God became united and yet retained their separate natures.

He had the text from St Teresa's autobiography in front of him:

> I saw in his hand a long spear of gold, and at the iron's point there seemed to be a little fire. He appeared to me to be thrusting it at times into my heart and to pierce my very entrails; when he drew it out, he seemed to draw them out also, and to leave me all on fire with a great love of God. The pain was so great, that it made me moan; and yet so surpassing was the sweetness of this excessive pain, that I could not wish to be rid of it.

He thought, he could not help but think, of his dream and the sweet pleasure it had given him.

Had he been visited by an angel? Had he, in his ignorance, denied it, because he was so ashamed of his sexual feelings? Could he not have accepted the erotic as part of God's gift to humankind? Perhaps he had been wrong when he thought that God had not spoken to him. For of course, it could not be that God had violated him as he feared. No, it must have been God who had spoken, and he who had not listened.

Relief swept over him, as he bowed in front of the statue. It was he who was at fault, for not listening. He had not been open to God's message, had been too wedded to his own idea of how God would speak to him. The Bible was filled with bridal imagery, from the Song of Songs to the Book of Revelation. *Upon my bed at night I sought him whom my soul loves.* Why should God not have spoken to him in this way?

Thomas came to see him after lunch. His face looked pale and haggard. 'I am sorry I was unwell, Holy Father. I have these migraines from time to time. You must forgive my outburst. I cannot understand it. It was the shock.'

'Of course, it is forgiven.' Patrick knew that, under stress, people reacted in strange ways. He had seen a mother who had lost her child acting with perfect composure as she had served him tea, going about the house as if nothing had happened. He had seen a man whose wife had been killed in an accident methodically smashing every piece of china in the kitchen.

They sat together in silence. Patrick asked Thomas to come with him into his study. They stood in front of the window, in the sunlight which cast square patterns on the floor. He knew he had to tell Thomas the whole truth; there was no one else he could turn to. But after yesterday, he was not sure that Thomas was stable enough to take it.

'Have you understood and accepted what I told you yesterday?'

'Of course, Holy Father.' There was certainly no trace of the hysteria of the day before.

'Thomas, you had better prepare yourself. I need your help, so I must confide in you. I have not yet told you everything.'

'Everything?' Thomas turned to him a face so anxious, so fearful, that a pain stabbed his heart.

'It is so hard to tell you. It is so hard to tell anyone. Perhaps I should not, after your reaction yesterday.'

Thomas fell to his knees in front of him. 'Forgive me, Holy Father, I was not myself. I cannot explain why I laughed like that – it will not happen again. If you tell me what you wish to confide, Holy Father, I promise I will guard it till death itself.'

A long moment passed, in which he looked at Thomas and Thomas looked at him, and he felt as if he was looking into the mirror of his own soul and seeing its reflection staring back.

'Well, this was a shock to me, as well. I was so innocent – I did not know that I was different. But there is something more. I am – I do not know how this could have happened, perhaps it is a miracle. It is because I was experiencing unusual symptoms that I went to the doctor. After tests they informed me not only of the intersex condition but also that I was – carrying a child.'

There was no other way he could think of putting it. A look of unutterable astonishment passed over Thomas's face. He knelt there, staring. He seemed to sway slightly, like a tree in a strong breeze. And then he turned ashen grey, his eyes glazed over and seemed to roll backwards, and his whole body limply toppled to the ground.

He hit the floor with a dull thump and lay there; for a moment it crossed Patrick's mind that the shock had killed him. He knelt down on the floor, shaking Thomas's shoulders. 'Thomas! Thomas! Wake up!' He lifted Thomas's head and held it in his lap. Should he call the doctor? Thomas began to moan faintly, then he opened his eyes. He seemed bewildered, confused; he did not seem to know where he was. Patrick took a cushion from the chair and rested it under his head.

'Don't get up... take your time... you must have fainted.'

Thomas rolled on to his front and lay there before him, face down, his arms stretched out, in a gesture of absolute submission. 'This cannot be, Holy Father. This cannot be!'

'It can be. It is. Nothing is impossible to God.'

Thomas was shaking his head from side to side. His face still looked strange, an almost putty colour.

'Thomas, it is a shock, of course. It was to me. But now I see that, in some way I do not yet understand, it can only be part of God's plan.'

'And what if it is not?'

'But, Thomas. What else could it be?'

He did not know how he expected Thomas to react; he only knew that it was not like this. His outburst last night, and now this. Yet, how could anyone say how a person would react to such news?

'Thomas, get up. Don't prostrate yourself like this. What is the matter with you?' He could not disguise his irritation.

Thomas scrabbled to his feet, looked away from him, his eyes cast to the floor. 'I am so sorry, Holy Father, I could never have imagined – I did not think – I cannot say – what are you planning to do?'

'Should I do anything? What do you mean, do?'

'Well – with the child. Do you – I am sorry – it is not for me to presume, Holy Father. I am so confused. I would have thought this was – impossible.'

'Well, it is not. It is possible, the doctors say, that I could have – fertilised myself. Either that, or it is a miracle. Thomas, let us not speak of this. I need your help. I need to find a family for the baby, a Catholic couple who will raise it as their own. No doubt such people could be found through an adoption agency but of course I need complete discretion.'

'Holy Father, I will look into it at once.'

A nun came into the room, carrying a tray of coffee. She looked at them standing there, at the expressions on their faces, and hastily turned and left the room, carrying the tray with her.

They sat at supper, he and Thomas and Alfonso. They did not speak. The nun brought them a little coffee but he declined it. They left the table and Thomas went to play the piano.

It was a melancholy piece, something modern that he did not know. Patrick sat and watched him play and felt an emptiness in his heart. His relationship with Thomas had changed. It was a subtle change, but it was there all the same. They had spent hours the previous evening in his rooms, talking about the situation. He and Thomas shared this secret and he could not help become more intimate with him. Yet at the same time, something about Thomas seemed more distant. He did not feel that easy companionship that he had felt before. Had he done the wrong thing? Had he spoiled everything between them? Perhaps Thomas could no longer regard him in the same way as before. But who else could he have confided in, appealed to for help, except Thomas?

It could be there was another explanation for his change in manner. Perhaps Thomas was simply trying to conceal their increased intimacy from Alfonso.

When he had finished playing, Thomas went to the window and stared out, his back towards Patrick. Alfonso came in, peering at them through his thick glasses. He said, 'The Cardinal Secretary of State is back, Your Holiness. There are two other cardinals with him. They are demanding to see you, now.'

'Demanding?'

'Yes, I tried to put them off, but they are insisting, Your Holiness.' He looked across the room at Thomas, standing with his back to them against the light from the window. 'And they are asking to see you alone.'

Thomas turned and looked at him, and he gave a slight nod. Thomas swept out of the room, his black silk robes swishing angrily against the marble floor.

Patrick went to the window where Thomas had been standing and stared across the gardens at the setting sun. The red ball of flames, like a malignant eye, was sinking into the clouds behind the rooftops. He heard footsteps coming along the corridor. He wanted to return to his desk but he could not bring himself to move. He was still standing at the window when the knock at the door came.

'Come in.'

It was not just Romano. There were three of them, Romano himself, Paolo Mancini, the Head of the Council of Cardinals, and

Cardinal Wolf, the Prefect of the Congregation of the Doctrine of the Faith.

He sat at his desk and gestured to them to sit on the chairs, which they had to bring forward from where they had been lined against the wall.

'Your Holiness,' Romano bowed. 'We need to speak with you urgently. You were not frank with me earlier. I have had new information. I imagine you must know why we are here.'

'I do not have the slightest idea,' he said. 'Please, do enlighten me, Your Eminence. I have many gifts, but I cannot yet read people's minds.'

He regretted his sarcasm as soon as he had spoken; it would get the conversation off to a bad start, he saw. But Romano did not seem at all affected by it.

'Your Holiness,' he said, 'We know. I do not need to spell it out, you know what I am referring to. Someone – we do not need to tell you who it was – has told us. He said he could not keep this to himself any longer because he knew it would imperil the Church.'

He felt a sharp shock, as if something in the ground had trembled. So – it had begun. And who could have told them? The only people who knew were Thomas – it was inconceivable that he would have said anything – and the doctors. He could see now, that it could only have been a matter of time before one of them spoke out about it. There had been too many doctors involved. Perhaps they had left the files somewhere others could find them. His hand began to shake; he stilled it by resting it firmly against the edge of his desk.

'Everyone involved took a solemn vow. If they have broken it –'

'I know. We are sorry. But this is too important.'

Patrick remained silent. He fiddled with the pen in his hands, turning it over and over in his nervous fingers. He wondered if they'd had suspicions, had put some pressure on Dr Conti. He said, 'How many people know?'

'Only us.'

'I see.'

'Your Holiness, at first we could not believe it. It seems impossible. But we have seen the medical records. We are all in agreement with what must happen next. You must resign.'

His voice came out much louder than he intended. 'I cannot. I will not.'

'You must.'

'I have prayed about this. I do not believe that it is God's will for me, or for the Church, either.'

'Your Holiness, you are not being rational. You must see a psychiatrist. We are all in agreement with this.'

'You cannot make me see anyone without my consent, and I do not consent. I am perfectly sane. I am carrying out all my duties and am completely in command of all my faculties. You will not be able to make any convincing case against this.'

Silence fell in the room. They looked at one another awkwardly. He could hear the tiny movements as they fidgeted, uncertain what to do next.

'I will carry on. I believe this is God's will for me. Thank you for your concerns. I will pray about it.'

Romano spoke out. 'The thing is this. We need to know whether you are a man, or a woman. A woman cannot be a pope – indeed, she cannot be a cardinal, or even a priest. We need to do some tests. We need to know whether there are more female cells in your body, or male ones.'

Patrick did not know whether he was grasping at straws, but it occurred to him that they might not know everything, that they might know about the intersex condition, but no more.

'But this – this is absurd. How could you tell? How could you possibly examine every cell in my body?'

'We have discussed this. It is clear. We need to sample your blood, a number of organs, and then see what the percentage is.'

'But this percentage could be quite wrong.'

He thought he understood their plan now. This was a clever, Jesuitical route to get rid of him. They would say he was a woman, and then he would have to step down.

'I will not consent to any such tests. You must be mad to even think of this. I have been brought up a man, I am legally a man, this cannot be altered.'

Now Cardinal Mancini spoke up. 'It can be altered. You may not know this, but in 1982 Italy became the third nation in the world to recognise the right to change legal gender. And in September 2015 in Ireland, the Gender Recognition Act provides a process enabling people to achieve full legal recognition of their preferred gender and allows for the acquisition of a new birth certificate that reflects this change.'

A feeling of complete, unutterable exasperation came over him. 'I am aware that in some countries, this is possible. But it is beside the point. And besides, we are not in Ireland, or even in Italy, this is the Vatican. In any case, this is a ridiculous conversation to be having. I am not going to apply anywhere to change my gender. I do not wish to change my gender, this legislation is only for those people who voluntarily wish to change their gender! There is, I am sure, no question of anyone being coerced into it. Whatever my physical condition, I am, I consider myself to be, a man.'

Now it was Cardinal Wolf who spoke up. 'This is all an irrelevance. We are missing the main point. Your gender must be what you are in the eyes of God, not in legislation made by man.'

'So, why have you been quoting the law at me? It will not do. Well, what would you have me be in the eyes of God? A monster? A – hermaphrodite? Supposing I am equally male and female? What will you do then?'

He had never seen anyone look so uncomfortable. 'It is not likely, Holy Father, that it would be so exact.'

'But it seems you have already made up your mind what the result will be. Why not call me Holy Mother?'

Romano gasped. '*Santità*, such a thing is not possible.'

'I will not consent to any blood or tissue samples.'

'Then we will have to go with the results that we already have, Your Holiness.'

'And what do they show?'

'They show a slight preponderance of female cells.'

He felt enraged. What games were they now playing with him? Was this a trick to force him into having further tests? 'I need to see the results. I need to be sure that you are telling me the truth.'

'You insult me, Your Holiness. We are trying only to do what is theologically correct. You yourself have spoken out many times against the possibility of women priests. Only a baptised man can receive holy orders – it is a matter of divine law. The Holy Father John Paul II infallibly and irrevocably decided that the Church has no right to ordain women to priesthood.'

'And I need you to tell me this?' It was beyond belief. 'But, this does not apply to me. I am a priest. That part of me that is male, whatever the precise proportion, has been legitimately ordained. Once this has been done, you know as well as I, that it cannot be undone.'

Romano glanced at Wolf, who nodded. 'We recommend that you have the tests.'

'I will consider it. Now, please, this is enough. Is there anything else that they have told you about me? Let me know it all now, so that we can discuss this matter fully.'

They were silent, staring at the floor. It was impossible to know whether they knew or not. Perhaps they were proceeding, one step at a time.

'In that case,' he said, 'please leave me.'

They were dismissed, and rose, but still they hovered in the room. 'Do you not understand?' said Romano, stepping forward suddenly,

202 • Virgin and Child

his arm touching the edge of the desk. 'Can you not see what will happen? This will be the end of everything. The Church will become – it will become a – what do you say? A laughing-stock. It will be – ridiculed. It will – do I have to go on?'

'Yes, please do.'

But Romano could not speak – this invitation seemed to have completely disarmed him. He walked to the window and back again.

'We must talk again,' he said, 'tomorrow. I will ring the doctor, and arrange for you to do the tests.'

He bowed, deeply, with the others, and swept from the room.

'What is going on?' asked Sister Veronica in the morning when she brought him his tea. 'The cardinals seemed to be in a terrible confusion yesterday evening.'

'They are always upset about something,' said Patrick.

'You must be firm with them, Holy Father. They do not respect you enough.'

He went for the tests. He had to see the doctors in any case, for a scan. He agreed to any test that was not invasive; it could at least buy time. They took more blood, and swabs from the inside of his cheek and nose.

De Luca, looking even more dishevelled than usual, did the ultrasound scan, and then he returned to the doctor's consulting room. Sitting at the desk opposite the three of them, Dr Conti, Professor Moretti, and De Luca, he could not help wondering which one of them might be the man who had betrayed him. And yet, if they had, why had they not told Romano about the pregnancy?

'The placenta is still very low,' Moretti said. 'This is a matter of some concern, but we will see. The foetus seems to be developing normally, though it does seem a little small for the dates.'

'Is that unusual?'

'Well, we must take great care. It is something we must keep monitoring.' He paused. 'I take it you are still against an amniocentesis.'

He hesitated for a moment. If the test provoked a miscarriage, would that not be a way out of his situation? He did not know why he so strongly resisted it.

'If there is any risk to the baby, yes.'

De Luca sighed. 'Well, we will continue with the monitoring, the scans.' He tapped his fingers on the desktop. 'If you refuse to let us investigate further, Your Holiness, there is not much more we can do.'

Patrick felt uneasy. Was he, in his desire to resist them, putting the baby at risk? 'You are worried.'

'Well, as I have repeatedly said, it is a high-risk pregnancy. There are many things that can go wrong. We have recommended certain actions, but since you disagree...' his voice tailed away.

'Well,' said Conti, standing up and bowing to him, 'we will see you in a fortnight.'

It was as if they wanted to be rid of him as quickly as they could.

Chapter Fourteen

It was just after eight o'clock. Supper had been cleared away, and Alfonso and Thomas headed with him to the living room. Thomas, unusually, did not go to the piano; instead, he went and stood by the window, fiddling nervously with the chain of his pectoral cross.

Alfonso asked Thomas if he wanted to watch the news but he declined. Again, Patrick sensed an awkward atmosphere between his two private secretaries. He thought for a moment of raising the subject, but he was too tired.

Alfonso suddenly excused himself and left the room. At once, Thomas left the window and came over to sit down opposite him.

'Holy Father, we need to talk.'

'Of course.'

'Perhaps we should go for a walk.'

'It is rather late.'

'Yes, but it is still light.'

They went up on to the roof terrace. The sun had set but the June sky was clear and still full of golden light. As they walked a cool breeze stirred his robes. They sat side by side on a stone bench. The warmth from the floor tiles was reflected back at him, and where they sat, they were sheltered from the breeze.

In the silence, Patrick heard a mobile phone start buzzing in Thomas' pocket like an angry wasp. Thomas looked embarrassed, slipped his hand into his pocket and the noise stopped.

Thomas turned towards him; he was very close. He spoke in a low voice.

'There is a group of cardinals, headed by Romano. They are plotting to remove you. They asked Alfonso, and he refused to join, but he told me about them. So I went to them, Holy Father, and I told them I was with them.'

'You did what?'

'I thought, Holy Father, that if they thought I was with them then I would know what they were planning and I could protect you.'

'But surely, they would suspect you. Thomas, this is dangerous.'

Thomas told him what had happened the previous day, relating the events with extraordinary detail. They had met in the late afternoon at Cardinal Rinaldi's apartment in the Via della Conciliazione. The apartment, he said, was old-fashioned, full of ornate gilded furniture and heavy drapery. Despite the heat, the windows were kept tightly shut, perhaps because of fears that they could be overheard. A solitary fan blasted hot air around the room. It was suffocating in there, Thomas said; probably that had not helped the debate that followed.

There were four of them, he explained; himself, Romano, Cardinal Wolf, and their host, Cardinal Rinaldi. They all sat on red brocade chairs gathered around a coffee table, on which sat an elegant silver coffee-pot and some small cups. Rinaldi seemed to be in no hurry; he poured the coffee and handed out the cups, then passed round a tray of sugared biscuits. They were all impatient to know why they had been summoned.

Eventually, Rinaldi got down to business. He told the group that Romano had informed him of the gravest matter affecting the health of the Holy Father and his ability to carry out his role. He thought they should go and urge him to resign.

Cardinal Wolf objected. He pointed out that Pope John Paul II continued as primate even though, at the end, he was extremely handicapped. Wolf recalled how he even used to fall asleep at his Wednesday audiences. They could not remove a pope because of this.

'But there are signs of mental disturbance as well,' said Romano. 'Is this not true, Archbishop Thomas?'

Thomas explained to Patrick that he had to answer. He admitted to them that the Holy Father had not been quite himself these days.

Romano then demanded to know whether His Holiness had confided anything to him.

Thomas admitted that this put him on the spot.

'What could I say, Holy Father? I am afraid I lied to them. I said that you had not. I don't think that they believed me, but they didn't press me any further.'

A shadow had crept across the bench; Patrick shifted away into the last of the sun. Thomas moved towards him, and then, after a quick glance around him, continued with his story.

He said that Wolf then told them that His Holiness had made some statements recently that could not be allowed to go unchallenged. Romano agreed. Many of the statements which the Holy Father had made in recent weeks, he said, clearly bore the mark of heresy, or at least, a tendency to mislead the faithful.

Thomas said the room fell silent at that point; they were all aware of the seriousness of what had been said. He recalled Wolf putting his cup down delicately on its saucer and placing it on the edge of the table. 'A private heresy is one thing,' Wolf had said. 'Has he been given the opportunity to examine and retract these statements? It would have to be some grave public heresy before we could become alarmed, and I have not been aware of this.'

Romano put a sheaf of papers on the table. 'I have some public statements His Holiness has made which, in my opinion, come very close to being heretical.'

Cardinal Wolf picked up the papers and read through them. 'Of course,' he said, 'papal infallibility does not mean that the pope cannot err when writing papal documents. Papal infallibility only applies to safeguarding and explaining truths already revealed by God and contained within the deposit of faith that was closed with the death of the last apostle. I agree, these statements are unwise, but I do not think we can call them heretical unless the Holy Father has had an opportunity to acknowledge his error and correct himself. It is only if he intentionally and wilfully proclaims a doctrine that is heretical that we can act.'

'Natural law allows us to correct a superior, when he is clearly in the wrong,' said Rinaldi. 'And St Paul rebukes St Peter in 2 Galatians. We should go to see him and explain our concerns.'

Romano disagreed. 'No, it is more serious than this. I have seen – I no longer have it in my possession – a document that shows that His Holiness is planning to allow the ordination of women priests.'

Patrick interrupted Thomas's monologue. 'Where did he get this idea?' he asked. 'There is no such document. He is fabricating information.'

'Holy Father, I think that they believed him,' said Thomas. 'They seemed inclined to believe everything. Romano clearly felt extremely threatened. He said – these are more or less his exact words – he said: "I need hardly add that this pope is very popular and that this move would be very popular with many of the faithful. We cannot risk an open battle on this subject. I propose to hold an Imperfect Ecumenical Council. While the pope is supreme in law, the decrees of such a council have a force like papal edicts. In effect, they are above and can set the law."'

Thomas said that they had all started talking at once. Rinaldi thought that a Council could not be convened without papal authority. Romano thought that, if there was sufficient support, it could. 'We must act,' he had urged them. 'The Church has a right and a duty to separate herself from a heretical pope.'

At this point, Thomas stopped. He lowered his voice. 'I could not discover, Holy Father, how much they know. But I had the feeling that this charge of heresy is just a blind. I know you never have supported women priests. That is unthinkable.'

He shook his head. There was nothing to fear. He knew there wasn't any way that he could be removed, even if it were to be declared that he was *non sui compos* and incapable of making rational decisions. In fact, looking back at history, if they wanted to be rid of him they were far more likely to murder him.

A cold breeze sprang up and made him shiver. The sun had long gone down and it was now completely dark, save for the light from a gibbous moon which was rising behind St Peter's. He wondered whether, at that very moment, they were trawling through the things that he had written when he was young, for any small signs of heresy. He thought in particular of his dissertation, on Meister Eckhart, in which he argued that, contrary to what had always been upheld, Eckhart's views were utterly orthodox.

Well, he would be like the Master himself, and repent of anything he had written then, and confess he might have been in error.

No, they could not get him on heresy.

'So it is Romano, you say, who is taking the lead?'

'That is right, Holy Father.'

'Then I should dismiss him.'

Thomas was silent. 'Holy Father, that might be the worst thing you could do.'

'Why? It would send a powerful signal to the others.'

'But it might force them to more drastic steps. He may be more dangerous if you remove him –'

'Not if I send him somewhere far away, some monastery in South America, perhaps. Let him try to scheme from there.'

'This will not be possible, Holy Father. What will people say?'

'Whose side are you on, Thomas?'

Thomas blushed a deep red. 'Holy Father, I am trying to advise you for the best.'

'It can hardly be a secret that Romano and I do not get on. I should have asked him to resign long ago.'

'Please, Holy Father, do not rush into this decision. Think and pray about it.'

He looked into Thomas's anxious face; his eyes seemed to gleam unnaturally bright in the deepening twilight. Why was Thomas so upset? Did he also feel the danger? He rose from the bench and they went back to his rooms. He looked down into the vast space of St Peter's Square, where a few candles lit by pilgrims flickered in the darkness.

Romano brought him the medical documents and laid them on the desk in front of Patrick. He could make no sense of them.

'I need a doctor to interpret them.'

Romano nodded. 'We can of course arrange this. This second set of tests shows a slight excess of male cells. But, still, when we put the two sets of results together it is uncertain. Perhaps it would be wise to have another set of tests.'

'I refuse. There will be no end to this, it is ridiculous. You cannot test every cell in my body. This is enough. We cannot keep going over and over the same ground. These latest tests, as you say, show more male cells than female. So, I am male. This is my last word on this.'

Romano gathered up the papers and, bowing deeply, left the room.

Well, at least the fact that Romano was concentrating on this meant that he could not know about the more important issue.

Why was he determined not to give in to them? It might be the easiest way. He would resign, on grounds of ill-health. Yes, there would be speculation, especially since it was so soon after the resignation of the last pope, and it might lead then to a change in the way the papacy was viewed, as a job which could be left at any time, rather than a role performed until death. But this was not his way, not his position. He had spoken out against papal resignation many times.

It remained, of course, a temptation. If he resigned, he could go to live somewhere in obscurity, could have the baby and keep up contact with his child, whoever he was with. He had an image of them in his mind, an ideal couple, young and healthy, smiling at one another, like those depicted on one of the leaflets promoting a conference about Catholic family life.

He asked Thomas how he was doing in his search.

'I have a list of three or four couples. I am going to go and talk to them first, and then you can speak to the most promising.'

'You will keep me informed.'

'Of course, Holy Father.'

He did not understand his own reluctance to engage with them. He felt ill whenever he thought of the family. When he prayed, he felt no impulse to pray for them. Rather, he felt more and more a desire to hold on to this baby.

His daily routine continued unchanged. Breakfast with Thomas; the daily papers. *La Repubblica* had always taken a critical stance against the Catholic Church, but recently, to Patrick's surprise, they had run one or two positive pieces about him. Today, there was a piece about the steps he had taken to resolve the sex abuse crisis. It was, on the whole, favourable.

He turned the page.

He saw the headline: 'Senior Doctor Killed in Hit-and-Run.'

Professor Moretti, a geneticist from the Salvator Mundi International Hospital, was killed yesterday in an incident on the Via Gabriele Rosetti. He was run over by a car on his way to work at the hospital. The driver of the car, a white Fiat Punto, appeared to lose control and the vehicle mounted the pavement. Professor Moretti was pinned against the wall by the vehicle and sustained terrible injuries. He was given medical aid on the spot, but died on the way to hospital. The driver fled from the scene and has not been identified. The police are appealing for witnesses.

Patrick felt the newspaper slide from his fingers. His hands were trembling. What was happening? It could not be an accident. It was too extraordinary a coincidence for it to be an accident. It was a punishment, or a warning to others. This was how they bought people's silence.

'Thomas.'

'Yes, Holy Father?'

He pointed to the paper. Thomas read the article and looked up at him. His face looked white beneath the dark curls.

'We are not safe.'

'What shall we do?'

'We could go to Castel Gandolfo.'

'I have said I will not go. They are opening it to tourists.'

'You can change that, if you wish.'

'Let me think.' For weeks he had been agonising over what to do with the baby. He had made no decision whatsoever. He had weakly allowed himself to continue, vacillating from one solution to the other, while this child grew within him.

He looked at the icon of the Virgin and Child above his desk. The mother's head tilted so gently against the sleeping baby, he rested his head so trustingly on her chest. Her cloth headdress hung down to shield him. His little hands sat so softly and gently on her blue robe; her lips were slightly parted. A sudden conviction came to him.

'I should announce it to the world. That is the only way to be safe. Once people know about it, these people will not have any power over me.' An announcement was the only way to be certain that the baby would be safe – and he must protect the baby at all costs.

Thomas took a step away from him.

'Holy Father, we have spoken of this before and agreed you cannot do this! Think of what will happen if you do! The secular world will not understand. It will be the scandal of scandals!'

Thomas turned and started walking up and down, up and down, his hand clutching his pectoral cross, a pleading expression on his face. 'Let me go and talk to them. Let me find out what they are thinking.'

'It would be better if you avoided them.'

'I cannot avoid them. They think I am on their side. I will go, tomorrow. Please do not do anything until I have spoken to them.'

He stared at Thomas. What was wrong? Why was Thomas so emphatic about this? Surely he should trust his own view on this. Or was Thomas right? He could wait another day or two. He should continue to think and pray.

'Very well.'

Thomas came over and bowed deeply, kissed the ring on his hand. The warm lips left a burning sensation on his skin which lingered even after he had left the room

He hated the way his body was changing. His voice seemed to have slid a few notes higher; he had to fight to control it. The hair on his chin, when he came to shave, seemed wispier than ever and he was sure that he could see his belly slightly swelling. And his breasts were growing too – not noticeably, he hoped, but to him, it was clear. The nipples darkened and there was even a dark line that started to form along the mid-line of his body, below and above his navel.

Was he right to hang on as pope? God, after all, did not choose to have his Son born to an emperor or king, but to a humble maiden in a stable. He must make his life a living sacrifice; if that meant giving up his position, then so be it. For what is the meaning of Christ's sacrifice? It is the gift of self. And it is this same gift of self that is involved in every loving act, no matter how large or how small.

He thought of the story of Moses. How a humble baby had been hidden by his mother when it was decreed in Egypt that Hebrew boys should be destroyed, and had been found and protected by the Pharaoh's daughter. And how Christ, in a mirror-image of this tale, had been raised as the humble son of a carpenter. He knew he had just two choices; he should step down and have the baby in obscurity, or he should give the child to a humble couple who would raise it as their own.

Siobhan wrote to him again.

Dear cousin Patrick,

I hope that you are recovering from the shock of your father's death. I have seen your mother a few times and she is bearing up. My mother sees her often, I'm sure you know that.

I wanted to let you know that I am much better than I was. Something has changed. I have been seeing a therapist, and for the first time she helped me to realise and come to terms with the fact that I will never be a mother. There! I have said it. It was like facing an abyss. But after the tears, finally there came peace. I realised how much I was allowing my desire for a child to eat up every aspect of my life and destroy it. Now I can start planning my life ahead – a life without children. My mental health has been much better since then and I am coming off the drugs.

I have also started seeing my husband, Jan, again. We are going very slowly because we both want to be cautious and be sure that this is the best thing for both of us.

I hope all goes well with you, cousin Patrick. I still think of our conversation that day in the hospital and I wonder if you have done anything yet about the question of miscarried babies. Somehow, I doubt it, but I still have hope.

He laid the letter carefully on his desk. Well, he had nothing to report to her on this last point. He had failed, completely, in this regard. He had been taken up so much with his own situation that he had not had time to take this forward.

And how kind of Siobhan to visit his mother! He had not even thought to speak to her since he left Ireland. He must write to her at once. He scribbled a quick note to his mother, saying she was in his thoughts and prayers. Then he wrote to Siobhan, thanking her for her kind visits to his mother and saying that he had raised her question at the Pontifical Council and that he would come back to it again. She must rest assured that he would pursue clarity on this, and on other related issues.

He trusted that she was well and that Ireland was as beautiful at this time of year as it should be.

He put down his pen. In this Roman heat, he longed for the cool Irish rain, for the green fields and hills and the wild flowers. If only he had never left his native land! Everything here was stultifying. He was watched, judged, criticised every moment of the day. It was hard not to feel that everyone was staring at him, that they knew something was wrong.

At least the faithful still stood by him. Every Sunday, they packed out St Peter's Square. He gave his address from the window high up in the apostolic palace, behind the plastic screen which would stop any bullet fired from below. He prayed with them and blessed them. Their faces turned up towards him, rapt and adoring. He wondered what they would think if they knew what he was hiding.

6 August; the Feast of the Transfiguration. A huge open-air mass at Turin for Catholic Youth. It was all to be televised. He had travelled there by train and was already exhausted. For three hours he sat on the throne on the platform, praying, speaking, saying Mass, in the glare of the spotlights. At one point in the prayers, he could not bear the sight of the cameras and the crowd any longer and he put his head in his hands to shield himself from them. A strange sigh went through the crowd and then an extraordinary hush fell as they

all prayed in silence with him. At the end of the Mass darkness fell and candles were lit, tiny points of light shimmering before him like sunlight flickers on the surface of the sea. The crowd sang hymns, some loud and joyful, others quiet and solemn, linking arms and swaying back and forwards in time to the music. He felt the power of the crowd and was swept up by it; this gave him strength to go on till the final blessing.

He was shaking with fatigue as he descended from the platform. Several of the cardinals greeted him, shook his hand. He had been, they said, masterful. The moment where he had covered his face with his hands was inspired. He could not tell them that the only reason he had done this was to hide himself from the intense scrutiny of the crowd, because he was afraid that when he made himself vulnerable in prayer they would somehow discern his secret.

'It is worse than I thought,' said Thomas, standing in front of the window in his office. His face was screwed into a look of anguish and he was actually wringing his hands.

'They know everything,' he said. 'Moretti told them. Perhaps he was going to tell others. But they – they are horrified that you might broadcast this news. They have decided this must be stopped, somehow. I had to pretend I agreed with them,' he said, 'Or I would cease to have access to them. I felt like St Peter, denying you, and that gave me some small comfort, but even so...'

'Calm down, Thomas, sit down here. Collect yourself. Tell me exactly what happened.'

Thomas spoke in a low, clear voice. Professor Moretti, it seemed, had decided that someone in the Vatican had to know what had happened. It must be handled with total secrecy, so he had gone to tell the Cardinal Secretary of State. Romano told the meeting that the doctor had arrived late in the evening, having clearly been drinking, and that he had stood in Romano's study and demanded that he swear an oath of total secrecy on the Bible before he would tell him why he had come.

Romano said he had at first resisted, saying that this was a ridiculous pantomime that had nothing to do with him – he thought he knew what the doctor was going to tell him and did not want the doctor to know that he knew about the intersex condition already – but in the end he had sworn a solemn oath, after which the doctor had told him everything, most importantly, about the pregnancy. He had brought with him the medical records, scans and the like, which he showed the astonished cardinal. Romano said he was beside himself. He told them that he had not believed it, that he had told the doctor that he would have him sacked from his job, that he would have him disgraced and struck off – but when the doctor insisted, when he asked him to re-read the scans, he slowly began to believe. But how had the pregnancy occurred? What could this mean? When the doctor could not answer, he dismissed him in a rage.

Romano had come to tell them at once. Thomas tried to describe the mood among the other cardinals. At first they, too, could not believe it, and denied that such a thing was possible. Then there was dismay and disarray – one of the cardinals collapsed and had to be rushed into hospital with a suspected heart attack. However, it was so fantastical that most of them were inclined to believe that no one could have made it up. One of them even quoted Tertullian in *De Carne Christi* – 'It is by all means to be believed, because it is absurd.'

Eventually they turned to Thomas. *He* must know if it was true.

'I have been sworn to secrecy by the Holy Father,' he told them. 'I can say nothing on the matter.'

'We understand this, of course,' they said. 'But if he has sworn you to secrecy, then he must have something to be secretive about. At any rate, we can see that you are not protesting.'

Thomas told Patrick that he had to give them something, to make them believe that he was on their side. He said to them, 'He believes that it is a miracle, that it is all God's will.'

At that, they were truly horrified. They began to talk among themselves, and he heard them say, over and over, 'Impossible!'

Thomas recalled that he had felt the same sense of horror among them at a meeting about child sex abuse, where the cardinals had refused to believe that what had been done was possible. And in the same way, their first instinct was to cover it up.

'He must be removed from office.'

'He must retire.'

'It must be announced that he is ill, too ill to continue.'

'No, this will not do. We cannot have two resignations like this, one so quickly after another. It will damage the papacy.'

'We cannot have the Church held up to humiliation and ridicule.'

The Cardinal Secretary of State took Thomas's hands. 'Are you with us, Thomas? You must swear. We in this room must swear that we will remain silent and share this with no one else – not even –'

Thomas told Patrick that he did not feel even the slightest twinge of conscience when he took the vow, solemnly, on the Bible. Did they really believe that he would conceal things from his pope? Would any of them, truly, stay silent? Something as big as this had a way of coming out – people could not help mentioning it, confiding to someone in a moment of intimacy, an unguarded moment. He did not know with whom they might share it, though he knew they would, above all else, want to keep it out of the press, keep it from public knowledge.

Their eyes had all been on him. He had sworn to keep them informed, to let them know what was happening.

Now, Thomas knelt down in front of Patrick, his eyes pleading. 'Did I do the right thing, Holy Father? I want only to protect you.'

'For heaven's sake, get up! But you must tell me everything they say, everything, do you understand me?'

Thomas, rising to his feet, nodded his head, once, emphatic. 'I swear it.'

'You know, if you betray me, that is the one thing I could not bear.'

'I will never betray you.'

Patrick looked at him. He thought that they both must be thinking the same thing, that St Peter himself had betrayed our Lord three times. He had done so because he believed himself to be in danger, because he did not see any point in taking the risk of identifying himself at that moment. And to be honest, if Thomas's life was in danger, perhaps he, Patrick, would not even mind if he betrayed him.

Thomas had not finished. He said, 'They plan…'

'Yes?'

'They have several plans. They discussed them for hours. The foremost is to announce you have an undefined illness and have you taken to a monastery where you will stay until… after the event. Whatever happens, they mean to make sure there is no announcement. So they may act quickly.'

'How quickly?'

'Within days.'

'And how can they do this?'

'They will find a doctor and they will bring him here and then they will drug you, I imagine. It is not so very difficult to do. And then they will say you were taken ill…'

'Then I must make the announcement right away.'

Thomas shook his head, 'There is another possibility. That you leave before this happens. That you go somewhere they cannot reach you. Where you will be protected.'

'You mean, where I can hide away? This is impossible. On the contrary, it is better if I make the announcement sooner. I can call a press conference for tomorrow. Or, I can make the announcement after the Sunday Mass or the Angelus prayers.'

'Please,' said Thomas, falling to his knees again in front of Patrick and grabbing the hem of his robe, tugging on it in a way that caused him to draw back with irritation and jerk it out of his hands. 'Please don't do anything without thinking it through first. Don't you see how the media will react to it? Don't you see what they will think? We live in a secular world, now, Holy Father. People – the press, the world at large – do not believe in miracles.'

He knew that it was true. The tide of secularism was sweeping right through the western world, leaving religion in the hands of the primitives, the fundamentalists. What hope was there? And yet if it could be proven that this was a miracle, an act of divine intervention – what then?

'Let go of me, Thomas. Let me be alone. Let me think.'

Thomas stood staring at him, his eyes following him, like a loyal dog's. Patrick felt for him, and yet he could not help it – at this moment he felt only anger towards this man who was devoted to him.

Whatever happened, he was tired of this subterfuge. He might not be ready to announce this to the world, but he could take away the power of this cabal. He would at least summon Romano and some other of the leading cardinals. And he must increase the security for the papal apartments, and make sure that extra people were on guard at the entrance day and night.

Chapter Fifteen

He met the cardinals in the papal library. His feet rang out on the marble floor as he crossed the room. He felt a great dislike for this cold, formal place with its high ceilings and heavy brown furniture; it made him feel exposed and vulnerable.

He stopped in front of the painting of Mary, crowned as Queen of Heaven.

Romano bowed his head, with the other cardinals. 'Let us pray for the spiritual and physical well-being of our Holy Father, Pope Patrick.'

He bowed his head.

When the prayer was over and he raised his head, he saw them looking at him. He supposed that he must speak.

'You are all wondering what is going on. Well, it seems that a miracle has occurred. I have seen the doctor and he has undertaken a number of tests. Everything has been checked and double-checked, so there can be no doubt about this. The implication will, I know, be startling. It will be more than that – I do not have the words to say what it might mean. I do not know how you will react, but I beg you not to rush to judgement, but reflect on this first. I will give you the news, and then I would like us all to stay here, in silent prayer, for fifteen minutes before anyone speaks. None of you is to say anything. None of you is to leave the room. After that, you may ask me questions. I want to be guided by the Holy Spirit in this.

'What I am going to tell you will seem at first to be impossible. It will no doubt make you leap, at first, to certain conclusions. Most of these conclusions will be false. I cannot prove many of them now, but in time, everything will be able to be proved to your satisfaction. So, I ask you to remain open in trust, to believe the best, and not the worst.

'Finally, I must ask you all to be silent. You will understand at once when I have explained to you. There will be the most serious consequences if anyone disobeys this. I know I can trust you. I do not have to remind you that you have all taken a sacred oath of loyalty.'

He knew the oath. It was the kind of oath you gave to a despot or dictator. He knew that it could not overrule their conscience, and that their first loyalty was not to him but to God's Holy Church. But it might make an impression on them. He saw them looking at one another, uneasy.

He told them what he knew they already knew. He might have guessed, from their lack of shock at the news, that this was the case. He looked at their faces, all serious, all grim. As he had asked them, they were silent for fifteen minutes. He glanced at the clock on the wall opposite, and it occurred to him that he could keep them waiting, twenty, thirty minutes, and there would be nothing they could do about it. He had that power over them.

He waited sixteen minutes, seventeen, eighteen. He saw them begin to shift their weight uneasily, to try to make little glances at the clock. After twenty minutes, without allowing any questions, he dismissed them. Only Romano remained in the room.

'*Sua Santità*, I know all this,' Romano said. 'Moretti told me.'

'And now he is dead. I hope this is not something that is on your conscience.'

The tip of Romano's angular nose turned white with anger. 'That was an unfortunate accident, which has nothing to do with this. Moretti was a good man. He did not want to break your confidence, but he felt that it threatened the whole Church. We waited for you to tell us, we prayed that you would realise what must be done. But you said nothing to us.'

'That is because I knew you would ask me to resign.'

'Is that not the best solution, *Santità*? For yourself, and for the Church?'

'I do not believe so.'

Romano seemed to pull himself up to his full height. 'This pregnancy... we cannot assume it is a miracle. Indeed, we must not. You must tell me the truth, now – have you ever had sexual relations with anyone?'

It was incredible that he could ask this! He must crush this thought at once. 'I have never broken my vow of celibacy. You have no right to ask me such a question... you are not my inquisitor.'

'I have been told that Archbishop Thomas has been seen coming in and out of your rooms at night.'

'Archbishop Thomas!' This was absurd. 'I have called him to pray with me, some nights, when I cannot sleep. Is this what goes on, in this place? What else has your imagination come up with? Have you nothing better to do than indulge in these lurid speculations?'

Romano said, 'Your Holiness, we must take this to the Commission on Miracles. We cannot declare this is a miracle without it. We must investigate it as thoroughly as we would any other miracle.'

'As you wish.'

'It is absolutely necessary, Your Holiness. The correct procedures must be gone through. And you must tell us what your plan is. What are you going to do? Do you intend to resign later? Do you plan to go somewhere secretly to have – to give –' He could not continue.

'I do not know. I am awaiting God's guidance.'

'But this is impossible! We must know what is going to happen, Your Holiness. We must be able to prepare. You cannot be naïve about this, you must understand the implications. The Church must not be exposed to humiliation and ridicule.'

'You are stepping out of line, Your Eminence. It is God's will that we must discern, not mine. As I said, I will pray about it. Now, that is enough. This audience is at an end.'

In the night, he could not sleep. Had he defused the situation by telling Romano and the cardinals, or had he made it worse? And what were these rumours, of him and Thomas? How far had they spread? Yes, he and Thomas had prayed sometimes well into the night. And there was that time, he recalled, when Thomas had heard him calling in his sleep and come to his room. That they could imagine... his position was worse than he had thought. And he was not sure that Thomas had told him everything – did he know other things, which he had not told him to try to spare him worry? At three in the morning, he could bear it no more; he got up, and began to walk up and down. He could not bear to be alone; he longed to speak to someone. He would ask Thomas to pray with him – not in his room, but in the chapel, where they could not be accused of anything.

He opened his door and looked along the corridor to see if anyone was around. All was silent. He walked to Thomas's room, his slippers making no sound, and tapped quietly on the door. There was no response. He hesitated, not knowing what to do. Perhaps Thomas was so deeply asleep that he could not hear him. He was afraid of knocking loudly in case he disturbed anyone else. He opened the door, called quietly, 'Thomas,' but there was no response. He opened the door wider and took a few steps into the room. He was aware of his heart beating loudly – what would anyone think if they saw him? His eyes were now adjusting to the darkness. He could see, in the faint light from the window, an empty bed, with the sheets folded back, the white fabric glowing faintly. Thomas was not there.

The sense of disappointment was crushing.

He closed the door behind him and made his way back to the room. Where could Thomas have gone? Was there a midnight meeting of the group that was plotting against him? And for the first time he wondered – could he trust Thomas? What if even Thomas was against him?

Thomas stood outside his room, ready for Mass. He looked tired, and there were shadows under his eyes, as if he had not slept well.

At breakfast, as Thomas poured the coffee, Patrick asked, 'Where were you, last night?'

'Holy Father?' Thomas's hand moved suddenly and a little coffee spilt on to the tablecloth. He put the pot down carefully.

'I came to your room. I wanted to talk to you.'

'To talk?'

'Where did you go?'

'I couldn't sleep. Holy Father, I have hardly left this building in weeks, months perhaps… I wanted to walk outside, in the city, to see the world outside.'

'And how was it?'

'It was… strange. The city at night is a very different place.'

'Were you not afraid to be wandering alone?'

'Afraid?… No. I have nothing for anyone to steal from me.'

'People do not only steal.'

Thomas seemed irritated now. Patrick realised he must sound like a parent angry that their teenage child had stayed out too late. Perhaps he had gone too far. 'I am sorry. It is so long since I have done anything like going for a walk at night.'

Thomas looked at him and a fleeting smile crossed his face before it assumed its usual solemn expression.

'I am not sure that you would like it.'

'Why not?'

Thomas shrugged. 'It is too… worldly.'

Patrick did not know what to think. There was some subtle change in their relationship and he did not understand it, did not know what lay behind it. It was as if there had been a tiny, almost undetectable shift in power.

Another scan. Lying on the couch, the bleep of the machine, the pressure of the probe on his now swollen belly. They were taking a long time. Was something wrong? De Luca looked at his medical notes, then back at the screen again.

The doctor stood up, asked him to get dressed and go to his office. Patrick sat opposite the desk in the sunshine, unable to speak.

De Luca tapped his fingers on the table, frowning. 'The baby is very small,' he said. 'I'm concerned that it may not be getting enough nutrition through the placenta. This can happen in some cases, especially, Your Holiness, with older mothers.'

'What does this mean?'

'Well, the baby is often underweight, often born prematurely, sometimes with birth defects.'

'What kind of defects?'

'We can't say. There is an increased risk of cerebral palsy, of the child having learning difficulties. Do you feel the baby moving much?'

He thought about this. 'Yes, I do feel it move.'

'Every day?'

'Yes, every day.' He began to feel more reassured. If the baby was moving, there couldn't be anything so wrong with it, surely?

'How vigorously?'

'I don't know.' What an idiotic question. He had never been pregnant before; how could he know what was normal or not?

The doctor took his blood pressure. 'Any headaches?'

'No, none.' He looked at the doctor. 'Can anything be done?'

'We need to monitor this carefully. You will need regular blood, urine tests. It might be wise to keep a diary, to record when you feel the baby move. We advise you to rest as much as possible.'

'How can I rest?'

The doctor looked at him sternly. 'If you care about the baby's welfare, it is essential.'

The anger that he felt was astonishing. That he should become an invalid! That he should go through all this in order to have a baby that might have something wrong with it! Could this be part of God's plan? If it was a miracle, it could not happen like this. A miraculous, a divine child, would be perfect. Or was this an error on his part? He must not presume he knew God's will for him. Again, he felt his faith was being tested. And why did this matter to him so much? Every human being, no matter how flawed, how disabled, was equally loved and valued by God. And he was not, after all, going to keep the baby. It would be for another couple to care for it.

But how would that look, in the eyes of the world, if it came out? That he had abandoned his disabled baby? He did not know what to think. With every step, this became more and more difficult. Again, there came into his mind, just for an instant, the terrible temptation to abort, and then the shame and guilt at his weakness.

That night when he prayed, he thought of all those who were pregnant and were suffering, now, at this moment, throughout the world. He thought of those who had become pregnant against their choice or will; women who had been raped, women who had been overpowered by stronger husbands, husbands who might have been chosen for them in arranged marriages and whom they might detest. He thought of women who had given in to their boyfriends' demands, women who had been tired, foolish, distracted, who had got their dates wrong. Perhaps the women had been abandoned by the father of the child, perhaps their community would ostracise them. Or there might be something terribly wrong with the baby. There had been a couple who had come to him, a woman carrying a baby that the scan had shown to have no brain. The mother had been told that the baby had no chance of life, but as a good Catholic she was advised to continue with the pregnancy, even though the baby would not survive more than an hour after the birth.

Why, in his arrogance, had he thought his situation was any worse than theirs? He closed his eyes. He felt as if he now suffered with all these women; for the first time, he truly felt their pain.

He reflected on this for a moment. He had been blameless – he had done nothing. Nor had many of them. And even if they had been reckless, immoral, had affairs or secret lovers or given in to lust – still, they all came to this place. This fear, this suffering.

Thomas was ill. He had a bad cold, with a temperature, and said on the phone that he did not want to risk seeing Patrick 'in his condition'. Father Alfonso worked with him instead.

It was good to work with someone who did not know about his pregnancy. It made him feel more normal. He could clear his head and concentrate on what he had to do.

On the second day they went for a walk in the gardens, to say the rosary prayers together. When they came back towards the Apostolic Palace, past the Medici fountain, Father Alfonso stopped and asked, 'May I say something to you, Holy Father?'

'Of course.'

'I don't want to say anything in criticism,' he said, 'but people have noticed. You are too partial. You have been too close to Archbishop Thomas.'

What should he say? Had the rumours about them spread everywhere?

He hesitated. 'It is true. It is, perhaps, just a matter of personality. I have always found it easy to confide in him.'

'He may,' said Father Alfonso, looking at the water splashing in the basin, 'be unworthy of your confidence.'

'What do you mean?'

'It is just what people say about him. It may be idle rumours – I do not want to repeat them. I do not wish to say any more, Holy Father. Forgive me. It was just that I thought it better to speak than to remain silent.'

'Thank you.'

After Father Alfonso had gone, he sat in his office, bewildered. What were people saying? Which people did he mean? Why did he not know anything? He had heard time and again people say ridiculous things about Vatican secrets, secrets that he himself knew did not exist. In his experience, people in the Vatican talked too much rather than too little. It seemed to him that a Vatican secret was something known by everyone else inside the Vatican but himself.

'We need to check the placenta is providing enough nutrients to the baby. We cannot delay any longer, the baby is at risk. We will do some scans, and some other tests.' It was clear that De Luca's anxiety about the baby had grown.

'What other tests?'

The doctor did not answer, but stared into space, tapping his pen repeatedly on a pile of papers on his desk. Without looking up, he said, 'I am referring you to someone who specialises in this area. I can't say for sure, that will depend on what the doctor considers appropriate, after he has seen all the scan results.'

Patrick was instantly suspicious. 'Supposing I disagree. Supposing I do not want these tests. Besides, I do not want any more doctors involved. Enough people know already.'

De Luca looked at him with a severe expression. 'He has already been briefed. If you refuse, you are putting the baby at great risk. Let me be clear to you; the child could be stillborn. Is this what you want?' He stared at Patrick over the rim of his glasses. 'These tests will enable us to give the appropriate treatment, to ensure the baby's optimal development.'

Why was he so suspicious of these doctors? Had they not taken the Hippocratic oath, or something like it? 'As I said, I will think about it. I will let you know.'

'The tests should be carried out urgently. There is no time to think about it. I have scheduled the tests for late this afternoon, at Dr Salvatori's private clinic, where there is better equipment than we have here. Most of the staff there will have gone home but you might like, Your Holiness, to dress yourself as an ordinary priest so that you don't draw attention to yourself. I must strongly advise you to go ahead. The baby's life may depend on it.'

Was he paranoid? Could he trust no one? He sat in silence for a few moments. It seemed to him that the baby's health must come first, and that he had no choice but to trust De Luca and this other doctor. He nodded his head in assent.

They came to collect him, in a private car, with his bodyguards. He dressed in a plain black cassock as de Luca had suggested; what they thought of this, he did not know. It was not far to go, up the hill to the Gianiculo. The clinic was in what looked like a residential building, but he noticed a doctor's plaque at the side of the door as he went in. Everything was very clean and modern and no one seemed to be around. When he arrived at the desk, the receptionist stood up, all smiles. He noticed that, though she was immaculately dressed, she had a small tattoo of a snake curling round her neck. Why did the sight of it make him so uneasy?

'Please,' she said, 'come this way. *Dottore* Salvatori is waiting for you.'

They walked along the corridor and she showed him into the room. The doctor stood by the window, looking out at the view, and turned round when he entered. He had a long, thin face, receding hair, and a reassuring manner. He shook Patrick's hand and pointed to the chair.

'I have had the reports. It seems to me that we must investigate further.'

Patrick looked around the room at the couch, covered with green cloth, at the now familiar ultrasound screen, at a table next to it, on top of which sat a steel tray covered with metallic implements, and, lying next to it, a syringe with an extremely long needle.

At the sight of the needle, he felt suddenly sick. He had told them repeatedly he did not want to have – what did they call it? – an amniocentesis. He wanted to turn and walk out at once, but he felt as if all the strength had gone out of him. He began, involuntarily, to tremble. It took a great effort to control himself.

Dr Salvatori bowed to him and then went and sat behind his desk. 'Please,' he said, gesturing to a chair. 'Sit down.'

He sat down. As long as he was here, sitting in the chair, nothing could happen to him. It was still his choice. He still had time to change his mind and refuse the tests.

The doctor, looking down at his file, did not seem to realise that there was anything amiss. 'I understand you have been advised about this test,' he said. 'We are going to draw a little fluid from the sac surrounding the baby, so we can ascertain what is going on.' His voice was calm, matter-of-fact. 'We use ultrasound to guide the needle so there is no danger of it causing any harm. The procedure will only take about ten minutes. You may find it a little uncomfortable, a stinging sensation and a little cramping, but it will not be painful. We don't usually recommend a local anaesthetic, though you can have one if you wish.'

A feeling of dread had come over him. 'I was told there is a risk of miscarriage?'

'Yes, but it is a small one, less than one per cent. The risk to the baby of not investigating will be far greater, let me assure you. Please, if you would like to undress over here, and then get on the couch.'

He did not know what to do. He didn't want to go ahead, but, having agreed to come here, didn't feel he could back out now. Perhaps, after all, it was for the best. He would place himself in God's hands. He walked round behind the screen and began to take off the cassock.

There was a sharp knock on the door. The doctor did not reply, but then the sound came again, louder and more urgent. Patrick watched from behind the screen as the doctor stood up and went to open the door.

The receptionist stood in the doorway, holding a cordless phone. 'There is a call for your patient. I'm sorry to interrupt, but he insisted. He is calling from the Vatican.'

The doctor was angry. He said, 'Please. Not now. We are in the middle of a consultation. Take the number and he will call back.'

Patrick was going to protest, but the receptionist had gone. Who could be calling him? Who even knew he was here? Perhaps it was de Luca. What could he want?

Doctor Salvatori asked if he was ready. Patrick stepped forward in his under-garments and climbed awkwardly onto the couch.

A male nurse entered, in a white coat, nodded at him then turned his back and began to arrange the implements on the metal tray, making sharp clatter.

Salvatori sat on a stool beside him. 'Now lie back, and relax. This won't take long. Just expose your abdomen for me.' The doctor took a swab and wiped his skin with something cold, that smelled like disinfectant. He passed it to the nurse who took the swab and moved away, then came round to stand behind the couch. Patrick lifted his head, looked again at the table-top, at the metal tray and the syringe with the long needle. Now that he looked at it more closely, he could see that there was some fluid already loaded in the syringe. Why should that be the case, if it were to draw something off, not inject something in?

He had read about these things. In a late abortion, they used to inject saline into the fluid around the foetus. He understood that it took hours to kill the baby. Who knew what torments it might suffer? Then there were worse methods, methods where the baby was cut up and removed piece by piece. He could not even bear to think whether it was still alive when this had happened. And the doctors who did the procedures could not bring themselves to say that they had killed a baby – they spoke of 'removing' the 'products of conception'. And then there was this doctor, the doctor in

America who had been killed by pro-lifers, who had come up with a drug that killed the baby 'instantly', from a heart attack. Could you really die 'instantly' from a heart attack? He had understood that dying this way could take some time and be extremely painful. And the thought that they would do this to an unborn, innocent child!

Patrick tried to sit up and the nurse put his hand on his shoulder, gently but firmly pushed him back down. Patrick's body seemed to act on its own volition; he jerked forward, freeing himself, forced himself upright, swung his legs around so that he was sitting on the edge of the couch. He said, 'I am sorry, I have changed my mind. I want to leave now.'

'Excuse me?'

His voice was stronger now. 'I don't want to proceed. This test is not what I thought.'

'I'm afraid that won't be permitted. This is a Catholic clinic. We must put the unborn child's interests first. You cannot act in a way that is prejudicial to the baby's health or life.'

The remark stung him. He felt an echo in it of something he had said himself, sometime. Was it about the woman who had died, in Ireland? He could not remember.

He tried to keep calm; he did not want them to suspect that he had noticed anything amiss, would simply ask for more time. 'You cannot proceed without my consent. I am not ready for this, I need to reflect.'

The doctor hesitated. He had the needle in his hand; for a moment Patrick thought that he might jab him with it. But then he turned and lowered in onto the tray. He said, 'Take a couple of minutes, then. I understand your nervousness; but it will be over very quickly. You are only making it worse for yourself if you delay.'

'I'd like to be by myself, just for a few moments. I wish to pray in private.'

'Of course.' Salvatori nodded at the nurse and they withdrew through a side door.

Patrick climbed off the couch, went behind the screen and dressed hurriedly. He thought, if I can just get outside this room I will be safe. He walked to the door. The handle would not turn; was it locked? He jerked at the door handle again, and this time it turned. He stepped outside and started to walk as fast as he could along the corridor. He could not move too fast: he was afraid any undue exertion might trigger labour. He heard footsteps behind him and turned to see Salvatori and the nurse advancing towards him.

He turned the corner above the stairwell and saw Thomas rushing up the stairs.

'I tried to ring you, to warn you. Is it –'

'No, it's not too late. Thank you.' He grabbed Thomas and embraced him for a moment. Just feeling Thomas's body pressed against his own made him feel safe. 'Please, get me out of here.'

The secretary came into view, joining Salvatori and the nurse. Another door opened further along the corridor and a face looked out, another doctor, perhaps.

Salvatori took a step towards him. 'You will regret this,' he said, 'If your baby dies.'

He was afraid that they would take hold of him and force him back to the consulting room. But Thomas grabbed his elbow, said, 'Quick, come this way,' and pointed down the staircase.

Two flights of stairs led to a small doorway at the back of the building. A taxi was waiting outside, its engine running. Thomas opened the back door for him and he sat down on the hot leather seats with relief. Thomas slipped in the other side, slammed the door and leaned over to speak rapidly to the driver in Italian. The driver nodded and the car's engine revved, then the driver reversed out, spinning round on the gravel in the main driveway. Patrick caught a glimpse of his bodyguards still standing in the sunlight by the front entrance.

He gestured towards them. 'My bodyguards –'

'And whose side are they on?'

Patrick glanced at Thomas. He did not know what to think. He was alone, entirely in Thomas's hands. He wondered again if he could trust him.

He pushed the thought aside; that way madness lay.

The taxi headed rapidly down the hill. Awkwardly, Patrick jerked at the seatbelt; Thomas leaned over and pushed the buckle into its slot. The strap stretched over his now-expanding belly; he wondered if a sudden jolt would damage the baby. At the traffic lights, the driver tapped his hands impatiently on the wheel. He looked several times into the rear-view mirror. They moved again, and the driver took several twists and turns down streets he didn't know. They were not heading for the Vatican. Perhaps Thomas had some plan; Patrick felt unable to ask him. The driver said something quietly and Thomas turned round to look behind them – again Patrick heard a sharp intake of breath. He turned to look but Thomas took his arm and whispered, 'Don't.'

'What is it?'

'I think there's a car following us.'

'Are you sure?'

He caught a glimpse of it in the rear-view mirror; a black four-by-four with tinted windows. He could see the driver wore dark glasses, and a rosary was dangling from the mirror. Patrick's hand reached instinctively for the rosary in the pocket of his cassock, and felt the wooden beads slip between his fingers as he prayed silently. The taxi lurched suddenly to the right and down a narrow side-street. They were in Trastevere; he recognised the bistros and tourist shops. He prayed that they would lose their pursuers in the network of narrow streets.

The car swerved suddenly to avoid a group of people wandering along the side of the road. The driver sounded the horn and Patrick caught a glimpse of bare arms, of startled and angry faces. They turned again and hurtled down another long, narrow road and then came to a sudden stop in a queue of traffic heading for the bridge. Thomas leaned forward and looked in the mirror.

'Are they still there?'

'They're a few cars behind.'

'This is absurd, Thomas. Why are we not going to the Vatican?'

'I've asked him to head for the police station.'

They crossed the river and hurtled along the Lungotevere through the heavy traffic. The driver constantly used his horn, wove in and out of the traffic, cursing at the other vehicles as if he alone had the right to drive like a maniac through the Roman streets. Thomas leaned forward to give him instructions, arguing in Italian, making vivid gestures with his hands. The driver slammed on the brakes and Patrick jerked forwards, steadying himself as the car veered sharply to the right. He heard the shriek of tyres on the hot surface of the road.

He could not help glancing back. The four-by-four was behind them now on the three-lane road, trying to move up on the outside.

The driver spotted a gap in the traffic and shot forward, accelerating as it carved its way between a bus and a large van. As they swung across the carriageway, Patrick put his hand out to steady himself and Thomas grabbed it and held it so tightly that it hurt. He looked down and saw the white knuckles; Thomas looked down, must have seen it too and abruptly let his hand drop. He turned and said something sharply to the driver.

They passed by the white church of Santa Maria dell'Orazione e Morti, gleaming in the sunshine. The car swerved again, across the path of a lorry whose horn blared like a foghorn. Then it slowed, moving into the outside lane.

Patrick began to feel nauseous. It was a nightmare. Could the men really be following them? What would the men do to them, if they caught up with them? They surely could not mean to kill them? If they had intended that, why not have simply killed him in the clinic when they had him on his own?

Because they had hoped that killing the baby would be enough.

Perhaps they meant to catch him and return him to the clinic. But perhaps only he needed to be kept alive.

Perhaps all this stress would kill the baby anyway.

The lights turned red in front of them but the taxi shot through, took a sharp right turn and plunged into a dark side-street. They were in the maze of little streets that lay between the Tiber and the Piazza Navona. This could not end well. Sooner or later a vehicle would block their path or they would take a wrong turn and come to a dead end. The driver seemed to know his way but now, after a sharp left turn and then a right, the street narrowed to a tiny entrance that looked too small for the taxi to pass through. He heard a scraping sound, this time of metal against stone. The engine revved loudly and then the car jumped forward and they came out into the bright sunlight of a square.

Thomas urged the driver to keep going, through the square and into a long avenue beyond. He was travelling at a normal pace now, glancing regularly in the rear-view mirror and clearly seeing nothing to alarm him. Patrick tried to fight his nausea. If he didn't get out of the car soon, he would be sick. He whispered to Thomas who asked him to hold on. They drove for a few minutes more before Thomas made the driver pull over and they stepped out into a side-street where he stood shaking, leaning his hand against the wall.

The taxi driver got out and stared at the long scrape-marks along the whole length of the car where the metal trim was pulled away. He began shouting at Thomas, gesticulating wildly with his arms. Patrick watched, detached, as Thomas answered, his arms also waving about in violent, almost obscene gestures as the torrent of Italian poured from his lips. He'd noticed this before; when Thomas spoke Italian the language seemed to take over his whole being, he was like another person, someone he didn't understand. Finally Thomas shoved a quantity of money into the driver's hands and wrote something down on a piece of paper which he handed over. The driver seemed satisfied and drove away.

Opposite them was a small café with some tables and chairs on the pavement where people were sitting in the bright sunlight. Thomas crossed the street, took hold of his arm and steered him through the dark interior into a dingy back room. Patrick felt a little less sick now; he needed something to settle his stomach. He asked for a glass of freshly pressed orange juice and it came, made with fresh blood oranges, red and sweet.

Nobody would know who they were, here. Thomas was just another cardinal, an everyday sight in Rome; he an ordinary priest. The waiter, busy with the tables outside, did not seem to look at them.

'Did you know what they planned to do?'

'They said they would induce an abortion.'

'What can we do?' It was exhausting even to speak.

Thomas leaned forward over the table. 'I have been thinking of this. We should go to Castel Gandolfo. It is closed for repairs the second half of August. You can say you are on retreat. You will be safer there.'

'But would it not be better to stay, to carry on as usual? There will be so much to rearrange.'

'I am afraid that you are not safe in the Vatican.'

'Could I not stay somewhere else? In the Domus Sanctae Marthae, for instance. Where there would be people around me.'

'It would be a strange precedent. People would wonder what was happening.'

'Well, why not? To be an Irish pope is a strange precedent. To keep my own name is also a strange precedent. I am the pope, I can do as I please.'

He thought for a moment about what it would be like to stay in a community again, as in his training days at Maynooth, at St Patrick's College. He could see it in his mind's eye now, with its huge grey-stone building with the pointed spire of the chapel at the far end. Mass every morning with the monks, prayers in the chapel last thing at night, prayers before lunch at the long refectory table. The discussions they had had, the feeling of companionship. He realised how isolated he had become.

'You must stay close by me.'

'I will.' Thomas put out his hand and took his briefly; then, as if thinking this was a breach of protocol, snatched it away. 'But there is another thing that concerns me, Holy Father. There is another meeting of the cardinals tonight, but this time I have not been invited to it.'

He had to return to the Vatican, despite the danger. It would not be for long. In the chapel, late in the evening, he lit a candle. It burned quietly in the darkness, flickering now and then in a little breath of air, a fragile, wordless prayer. A dreadful thought had occurred to him. Would it have been better if he had not guessed what was intended, and so had said nothing, and they had gone ahead with the abortion? It would not have been his fault; there could have been nothing for him to reproach himself with. It would soon have all been over; everything would have returned to normal. How fervently he wished for this! He prayed for forgiveness. He could not understand himself. One moment he felt an overwhelming sense of protectiveness for his child, the next he wished to be free of it.

Chapter Sixteen

Rome was unbearably hot. The sun beat down day after day. A dusty hot breeze came in through the windows of the papal apartments, bringing with it the sound of snarled-up traffic; a haze of exhaust emissions hung across the city. Even when he walked in the gardens under the trees in the early morning he could feel the heat mounting, ready to pounce. The trees, the shrubs, the flowers looked limp and exhausted as if they no longer had the energy to force themselves upright. He longed again for Ireland, for the grey skies and cool sheets of slanting rain, the greenness of the hills and fields.

Papers piled up unattended on his desk. He postponed decisions. Thomas was anxious, fearing something terrible might happen, that there might even be an attempt on his life. Patrick hung on for two weeks, carrying out his duties as best he could, but his ankles began to swell; the heat was bad for him. He had the perfect excuse to leave for Castel Gandolfo.

The palace stood high up above Lake Albano, the round volcanic lake that lay in its rugged crater. Above the city, there was a cool breeze and in the evenings the temperature became quite pleasant. The cool marble floors and the breezes which blew in through the open windows refreshed him. He felt himself removed from the febrile atmosphere inside the Vatican, the sense of everyone talking behind his back and plotting his downfall.

He stood with Thomas on the terrace looking out across the lake. The perspective disorientated him; on the parapet where he rested his arms, tiny red spiders crawled over the hot, lichen-covered stones, while beneath them was a precipitous drop down to the lake, its surface rippling gently, shaded from pale green through turquoise into blue. The little waves caught the sunlight and sparkled, except where small dark patches lay under the fluffy clouds. Birds soared beneath the terrace, high over the lake, and in the distance, the mountain bristled with radio masts among the tall trees. On the slopes villas lay basking in the sun. A small boat set out from the shore, two men rowing, black dots with arms like those of insects.

He intended to spend the time in prayer and contemplation, visiting the Barberini Gardens every day. In the garden was a statue of the Virgin by a little lake. He liked to sit there in silence, but it was hard to concentrate. Time and again, his body drew attention to itself and he found that his mind had wandered from his prayers. He was becoming heavier; he could see now the convex curve of his belly. A heaviness and lassitude overcame him. He would sit in the courtyard under the shade of the tree, trying to read, and all he was aware of was the child's movements inside him, demanding attention.

Thomas had found him a doctor he trusted, from outside the Vatican. He was an old-fashioned doctor, a man of profound faith who had a gentle manner and who seemed amused and not at all shocked by what he had to tell him. Dr Lombardi came every few days to examine him.

They went inside, into a cool room within the palace, and he lay down on the bed.

As always, there was the feeling of shame and embarrassment at removing his clothing, of allowing the doctor to touch him, despite his every effort to preserve his modesty.

'The baby seems to be coming on well,' Lombardi said. 'I do not think that they were right about the baby being too small. They rely too much on machines, these people, and they forget that it is possible to know as much if not more with their hands.'

Patrick nodded, and silently gave thanks. He now trusted God that all would be well. It seemed to him shameful now that he had once found himself worrying that something would go wrong, half hoping that they might have told him the pregnancy had failed.

He sat outside, in the courtyard. Thomas sat beside him, reading. He could not help noticing the shape of Thomas's wrist and the fine down of hair that sprouted from the back of his hands and wrist. He wanted to take his eyes away from it but he could not; the sight gave him a strange sensation, almost like those days at school when he had struggled with differential calculus and his eye was irresistibly drawn to the sunshine in the trees outside his classroom window.

A sudden breeze stirred the trees and he heard the clear, sharp sounds of a bird. He looked at Thomas, his head bowed over his book. It seemed strange that Thomas should be so close and yet so unaware of what was going on inside him.

'Thomas,' he said.

'Yes?'

He reached out and took Thomas's hand, and placed it over his belly. He felt the child move, and Thomas's face suddenly changed its expression – he could not read the emotion that passed across it. Was it awe or horror? Thomas snatched his hand away and threw himself down at his feet.

What had happened? He felt hurt – perhaps the gesture had been too intimate, perhaps he should not have done it. He asked, 'What is the matter? Did you feel it?'

Thomas lifted up his face. 'I – I am overwhelmed. If this is –' And he turned his face away again and stared down at the dust.

Thomas had not been idle. He had approached someone he knew from an adoption society in confidence, and been recommended some couples who might be suitable parents for the child. He told Patrick he had spoken to them personally and there was one couple who seemed to be outstanding – mature, devout, and intelligent. He was an engineer; she had trained as a paediatric nurse; both were deeply involved with their local church community. They were invited over to the palace for an interview that day.

They were a young couple. He was a little older than her, a good-looking man, but not unduly so; he knew from their letter that he was thirty-five, and she was thirty. She had streaked blonde hair, cut neatly in a bob, and wore no make-up; she wore simple, plain clothes, a grey sweater and a black skirt which came down past her knees. When they came in they both bowed low, and kept their eyes to the ground; they stayed like that for a few moments until he called them by their names and told them to sit down.

They sat by the open window. The breeze gently moved the curtains and he heard distant sounds coming up from the lake.

Patrick spoke slowly, in Italian. 'Archbishop Thomas has explained to you,' he said. 'There is a child to be born, who will need parents. I am to be his godparent and his legal guardian.'

He knew Thomas had lied to them, but he could not bring himself to say something that wasn't true. Of course, they might have their suspicions, that he had fathered an illegitimate child. But let them think it; he no longer cared what people thought.

Thomas, standing beside him, spoke fluently to them. 'I cannot explain all the circumstances but the task of making all the arrangements has been entrusted to me. It must be done in complete secrecy.'

'We understand, Holy Father.' The man spoke quietly but firmly.

'The child will be born in January,' Thomas said. 'The plan is that he would be brought to you straight away. It will be a private fostering arrangement and I will be the legal guardian of the child. It may be that later we might proceed to a full adoption but this would not be guaranteed.'

The woman glanced at her husband, then spoke, nervously. 'We do not know what to say. We have said everything in our statement.

If this happened, we would love the child as our own. We would raise him in the Catholic faith. We would be guided in everything by the legal guardian.'

'It would be the greatest honour for us, as well as fulfilling our deepest wish and longing,' said the man. 'Please, ask us anything you like.'

Patrick had a list of questions to ask them, which Thomas helped express to them. Questions on discipline, on morals, on the child's routine. He found their answers on every point to be exemplary. They were honest, too. When he asked the would-be father if he would ever strike the child, he said that he did not believe in physical punishment, but that he was not a saint; there might be occasions where he might lose his temper for an instant and slap the child, or that he might strike the child to prevent something terrible, such as the child running out in front of a car, but that he did not believe he would ever use force enough to injure the child.

She explained that she had been devastated to discover that she would not be able to have children. She'd had two ectopic pregnancies; the embryos had lodged in her fallopian tubes and she had haemorrhaged and nearly died. Both tubes had been removed and she was offered IVF. 'I was tempted, but I felt that it was wrong,' she said. 'I felt that God must have had some purpose in this. I would not go against God's will. Perhaps God did this in order that this might happen now, that I might become the mother of this child.'

'I am afraid to say this,' said the husband, 'but I feel that God has chosen us. I have prayed about this many times and in my heart I feel that this is what God wants for us.'

The couple looked at one another for a long moment; then they turned back to him again. They sat in silence, waiting for him to speak.

He wanted to say something to them, something that would not give them too much hope but would not seem too dismissive either.

He was not able at the moment to make a decision. If this baby was a miracle, some kind of new incarnation, then a theological problem had occurred to him. Mary had been immaculately conceived, born without sin. If this child of his was a miracle, how could he be raised by a mother who was sinful? How could she set the right example to him?

And yet of course he himself was a sinner.

He could not think about this now. He had nothing else to say to the couple. 'I will be in touch,' he said. 'I too will pray for the right decision.' He felt their yearning for the child; he could not bear to disappoint them. And yet he could not deny that there was something about them that troubled him. They were too watchful, too guarded. The woman looked to the man sometimes as if she was afraid of him. And there were more couples to come. He knew he would cause grief and suffering to the ones who were not successful, and he hated to feel like this. This couple seemed ideal; and yet, could they be concealing something from him? Would they over-protect the child, spoil him, make him insufferable? How could he hand over his child to someone on such slight acquaintance?

Perhaps he had been wrong, to want to give the child to a childless couple. Perhaps it would be better if the child was part of a bigger family, given to parents who had already proved they could raise children well. He felt an impulse to get this over with, to simply choose them. It was not going to get any easier. If he saw more people, people who would be disappointed, there was always the risk that one of them might talk to someone, and that something would leak out. And yet – he could not choose this couple. He must trust his instinct, no matter how irrational it seemed.

The nights, at least, were cool. As he knelt in prayer before the little statue of the Virgin, seeking guidance, a strong breeze blew in through the open window, stirring the glass drops on the chandelier lamp on the desk which touched one another with a little tinkle, and ruffling the papers on his desk. He felt, suddenly, a presence in the room. He was afraid to lift his head, to see if there was someone there beside him. He saw a shimmering in the room, specks of light which seemed to dance before his vision, but then became still. He waited, expectantly.

It reminded him of the time – he was just a young priest then – when he had been out walking in the woods. The sun was sinking low in the west and the tall trees stretched their bare boughs up towards the sky. The leaves were just starting to swell at the tips of the branches, and here and there he saw a touch of green. As the sun turned a deeper gold he saw the insects flying in the air, tiny dots swimming and drifting in the brightness, each one a shining point of light. And then he had the feeling. A feeling of immensity and beauty and clarity, an intimation that this was just the surface of the world, and behind it there was something else, so big and powerful and tremendous that he could only sink to his knees and call out to it.

The feeling was the same. But now it became stronger, and began to change. It was not sweet, but overpowering, the sense of an awesome presence. It grew and grew until terror overwhelmed him, as if he might be crushed or annihilated by its intensity. It speared him and fixed him to the spot as if he were an insect pinned to a board, unable even to struggle. And then, just as it became unbearable, it faded, and he felt himself tingling all over, a warm feeling that swept through him and dissolved away the fear. Now he felt God was there, no longer outside, but inside him. He realised that when he breathed, it was God breathing in him, and that the feeling of love flooding through him was the love of God moving in him. And he felt an immensity of love for this child, his only son.

Yes, it was a divine birth. He knew it now, without any shadow of doubt.

In the morning, Thomas was sitting at the table, having breakfast. When Patrick sat down, Thomas poured out the coffee and passed him the jug of milk, and apologised for not waiting for him. He, in turn, apologised for having slept late.

'I had a visitation last night,' he said. 'Thomas, we have discussed this before. We will have to return to the Vatican at the end of the month, we cannot stay here forever. And soon, it will be impossible for me to conceal my condition. It will be obvious to everyone. I will write that speech. I must announce it to the world.'

Thomas's face turned white and he choked on his coffee. 'Holy Father, we have discussed this before. We will find a family, the child can be safe, and everything will go on as it was before. You cannot make this announcement and remain pope. It would be suicide. Most people today do not believe in miracles. The faithful would believe, but the world at large – the media – we have talked of this before. It would expose you to too much risk, and the child, too.'

'Thomas, I am determined. I must do God's will, no matter how difficult.'

'And you are sure that it is truly God's will?'

'You ask this of me?'

Thomas looked down, and answered quietly. 'Forgive me, Holy Father. I did not mean that.'

'I need your support, Thomas. I must have it.'

'It may be right, as you say, to make the announcement. But then, can you remain as pope? Christ, after all, was born of someone humble. Perhaps this was necessary to protect the child Jesus. Had the news been broadcast, how could he have escaped as a child the terrible effects of fame, let alone the attempts from those, like Herod, who would want to kill him? If you announce this birth, you surely must resign. The holy family had to flee into obscurity. Isn't it safer for you to do the same?'

'I don't know, Thomas. I have prayed for guidance, and this is the answer that came to me.'

It was impossible, now, sitting in the sunshine, face to face with Thomas, to be certain of what he had felt last night. Thomas's argument, as before, made perfect sense. He must think, above all, of the child.

In the late afternoon, he went with Thomas to the Barberini Gardens. Long shadows from the tall cypress trees fell across the grass, crossing the parterres with their neatly-clipped box hedges set with multi-coloured flowers. In the distance, he heard a church bell ringing, the sound drifting through the cooling air. Below him, the rich plain stretched out, and in the distance, there was a band of blue sea.

He went to the statue of the Virgin, a white figure perching on the crescent moon. He looked down into the pond. Two dark carp swam among the goldfish, moving like shadows under the lilies. It was like the hidden life inside him, moving in the waters of the womb.

He thought of the motto of the Marian order, *Ignoti et quasi occulti in hoc mundo*, unknown and partially hidden in this world. Yet he thought also of Luke 12:2: 'Nothing is covered up that will not be uncovered, and nothing secret that will not become known.'

As long as he kept it secret, there was a chance that they would act. They might come and take the child away, even harm or kill it. Once he had made the announcement, it was done. There would be no more need to act. It would be too late to act. They would be safe, he and the child. No, he must make the speech, as soon as he returned to the Vatican.

As the helicopter cut its engines and Patrick climbed out on to the Vatican pavement, he saw Romano was waiting for him.

'*Santità*, I trust you are rested?'

'Thank you, I am.'

'I must speak with you in private.'

'Come to my office at six.'

As the little clock on his desk struck six times, Romano was shown in. He stood before the desk like a hawk ruffling its feathers, bristling with suppressed rage.

'We must know your plans.'

'It will be announced that I am ill or that I will go on a retreat. I am sure some explanation can be given.'

'Secrecy in a matter like this will be completely impossible. Already the secret is leaking out. There are – rumours. Every day it seems to spread to someone else within the Vatican. How long before the secret leaks out beyond it?'

'If there is a leak, it will not come from me.'

'Your Holiness, this situation is intolerable. In the middle ages, perhaps this situation could have been managed. But now, in the glare of twenty-four-hour news, I do not see how this can be kept a secret.'

'Well, if you are so sure, then let me announce it first. It will be better if we are open with the faithful. They will understand that a miracle has occurred.'

'*Santità*!' Romano's eyes looked as if they might fall from his head. 'Impossible!'

'Well, I will consider this. I will pray for guidance. Please, I have had enough of this matter, there are so many other things we need to discuss. Do you have a list for me?'

Romano opened his mouth and then closed it again. After a pause, he said, 'There is nothing more important than this, Your Holiness. If we cannot resolve this situation, then nothing else is of any significance.'

'And how do you propose resolving it? Even if I resign, it will make no difference now. A scandal will, it seems, occur. Even if I were an ex-pope, joining with my predecessor, would it not still be a problem for the Church?'

Romano was practically grovelling now, so eager was he to persuade him. 'It is a problem that could be more easily managed, Your Holiness. All the publicity would be on the conclave, on the newly elected pope. I put it to you one final time – you must resign.'

It was tempting; he had to admit it was tempting; he closed his eyes. Then he thought again of the moment in Castel Gandolfo when he felt the force of God. 'No,' he said, firmly, 'I will not.'

His mind was made up. He would make the speech after the open-air Mass on Sunday. He would let the head of the Vatican news service, Bianchi, know the day beforehand that there was to be a special announcement, so the news media would all be there. It would not be necessary to give any further details.

He would say nothing to Romano about the timing; it was safer that way. He dismissed him and Romano turned and left the room without a backward glance.

Sunday dawned sharp and clear. He had hardly slept; excitement and terror at what he was about to say kept him awake for most of the night. The air had changed – no longer the oppressive heat of summer but a fine autumn light. Small white clouds broke the intense blue of the sky and, as he watched, a tiny shadow passed swiftly across the square.

He was ill at ease. He and Thomas had argued for hours beforehand, both far into last night and again in the morning, with Thomas speaking to him in ways no private secretary should be allowed to address his pope, begging him, pleading with him, warning him of the danger. He had dismissed Thomas with strong words, but Thomas's words were not so easily dismissed. Thomas said that he had found the perfect couple, that there was not long to go, that his – what did he say? – his egotistical self-identification with both Christ and Mary would imperil everything he had worked for and destroy the faith of millions of Catholics. Why had he allowed Thomas to become so over-emotional? It was becoming apparent that he was unstable. But he needed Thomas now more than ever.

Now, as Thomas stood in his usual place beside him with a heavy, sullen face, there was still animosity between them. The words from Matthew 5:23-24 came to his mind:

> So when you are offering your gift at the altar, if you remember your brother has something against you, leave your gift there before the altar and go; first be reconciled to your brother, and then come and offer your gift.

He should not be celebrating Mass before he was reconciled with Thomas. But now, there was no time.

He stood before the altar. A little wind blew up, and flapped his short cape, the mozzetta, up over his shoulders. Thomas stepped forward and gently adjusted it, smoothing out the folds. Then he fell back to stand obediently by his elbow.

Patrick said the Mass. The bread and wine were distributed. While they stood still, bathed in sunlight, dark clouds were gathering on the other side of the river. He heard in the distance a low rumble of thunder.

It was time. The crowd stood in front of him, densely packed. He could not quite bring himself to focus on their individual faces; it was better for them to be an amorphous mass so that he would not think too much about their reaction to him. He could hear their voices begin to murmur, a sound almost like the sea emerging from the indistinguishable mass of faces. Each one was a soul, unique, beloved by God; he should love them, and yet he was afraid of them. How would they react? Some, he was sure, would believe, but others? Might they become angry, hurl insults at him? Could there even be a riot? The guards would be unprepared. He had told no one. When he looked around, there was no extra presence of guards or police in the square, though he knew there would be plain-clothes men within the crowds. Everything was as usual.

They seemed to rustle and sway in front of him as if they were leaves caught in a light wind. He unfolded his statement; his hands were trembling. Thomas leaned over and, without looking at him, quietly arranged the papers.

The cameras were on him, he could see them, the microphones pointed. He hesitated for a moment; he did not have to go ahead with this, even now. He felt as if a vast space had opened up in front of him, a moment where the course of history would fork, leading to utterly different outcomes. Did he, truly, have free will? This moment made him feel as if he did. It was still not too late to change his mind – he could make another announcement, declare a special Jubilee year, something like that.

Thomas nudged his elbow gently. He must have thought that he had gone into a trance, or forgotten what to say.

'I have,' Patrick said, 'a special announcement to make.'

A strange expectant hush fell over the crowd.

'This is something many of you will find hard to believe. Yet I beg you to believe that it is true. We must all trust in God, though his ways may at first seem strange to us. May I invite you, before I speak, to join me in a moment's silence, in prayer.'

The silence that fell now was so intense that he could barely hear a rustle from the crowd. He could no longer see their faces; every head was bowed, and he could see only the tops of people's heads, dark hair, brown and blond, the occasional bald skull, some women dressed in headscarves, the black or white veils of the nuns. In the distance, he heard the sound of a helicopter and the muted buzz of traffic. A page of his speech fluttered and blew from the stand; he moved sharply to the right to grab it.

He heard a sudden sound, a loud crack echoing around the square. Was it thunder? He glanced up at the sky, but above him, it was still blue. Or had someone let off a firecracker? There was a disturbance to his left; Thomas lurched towards him suddenly, taking hold of his arms and pushing him backwards, shouting at him to lie down. Another firecracker sounded; he heard a sharp intake of breath from the crowd and it began to part in front of him. He felt himself topple and fall heavily on his back; a sharp pain jolted him as he hit the hard stone. Thomas was falling on top of him, pressing down on to his chest, weighing him to the ground. Then the black-suited bodyguards moved in, crouching over him. He heard a woman screaming close by to him. High-pitched wails and loud voices clamoured around him, but he could no longer see anything. He was trapped on his back beneath Thomas, looking up at the sky, which seemed a long way above him, a clear, deep blue.

Thomas began to make jerky, convulsive movements above him; he lifted his head. He saw the robes of black and scarlet, and Thomas's hands making odd fluttering gestures near his throat.

Someone leaned over and grabbed him, trying to lift Thomas up and pull him out from under him. Hands lifted him up and he felt himself drawn backwards, his back scraping on the hard stone. Thomas too slipped backwards; his head was lying in his lap. Around his curly hair, like a halo, was an astonishing intense pool of orange-red, shining intensely bright in the sunlight, soaking his white robe. Thomas turned his eyes up towards him; His lips moved, but only a hoarse whisper came out.

'Forgive me.'

'Our argument – it was nothing. I –'

'No... not that. I am the... Father, forgive me.' Then he made a choking sound and a spray of fine red droplets flew upwards from his nose and mouth – his face and lips turned purplish blue.

No! This was not happening, it could not happen, he must stop it, now.

With frantic hands he pushed the others back and managed to sit up, still resting Thomas's head in his lap. Now he could see what was the matter; a gash high up on Thomas's chest, just below the neck, was gushing blood, and the blood was spreading out over his clothes and down on to the ground beneath him.

Two guards pushed forward, pressed some white cloth hard against Thomas's chest, shouting loudly in Italian, and then someone was pulling him back by the shoulders. He felt himself sliding out from under Thomas's body, dragging on the hard stones. He struggled against them, shouting, 'Stop! Let me go to him! Thomas! Thomas!' People grabbed and pushed at him from every side so that he could not see what was happening. With a wrench, he tore himself away and stepped forward. Thomas was lying on the ground; people were crouching over him, he glimpsed him between their legs. 'Let me go to him!' he shouted. 'Let me see him!' Had not Thomas asked him for absolution? Supposing he died and he had not been able to absolve him? He struggled again but they were pulling him away, men in grey suits, surrounding him. 'I order you to let me go!' he shouted, but they took no notice.

He felt them lift him under the armpits like a child and propel him forwards, his feet flying helplessly over the paving. He heard the sounds of sirens in the distance and for a moment felt relief; an ambulance was coming. Then the sounds abruptly stopped and he was in the cool interior of the palace. A voice in his ear said, 'Are you hurt? Can you feel anything? Is there pain anywhere? Let me look.' He realised, now, that they thought he too was injured; he looked down and saw that his robes were stained all over with blood, like the red robes he had worn as a cardinal to commemorate the blood of the martyrs. The sight of the blood, staining the whiteness of his robes, sickened him. They began to pull at his clothes and then a man came forward, an African in a dark suit, saying he was a doctor, asking again if he was hurt. He answered, 'I want to see Thomas. What has happened to Thomas?' He realised that he was shaking. The blood had penetrated right through to his undergarments; the doctor at first refused to believe him when he said he was unhurt. With a start, he realised the danger he was in. If the doctor saw him naked, surely he would realise at once that he was pregnant? He resisted, grabbing the blood-stained robe and clutching it tightly to him, demanding that they bring him clean clothes and privacy to change into them.

The doctor backed away. Two aides brought him fresh robes and, in a private room off the gallery, he dressed in them. He did not know where they came from – the robing room, perhaps – they were slightly too big. He went back into the hall; his hands would not stop shaking. He could think of nothing but Thomas; he prayed for him ceaselessly, dear God, let it not be too late, let them save him. People crowded in around him. Someone was talking urgently in his ear – it was Bianchi – a statement must be given out to the press. What did he want to say to them?

Patrick fought to control himself. He said he was praying for Thomas, he was praying for whoever had done this. He asked someone to go and find out what was happening, where Thomas had been taken. Then a policeman came with more information. Thomas had been taken to the Ospedale di Santo Spirito. He would be taken straight into surgery. There was no more news.

He thought back to when Pope John Paul II had been shot, and he had survived. He had been shot more than once, in the stomach, in the arm. If Thomas had been alive when he reached the hospital, there must be a good chance that they could save him.

But if Thomas died? Why had he not been allowed to speak to him? Thomas had said, 'Forgive me.' What did he have to forgive him for? It was not their argument, he'd said, an argument that Patrick realised now, was his own fault. Thomas must have feared this very thing. It was he, Patrick, who had said the harshest words. It seemed clear that Thomas must have saved his life, had stepped between him and the bullet. Why at that moment was forgiveness most on his mind?

It could not be a coincidence that they had chosen that moment. They had known when to strike. Only Thomas and Romano knew what he was to say, and Romano did not know for sure, though Patrick supposed he might have guessed.

He heard the door open and someone came to sit beside him; it was Alfonso. Patrick begged him to call the hospital again. After a few moments he came back and said that Thomas was being operated on and they were doing everything they could. He stared at Patrick soulfully through his thick glasses. 'But it is very serious,' he said. 'They think you should prepare yourself for the worst.'

'No.' He could not bear it. He stood up suddenly and moved towards the door. 'I must go to the hospital.'

'Holy Father, it is best if you stay here. You can do nothing to help him. It's safer here.'

'I want to be near him. He might ask for me. I insist on it. He may need extreme unction. Please, order a car to be ready for me now.'

'Holy Father, we will need security at the hospital. It will take time to set up. We need –'

'I will go now. You can telephone to the police. Don't argue with me, do as I say!'

Alfonso nodded, then turned and left the room. Sister Veronica came and knelt in front of him. She, too, pleaded with him to stay where he was. He should not take any risks, she said. The gunman had not been caught, the police were clearing the whole area. She pressed her hands together and murmured a prayer.

Patrick could not bear it. Every moment that went past risked him not being there when Thomas might need him.

He sent for the small, battered box that he still kept, which he had been given as a young priest and which contained all he needed to give communion to the sick at home – a little chalice; the pyx, the container for the host; a phial for the wine; a small purificator, two candles and a cross. He asked Alfonso to fetch the reserved sacrament from the chapel, and with shaking hands transferred it to the case. Thomas had asked him for forgiveness; he might need absolution. It was imperative that he went to him. They ordered him a car. Alfonso insisted on going with him, with two of the security guards. It was perhaps a brave thing to do, considering. The guards took them down to the entrance and got in the car with him, one on either side; Alfonso sat in the front. They went by a strange roundabout route, perhaps to avoid the traffic in the Via della Conciliazione.

The car seemed to move so slowly; the traffic was heavy. He stared out helplessly at the crowded streets. Life was going on all around him. He saw a cardinal, his red sash folded and held neatly in his hand, walking along eating an ice cream. He saw people on the pavements, shopping bags in hand, sitting outside at cafés, a woman laughing, mobile phone clasped to her ear, a woman grabbing her child's hand, a pair of lovers kissing at the fountain, the tourists with their cameras and phones, all ignorant of who was in the black car with its tinted windows and black-suited driver, passing by them like a harbinger of death. All the time, he prayed, passing the rosary through his fingers, seeking comfort in the familiar words that dropped like stones into his heart. He did not like to think of Thomas, laid out on the operating table, but images of him kept intruding into his mind, flashes of him falling in the square and his head in his lap with the halo of orange blood.

Alfonso got out first and opened the door for him, and he and the guards escorted him in through the back door of the hospital and up in a lift to the first floor. They hurried him along through narrow corridors, his head down, like a convict being kept out of sight. He was taken into an office room, a doctor's office, no doubt, with medical charts on the wall and a desk with a phone on it. Alfonso sat on a chair beside him; the two guards stood by the door. Someone in a doctor's coat came and told him there was no news, his Grace the Archbishop was still in surgery. Would he like anything to drink? He shook his head, then asked for a coffee. When it came it was in a plastic cup and so bitter that he couldn't drink it.

In the room, on the wall, was a plastic clock. He watched the second-hand ticking. He realised he would not be able to sit there, second by second and minute by minute, not knowing what was happening. He felt angry with Alfonso, who sat silently, looking at the floor. He should have stayed at the Vatican – at least he would have had the comfort of familiar things and people around him – he could have prayed with Veronica and the other sisters, which might have given him some comfort. And yet – if Thomas – if the unthinkable happened – then he wanted to be with him.

He sat with his hands in his lap, waiting for news. A doctor came again to ask if there was anything he wanted, and said there was still no definite news, it was too early to say.

If Thomas died, he would never know what it was he wished to be forgiven for. Wild thoughts went through his mind. He recalled Thomas's pleading that he did not give this speech – 'It would be suicide.' Yes, that was what he had said. But was it something more than that? Could Thomas have told them what he was about to say? Could Thomas even have known what they had planned to do? Was it because he knew, was expecting something to happen, that he had been able to intervene at that moment?

No. How could he begin to think these things?

The phone on the desk rang. He did not answer it; it was not his phone. Alfonso looked at him questioningly. Then he thought, perhaps someone was calling him with news; he snatched up the receiver, but just as he did so, the ringing stopped.

When they came to tell him the news he could not believe it.

'We are very sorry,' the doctor said. 'He is out of surgery but he has not regained consciousness.'

Did that mean that he might?

'They tried for an hour but could not resuscitate him.'

Did that mean, then, that he was on a ventilator, that he needed help with breathing?

'There was no more that could be done.'

He was bewildered. What could they mean? He could stand it no more. 'Enough of this!' he said. 'Speak to me plainly, for the love of God. Do you mean that he is dead?'

Their silence was his answer. Then one of the doctors, very slowly, nodded his head.

He insisted that he go at once to see Thomas. He knew that if he did not see the body he would be unable to believe that he was truly dead. He had an overwhelming desire to be with Thomas, to touch him and comfort him. He could not bear to think of Thomas alone in the hospital mortuary, cold and abandoned. There was still time to give extreme unction; it was allowed for a short period after death, perhaps thirty minutes, perhaps an hour, in case the soul might not yet have left the body. He wanted to anoint him, to grant forgiveness for anything he might have done. Even if Thomas were dead, the sacrament would take away all venial sins, and mortal ones if he was truly sorry for them, even if he had not been able to confess them.

Thomas was laid out in a small room, everything but for his head hidden under a white sheet. A bandage had been wrapped round his upper body where the bullet wound would be. His face, though pale, was unchanged, and his vigorous dark hair curled up from the forehead as it had in life. He looked almost as if he was sleeping; it seemed impossible that he would never wake again. If only there was some way that he could breathe life back in to his body.

'What did you mean, Thomas?' he whispered. 'When you asked me to forgive you? If there was anything to forgive, I have already done so a thousand times.' He wanted to weep, but he could not. Weeping would be too easy.

And to think that their last conversation had been words of anger, not of love.

Then he remembered the tender moment when Thomas had adjusted his cape.

He opened his little case, and spread a white cloth on the table beside the bed. Then he placed the crucifix, the two blessed candles and the holy water on the table. He prayed, sprinkling the holy water over Thomas's body. He took out the holy oil and made the sign of the cross on Thomas's eyes, ears, nostrils, lips, hands and feet, the organs of the five external senses. How strange, to touch him so intimately, when he had never been able to do so in life. He began the prayers, preceding them as was proper with the words, 'If you are now living.' No one could know when the soul departed; there was still hope that Thomas's spirit lingered. There was a time after death, he had noticed, when the person's spirit seemed near, and when the relatives would speak to the person tenderly, as if they were still alive; he felt the same, that Thomas was still close to him, that his body was not yet an empty husk. 'Through this holy anointing, and by His most tender mercy, may the Lord pardon you what sins you have committed...'

After saying the final blessing he sat, his head bowed, holding Thomas's hand. He sat there for a long time. He was aware of people coming to stand in the doorway, but no one came in to the room. He realised now that it was becoming dark outside. What time was it? How could the whole day have passed so quickly? It seemed that no one dared disturb him. Finally, he heard a timid tap on the door. A doctor stood there, holding out a small, transparent plastic bag.

'We thought you might like to have these – they are all that he had on him.'

He took the bag and stared at it. A key, a crumpled handkerchief, a little gold cross on a chain.

He tipped it into his palm. He knew it at once; it was his grandmother's cross.

He was still shaking when he returned to his rooms in the Vatican. Sister Veronica came and sat with him, she held his hand and they prayed together. Close up, he noticed Sister Veronica's habit for the first time, how worn it was, and frayed where it scraped along the floor. Clearly she took no notice of such things, in true poverty of spirit.

From time to time shudders overtook his body. One of the sisters came with a blanket to drape around his shoulders. Another brought him a hot herbal tea.

He held the small cross in his hand. Had Thomas taken it? Why? How could it have come into his hands otherwise? Had he taken it deliberately, or simply found it, on the floor perhaps, and taken possession of it? Why had he never said anything about it, even when he asked Thomas if he had seen it? He imagined what might have happened. Perhaps Thomas had come to his bedchamber, possibly to confide in him, even to pray, and he had been deeply asleep with the sleeping pill, and the little bottle had been by the bed. It could have been that Thomas had looked at it to see what it was, and seen the little cross. He might have picked it up and then, perhaps with a desire to have something intimate of his, taken it.

Was this also what he had sought forgiveness for?

Only now, when night had come and he was alone, did the full impact of Thomas's death strike him, like a heavy physical blow. He felt as if he was in pain and it took all his strength to stop himself from moaning aloud. His body, as if outside his control, rocked back and forth. He curled himself up like a foetus on the bed and wrapped his arms tightly around the pillow.

'O God,' he said. 'O God, help me to bear it.'

But he could not bear it.

He tried to calm himself, afraid of the effect his emotions would have on the unborn baby, but he was not strong enough.

He realised that it was the physicality of Thomas that he missed. He missed his thick curling hair, the way his skin around his eyes crinkled when he smiled, the way the light illuminated the hairs on the back of his hands, the sound of his distinctive footfall in the corridor. He had lived so much in his head that the sheer physical aching loss stunned him.

Without Thomas to support him, he could not go on. It was impossible. It was a sign; a sign that, as Thomas had argued, he should not have tried to announce this to the world. The world was not ready. And it was no accident that the assassin had struck now. They knew what he was going to say. They had tried to silence him. He could not stay in the Vatican. Everyone around him was his enemy, and now he had no Thomas to bring him news of what was happening.

The doors to the papal library opened and Alfonso swept in, followed by Inspector Giordano. Alfonso went and stood away from them, near the window; the two Swiss Guards took up their positions on either side of the door.

Giordano said that it was clear what had happened. Somehow, the marksman had gained access to the roof terrace of the Istituto Santissima Bambina, and managed to get away afterwards. Rigorous searches were being carried out. He said that three shots were fired. The rifle had been abandoned at the scene; it was being examined but, Giordano explained, in a professional hit of this kind, it was very unlikely they would find fingerprints. Tracing the weapon was also not an easy matter; guns like this were acquired illegally and often passed through many hands. Finding out who had hired the assassin was even more difficult; in such cases a series of cut-outs was normally used, even the assassin would not know who was behind it. After all, he said, the reasons behind the attempt on John Paul II's life were still a mystery, even though on that occasion they had arrested the gunman straight away.

'But how easy is it to be accurate over that range? Won't that help you narrow down the assassin?' He remembered standing up on that terrace and looking below him at the dais; his head would have been a tiny dot.

'With a modern rifle and sights such as he used, they can be accurate over twice, maybe three times that distance,' said Giordano. 'It is lucky for you that the first shot missed, and that the Archbishop intervened before the bodyguards could get to you.'

They had watched footage of the attack, Giordano said. It was obvious that Archbishop Thomas had deliberately thrown himself in front of Patrick. The Archbishop, he said, had undoubtedly saved his life. He was rightly being hailed as a hero in all the papers.

'This attack could be politically motivated,' he said, 'An Islamist, perhaps, though we cannot speculate. The Cardinal Secretary of State, Romano, has given me threatening letters which have been sent to you and we are going through them. Of course, we will pursue every avenue. But – is there anything you would like to tell us, anything that you are aware of, that could shed any light on this matter? You may know something that we do not.' He gave Patrick a searching look.

Patrick thought, for a moment, of telling him about what he knew of Romano, about the secret meetings, but he could not bear to. He could only make his own situation more insecure. He was convinced, himself, who lay behind the attack; the assassin was a mere pawn. And even if they found the killer, it would solve nothing, for nothing could bring Thomas back to him.

He would conduct the funeral himself.

In the great basilica of St Peter's, he saw the image of the *Pietà* as if for the first time. The anguished Mary holding the dead body of her son in her arms, as he had held the dying Thomas.

The choir was singing. *Lux Aeterna*. Let light perpetual shine upon him.

An image came into his mind, an image so strong it would not leave him. He saw himself and Thomas and the child at Castel Gandolfo. He saw the child, his son, running and laughing in the sunlight, and Thomas running after him, picking him up and lifting him in his arms, and they were there together, the three of them, a happy family.

He realised that he had truly loved Thomas. Not as a friend, a companion, but in another, deeper way.

What was so wrong with this? Why had he spent so much of his life in opposition to this idea? What was male, what was female? Why was it so terribly important? Why had he been so obsessed by such dualities? All his life he had been concerned with drawing a line, a clear line that separated good from evil, the holy from the profane. Everything had seemed so clear. He had not realised that everything was on a spectrum, that it wasn't always possible to draw a clear line, that one thing blended seamlessly into another. There were terrible things happening in the world, there was dreadful suffering, and he had been caught up with failed attempts to impose laws which in the end had only stopped people from being free to love one another. This image of a child, loved by them both, bathed by sunlight, he realised, was an image of fulfilment for him. He could not imagine anything more beautiful. And now, it would never happen. He had never been able to tell Thomas what he thought, what he hoped for. He had not even been able to recognise it himself.

Could he do something with this knowledge? Could he change the Church? He doubted it. He himself could do nothing. Only God could save the Church.

The funeral was over. He stood on the steps outside. Cardinal after cardinal came to kiss his hand. They murmured words of consolation. 'Our brother in Christ.' 'A holy martyr of the church.' 'Greater love has no man.' Then a dark-haired woman, veiled in black; Thomas's sister. She bowed and thanked him for the service. What could he say to her? His heart felt empty. He should grieve with her, give her words of comfort, but he found himself unable to say anything to her.

Chapter Seventeen

He took out his diary, but he could not add anything. Words would not come. He thought how now there was no one to destroy the diary should anything happen to him. Much better for him to destroy it now. He tore out the pages, took them into the bathroom and set fire to them in the sink, washing away the ashy remains. He thought it would upset him to destroy what he had written, but his heart felt like a stone.

He did not want anyone to replace Thomas. It was impossible to think of taking anyone else into his confidence. There was no one that he trusted. The isolation was appalling. He felt a prisoner within the walls of his papal suite. People walked around with quiet voices, whispering things he couldn't hear.

He now had the perfect excuse to retreat for a while. He could say that he needed the time and space to reflect. That he wished to refrain from public appearances until more was known about who was responsible. That he needed time to mourn. He must not make it too long, of course; that would be unseemly.

He had taken to walking with a slight stoop, bending over a little and leaning forward, so that his robes would completely cover the bulge in his belly. Even more hard to conceal, though, were his breasts, which he had to bind with a tight cloth that made them ache. He had decided to eat more, too. He could see the irony in this change from an abstemious man who had seen fatness as a sign of moral weakness.

Father Alfonso took over Thomas's role, and there was another, Cardinal Esposito, who joined him.

Father Alfonso now took breakfast with him and brought him his papers. Father Alfonso and Esposito accompanied him at Mass and to the shrine in the garden. Father Alfonso took all his meals with him. But he could not help it; he still did not feel comfortable with Father Alfonso.

One still morning they were walking in the autumn sunshine in the gardens. The sun was low, slanting through the trees, and the leaves dropped in a steady rain, falling on the path and crackling underneath their feet. Father Alfonso said, 'You must not grieve too much over Thomas, Holy Father. He was not what you think.'

'What do you mean?'

'I say this in your best interests, Holy Father. Believe me, it is not pleasant to talk of such things, or to tell you the truth at this time. But I know that he did not always act in your best interests. You confided in him, and he did not keep your counsel. Besides, even worse – there are rumours that he did not lead a celibate life. There are stories that he left the Vatican at night and went to –'

'Stop! I will not listen to these ugly rumours. They are based on spite and tittle-tattle.'

'Nonetheless I know some of the people concerned and I believe there to be some truth in them, Holy Father.'

'It is all hearsay.'

Alphonso hesitated. 'Holy Father, I must tell you that I have some evidence myself. One evening Archbishop Thomas left his mobile phone on the table when he went to play the piano. A message came in and I saw it – it was – I cannot repeat what it said but –'

'Enough! You will refrain from talking to me on such matters. I forbid it.'

'But it is not a secret among the people in the Vatican, Holy Father. It does not help you to show such feeling for someone, someone who is in no way worthy of the regard that you have shown him. You have conducted the funeral, you have mourned, and now you must move on.'

He realised that he was shaking with anger. 'Father Alfonso, it is quite clear that what you have told me is not appropriate for me to hear. I will not hear you speak ill of the dead.'

Father Alfonso nodded. 'I thought it might help you to get over your grief, Holy Father. I meant it for the best. Please, forgive me.'

That night, he prayed for Thomas. What if he had not led a moral life? Did it matter so much to him? Was the pain he felt now of disappointment, or was it jealousy, as any man might feel if the person he loved had been unfaithful? He did not know.

For a long time he could not sleep. Then he must have dozed off because he suddenly awoke, crying out, from a terrible dream.

In his dream, Thomas came and stood at the end of his bed, his arms outstretched. There was blood on his hands and blood gushing from the wound in his neck. He reached out to try to stem the flow of blood, but it came welling up between his fingers and flowed out, spilling down in bright-red rivulets on to the floor. The sight repelled him, so that when Thomas reached out his hand imploringly he could not move forward or step towards him. Patrick watched the long trail of blood spread out along the marble, moving like a snake, stopping and then advancing, finding its way into the cracks in the floor.

Then he saw Thomas's lips moving. He said, 'I am the father of your child.' Then he began to fall, like a statue, rigid, breaking into a thousand bloody fragments.

He woke up with a loud cry.

He put on the light and tried to wipe the image from his mind. But was that what Thomas had said to him when he was dying. 'I am... the father. Forgive me.' Was that what he had meant?

Could it have been that the dream he remembered, that night, was not a dream... that Thomas had come into his bed?

He remembered that discussion the doctors had said, when they had told him he was pregnant, about the couple who sought an annulment. They claimed that the marriage had not been consummated, although they had a child.

That night, Thomas must have taken the little cross. What had happened? Had he come into the room, seen him heavily asleep and seen the bottle of pills, taken an opportunity to climb into bed beside him, perhaps embrace him, and then become aroused and –

It was confusing to think about it. It should be shocking, horrifying, but he realised that he did not, after all, mind the thought of being embraced like this by Thomas. In fact, now that Thomas was removed from him forever, he realised that he might even have wanted this himself. What he had imagined now was perhaps not likely, but it was not impossible. Did Thomas know or suspect that it was not, then, a divine birth, but an all too human one? Did that explain all his strange behaviour? Was that the reason that Thomas had been so opposed to his announcement?

He wished he could tell Thomas that it did not matter to him, either way. Would the child, if it were safely born, be no less a miracle because of the way it had been conceived? He supposed there might be a way to know, after the baby had been born; they could test the DNA – no doubt Romano would want to insist on this. But would it not also be a miracle if something of Thomas had survived in his son?

If only he could speak to Thomas, to ask him what had happened. But now it was impossible. The chasm of death now stood between them and there was no way of crossing to the other side.

This time, in the confessional, he could not bring himself to say the usual formulas. He wished to forgive Archbishop Thomas, he said, for something that might have happened, and to ask forgiveness for himself, but now it was too late. Their last conversation had been a bitter argument. Thomas was dead, and he was grieving terribly. There was no possibility of finding out the truth.

There was a long silence, as if his confessor was searching for the right response.

'When there is a strong emotional component to the matter, it is hard sometimes to remember what absolution means. You must understand that when you ask for absolution, that must be an end to the matter. You must not cling on to it, must not dwell on it. You have handed it over to God and God, in ways we do not understand, will make everything well. You should believe also that there is some way in which Thomas himself will know that you have forgiven him.'

How strange that in all the times he had given and received absolution, he had never felt the full impact of it. The thought that Thomas might still in some way be in touch with him was overwhelming. He found himself weeping, silently. He felt no shame. The tears were of grief, but gladness also. The confessor silently passed him a handkerchief and he dried his eyes.

The confessor said the words of absolution. Together, they made the sign of the cross.

'Give thanks to the Lord for He is good.'

'For His mercy endures forever.'

As he walked along the corridor, his steps felt lighter. He must not cling on to his grief. Thomas knew that he loved him, and that love, he believed, was eternal. God's mercy was being poured out to everyone in a continual stream, no matter how sinful, how confused. And hardest to accept was that God's mercy extended even to himself. Well, he was forgiven. He must think now of the future, and the child who would soon be born.

A few days later, he received another letter from Siobhan.

Forgive me for writing to you, cousin Patrick, but I had a dream of you last night, and it prompted me to write. What a strange dream it was! I dreamed that you had a baby. It was your baby, I mean, not that you were holding someone else's. You were holding the baby on your lap and you were wearing a blue robe, like the Madonna in a painting. Perhaps it was because of that day when I so wrongly and foolishly attacked you, for you were holding a small baby then, I remember, and she was crying, and they could not find the mother.

Perhaps I dreamed of you because, by a happy coincidence, Jan has got a visual arts residency in Rome and so we are travelling to Rome shortly to stay for six months. We will be staying in Trastevere. If you want me to come and see you, let me know.

Anyway, I thought that you would like to know that I am no longer at all ill, and that I have been completely reconciled with my husband, Jan. We are very happy. Rome will be a new beginning for us. I have been thinking of you daily, of all the burdens that you must bear, all the work to do. And then this dreadful murder! I know there is no reason for me to say this, but I feel that perhaps God is prompting me, and if I can be of service to you in any way, please let me know.

He read and re-read the letter.

It was a sign. It must be a sign.

He wrote back, asking her to come to see him as soon as she could. She should liaise with Father Alfonso, he would sort out all the arrangements for her.

Siobhan came to see him with her husband, Jan. He was a handsome man, tall and dark-haired, towering over her. Patrick was struck by the change in her. She was neatly dressed in a modest white blouse buttoned up to her neck and her chestnut hair was drawn back from her face in a neat chignon. She had plucked her eyebrows and this gave her eyes an open, almost surprised look, as she looked at him serenely, calmly, from under an unlined forehead. She was no longer so pale; she had been in the sun and her freckles were darker, spread out across her nose. He had not realised before that she was beautiful.

She bent down in front of him and he took her hand and drew her up. He noticed the small pearl earrings that trembled as she moved her head. She turned to Jan, who came forward and kissed the ring on his hand; he seemed overawed, unable to speak.

They exchanged a few words of greeting and he apologised for the security screening they'd had to go through. Siobhan sat on the chair beside him and looked down into her lap. 'I am glad you wanted to see me,' she said.

Jan reached over and took her hand, and she squeezed it affectionately. Still holding her hand, he slipped his fingers between hers, and rested their hands together on his knee. She looked at him and smiled, and there was in that smile something – not exactly flirtatious – it was stronger than that, it was a look of real desire, of bodily hunger. With a shock that was almost physical, Patrick realised what had been wrong with the couple he had interviewed at Castel Gandolfo. They had not touched one another. He thought of his parents, cold and separate from one another, never sharing any physical affection. It was not what he wanted for his own child.

This then was the message that God had given him; that erotic love was good, that it was a necessary part of human life, that from it love and affection flowed, that it would bubble up from underneath no matter how much it was suppressed, and its suppression led to misery and harm. Why had he not paid more attention to the Song of Songs? This should have been the subject of his forgotten encyclical.

'Siobhan,' he said, 'There is something you can do for me. It ties in with your dream. Look at me.'

It was perfect. He was amazed that he had not thought of it before. She shared some of his genes, she even looked a little like him, with her pale skin and chestnut hair. Her husband he knew was a good man, a Catholic who had stood by her through all her difficulties, when he could have run off and found a woman who could bear a child for him. She would value his gift above all else, above her own life, even. Yes, it had all been for a reason, he saw that now, everything that had happened had been for a reason. She had been sent to him for a purpose, and that purpose would now be fulfilled. He wouldn't tell her the full story, not now, but he would have the papers drawn up and, in case the worst happened, make her a legal guardian in his will. He was going to give her the baby.

Twenty-eight weeks. The baby should now be able to survive, even if it came early. It would be difficult now to cover up the pregnancy, even under his robes. He felt in constant danger in the Vatican, felt that everyone's eyes were on him, especially Romano's. He did not know how many people knew.

He had an argument again with Romano, who came to him and again begged to know what he planned. He was afraid to tell him anything. Since Thomas had been killed, papal security was extreme. Romano had finally had his wish; the open-air Masses and audiences had been suspended, his appearances limited to the prayers from his window. Everything and everyone who came into the papal apartments was screened; Alfonso personally unlocked the doors to visitors, accompanied them in and stayed with him during their audiences. It would be difficult for them to kill him here. But even so, it would be possible. They could murder him in the papal apartments and announce it was a natural death. The previous popes, even John Paul I, over whom there were such suspicions, did not have an autopsy. And with every day that passed, the danger that they would do something terrible increased.

He must go into hiding. He would leave a message that he had gone into retreat for a time and would take up his duties again at the start of Lent. It was clear where he must hide, in one of the convents that surrounded the Vatican, somewhere he could be on solitary retreat. He would have to confide in Sister Veronica.

Sister Veronica came to his room with his infusion in the evening and he asked her to stay with him a while. She sat beside him and folded her hands in prayer. He told her that what he had to say was difficult to believe, and that she must prepare herself for a shock. She nodded and crossed herself.

When he told her, she did not blench. She looked up at him, her wide eyes open and trusting and said, 'Praise the Lord! It is a miracle indeed.'

She saw at once what was needed.

'It is like the Flight into Egypt,' she said. 'But you will not have to travel so far. I know a convent where you can stay, Holy Father, close by, where you will be quite safe. There is a gate and entry-phone, and I will tell the sisters that there is a guest who wishes to keep silence. I can organise everything for you, Holy Father. You can count on me, absolutely.'

With a little joyful laugh, which she could not suppress, she turned and rushed from the room.

Autumn came to an end; the leaves had fallen from the trees, revealing their skeletal branches. Storms blew in and the rain lashed down on the gravel courtyard outside his window. The moon waxed and cast bright patterns on the floor of his room and then waned again. The nights grew cool. Inside the convent, the nuns moved silently along the corridors; they did not look at him, practising custody of the eyes.

He prayed daily in the chapel, rising early every morning and staying late every evening. The nuns' simple, artless singing was enchanting. He knelt there to pray alone sometimes, watched the tallow candles gleam and quiver on the altar. He took a daily walk round the gardens, where late flowers bloomed. He saw the petals drop, the hips swell. The nuns brought him his meals in his rooms.

The baby moved inside him. Sometimes he saw a bulge under his skin that might be an elbow or a knee. He tried to imagine what this child, his son, would look like. He thought that he would know the truth if the child looked like Thomas. He hoped that it would, and that something of Thomas could be his.

Dr Lombardi had reassured him. It seemed clear to him now; that all the talk of risk, of low-lying placentas and the baby not growing had been to scare him into ending the pregnancy. Everything those doctors had said had frightened him. He wanted to avoid them, to let God bring this mystery to fruition inside him in stillness and in silence.

He did not know what was happening at the Vatican. He saw no news, read no papers, talked to no one. He felt at peace. Perhaps it was the pregnancy hormones washing over him, preparing him for the momentous event.

Winter came, the first of December. Patrick woke abruptly with the feeling that there was something wrong. He turned to look at his clock and realised that it was later than usual; he had overslept. The nuns said Mass at seven; he did not want to be absent. It was only just beginning to get light but the sky was clear and it had been cold in the night; when he turned his head and looked out of the window he saw the frost on the grass outside and the long dark shadows lying across the courtyard. He was reluctant to leave the warmth of his bed; perhaps there were just a few minutes before he had to rise. He leaned over and picked up the copy of Julian of Norwich's *Revelations of Divine Love* from his bedside table and opened the marked page. *And in the adoption of our nature he quickened us; and in his blessed dying on the cross he birthed us to eternal life…*

He meditated on the words for a few moments, put down the book and rose from the bed. As he dressed, he began to feel vague, cramping sensations in his lower abdomen, a feeling of heaviness there. Was this the beginning of labour? No, it was too soon, there was still a month to go. He felt uneasy, but he did not know who to ask. He did not want to call a doctor unless he had to, did not want to give his presence here away. He finished dressing and went towards the bathroom.

He felt a sharp pain and a sudden warm rush of fluid between his legs. Had the waters broken? He looked down and saw blood, it was coming out of him as if a tap had been turned on, spiralling down his leg like a twisting snake and splattering on to the marble floor. It was so bright, so red, there was so much of it! He thought, no, this is not happening. Something has gone wrong; I must get help. He thought – the baby will die. Then, he thought, perhaps I will die too. He snatched up a towel and shoved it between his legs, and, bending over, shuffled awkwardly out of the room. He could not call the nuns; they were all in the Chapel, two floors and a long corridor away. He moved slowly towards the landing where he knew there was a phone. The pain was getting stronger, it was like a vice gripping his lower abdomen; he could feel the blood still flowing down his leg; he had to force himself to keep moving. In the dim light he found the phone and picked up the receiver. What was the emergency number? It was not easy to find the right keys; his hand was weak and shaking. He dialled 112; someone answered almost instantly. He gave the address, said, '*Ambulanza.*' A woman's voice asked him a question but he couldn't understand. He said, '*Sto sanguinando*, I am bleeding. I think I am dying, *Penso che sto morendo.*' His legs did not have any strength in them; he realised that he was sinking to the floor. He thought that perhaps if he lay on his back with his legs folded up and kept very still the bleeding might lessen. The towel was already soaked. He gathered up the bottom of his robe and stuffed it between his legs.

He heard a strange whimpering sound and realised it was coming from him. Had he been through so much only for this to happen? He began to bargain, 'O God, let the baby live, at least. Let me live if it is Your will, help me, save me.'

He lay on the floor for what seemed a very long time. The marble was very cold and he realised that he was shivering. His head pressed painfully against the cold stone. The receiver had slipped from his grasp and was hanging down above his head, just beyond his reach, and he realised the distant sound he was hearing was a voice still talking at the other end, asking questions that he couldn't quite make out, in Italian and in awkward English. He didn't care that he couldn't answer; the sound of the voice was strangely comforting.

He heard footsteps and someone running down the corridor. A face looked down at him and he saw her expression, white and shocked; it was Sister Borgia. He turned his head away. He heard her voice, talking on the phone, and then the words, '*Subito, subito.*' Then she was kneeling next to him, holding his hand and murmuring soothing words to him. He heard more feet and then more voices around him, more footsteps running. Someone lifted his head and placed a pillow under it, someone else took his other hand, someone pressed a little crucifix into his hand and all the while, Sister Borgia went on praying.

It was getting light. Pale sunlight fell on the wall on the other side of the corridor, a thin strip. It began to widen and move across the wall. Through the window he heard the sound of the ambulance siren, that annoying peep-eee-pee-pee, peep-eee-pee-pee, followed by the scrunch of tyres below, and then he heard more footsteps in the corridor. He dimly understood the Italian. They were taking his blood pressure. They said they must get him to the hospital at once.

A man's voice explained that they would lift him. Several hands were slipped beneath him and then he was on a stretcher and moving down the corridor. He looked up at the ceiling, saw it passing overhead, the metal light fittings, the arches at the top of the stairwell. Then they turned with a jolting, clumsy movement, trying to keep the stretcher level, and were carrying him down the stairs. He heard more voices as he came out into sunlight so bright that he had to close

his eyes. He heard the sound of an engine running. They were load-
ing him into the ambulance. They asked him if there was anyone he
wanted them to call and he gave them Siobhan's number. He realised
that at some level he had expected something to go wrong; he had
memorised it for that reason.

The doors slammed shut; the ambulance began to move. He felt
that everything was very far away. He heard the siren sound, urgent
voices speaking. There was a sharp jolt. They were in the hospital.
How had they come there so quickly? It seemed to have taken no
time at all. People were crowding around him. He heard voices, first
in Italian and then English.

'It's a placental abruption,' the doctor was saying to him, peering
down from above. He had a kind expression on his face and his voice
was smooth and calm. 'The placenta is coming away from the lining
of the womb. It's quite severe, I'm afraid. We are going to get you
into surgery right away – the baby will be delivered by caesarean. We
need to see if the baby is OK; we will use a monitor to check for the
heartbeat.'

He felt them place something on his belly, cold and firm. He could
hear nothing, then a distant pitter-patter, pitter-patter. Siobhan's voice
came from his side – how had she got there so soon? He heard her say,
'Patrick, they've found the heartbeat. Praise God, the baby is alive!'

He turned his head towards her. She was standing next to him, her
face even paler than usual. She was wearing some kind of hospital
gown and a cap over her head. He felt her take hold of his hand and
squeeze it warmly, but he tried to pull it away. He had wanted her
there at the birth, but that was when he had imagined it all differently. Why had he told them to call her? It was cruel. She wanted the
baby to be alive as much as him, more than him, perhaps. If the baby
was born dead how would she be able to stand it?

Someone started rubbing his arm; he felt a cool sensation. Another
doctor in a green gown was looking down at him. 'I'm the anaesthetist,'

he said. 'We are going to put in a drip; you need blood and fluids. And we will give you spinal anaesthesia. There's less risk and also that way you will be awake when the baby is born.'

He felt a sharp prick in his arm and saw a bag of blood being hung up above him on a stand. He heard Siobhan behind him, telling him to hang on, it would be over soon. 'It won't be long now,' she said. 'Please God, it won't be long.'

The anaesthetist told him to roll over, to try to curl up and expose his spine so they could get the needle in. He could not move; two nurses came and helped him. He felt a sharp pain in his belly and more blood rushing out between his legs. He heard Siobhan's voice, high and anxious, 'He's bleeding, he's bleeding, is it all right?' and someone hushing her. He felt something ice-cold being rubbed into his back and the scratch of a needle, then, after a few moments, a strange sensation in his spine. He felt a tingle going down one leg, like a small electric shock. They rolled him on to his back again and after a few minutes his legs began to feel heavy and warm. The numbness spread gradually up his body. He could not feel his legs, his belly. His mind began to drift. Was this what dying felt like? The nurse at his side was taking his blood pressure again; he felt someone else take hold of his other hand. He realised that all sense of panic had left him, that they knew what they were doing, that everything that was possible would be done, that it was in their hands, in God's hands, too. He heard the doctors' low voices, the clatter of instruments being got ready. He heard a hissing noise, then someone was placing a transparent plastic mask over his face. The doctor said, 'Breathe slowly and deeply, your blood oxygen levels are low; this will help us get enough oxygen to the baby. Don't worry, it won't be long now.'

He breathed in the cool air gratefully, as if each breath was bringing life to the baby. He repeated the Hail Mary, over and over. It was the only thing he could think of. Hail Mary, full of grace. The Lord is with thee. Blessed art thou among women, and blessed is the fruit of thy womb –

His head felt very light. Was it the oxygen? Then came a strange sensation, as if something was pulling him, drawing him upwards out of the top of his head. He was floating, up, up, towards the ceiling, and he saw a faint light above him which seemed to illuminate the whole room. He saw the doctors leaning over him, the green operation cloths spread around him, a nurse passing an instrument, and then a bright red line of blood as they cut across his belly. He saw the crucifix, the tortured Christ, hanging on the wall above the door, and was it his imagination, or were His wounds running fresh with blood that dripped down on to the floor to mingle with his own? He heard distant voices too high to be human, a chorus like a shimmering curtain of sound so beautiful he thought he would die. And then he heard a voice right beside him, low and urgent: 'Patrick! Wake up! Patrick!' and knew it was Siobhan calling him back.

He felt as if he was falling then, and with a start he was back in his body and he opened his eyes. He was staring up at the bright ceiling. He felt strange sensations, a pressure and a tugging in his abdomen, and then he looked down and caught a glimpse of a head emerging with a slick of dark hair, and the baby was lifted out of him and he saw it, tiny and so fragile, held up vertically in the doctor's hands, its arms hanging limply by its side. He heard a gasp from behind him. The baby was covered in blood and its face and body were the colour of putty. It did not move and he thought, that's the end then, it's all been for nothing.

There was a long, still moment in which he saw the baby hang there, lifeless, and he heard the deathly silence in the room, broken only by the hiss of the oxygen and the distant beep of a machine. A nurse rushed forward with some instrument in her hand; perhaps they would try to resuscitate the baby. And then he saw the baby draw up its legs and its face convulsed and turned rosy pink, and it wailed, a reedy sound at first, then louder and more furious, and then they passed it to one side and he could see them examine it, heard them talking to one another as they repeated some numbers, and then he heard Siobhan's voice calling out with breathless joy, 'Oh! A baby girl! Oh! A baby girl!' and he looked and saw that they were holding up the baby to him and that it was a girl but he felt no surprise, only amazement as he gazed at the wriggling little creature, this fruit of his own womb, and he heard Siobhan crying and telling him that the baby was all right and she was beautiful and there was the sound of absolute wonder in her voice and he said, 'Let me hold her', and then the voices began to fade and an alarm sounded somewhere far away and he was slipping away into a great darkness as they put the baby on his chest, and then he felt his baby's skin against his skin and he felt himself melting into the baby and the baby melting into him so that at last he felt complete…

Acknowledgments

I would like to thank my publisher, Martin Goodman, for his unfailing support of this project and his perceptive comments on the work in progress. I must also thank Catherine Wynne, who generously donated her memories of her Irish childhood and gave her encouragement and help throughout. I owe Fabio Jephcott a debt for guiding me around Rome and taking me to Castel Gandolfo, as well as making the happy suggestion that my pope be named Patrick. I am grateful to those who made helpful and insightful comments on various stages of the draft, including Olivia Fane, Jane Havell, Charles Palliser, Gillian Paschkes-Bell, Andrew Rivett and Ross Thompson, as well as my husband Jeremy for his enduring support and patience. My dear friend Mary also needs a special mention. Without all this help, this novel would not have been completed.

CPSIA information can be obtained
at www.ICGtesting.com
Printed in the USA
JSHW010131300323
39675JS00005B/5